D0502164

SON OF
STONE

BOOKS BY STUART WOODS

FICTION

Bel-Air Dead[†]
Lucid Intervals[†]
Strategic Moves[†]
Santa Fe Edge[§]
Kisser[†]
Hothouse Orchid[*]
Loitering with Intent[†]
Mounting Fears[‡]
Hot Mahogany[†]
Santa Fe Dead[§]
Beverly Hills Dead
Shoot Him If He Runs[†]
Fresh Disasters[†]
Short Straw[§]
Dark Harbor[†]
Iron Orchid[*]

Two-Dollar Bill[†]
The Prince of Beverly Hills
Reckless Abandon[†]
Capital Crimes[‡]
Dirty Work[†]
Blood Orchid[*]
The Short Forever[†]
Orchid Blues[*]
Cold Paradise[†]
L.A. Dead[†]
The Run[‡]
Worst Fears Realized[†]
Orchid Beach[*]
Swimming to Catalina[†]

Dead in the Water[†]
Dirt[†]
Choke
Imperfect Strangers
Heat
Dead Eyes
L.A. Times
Santa Fe Rules[§]
New York Dead[†]
Palindrome
Grass Roots[‡]
White Cargo
Deep Lie[‡]
Under the Lake
Run Before the Wind[‡]
Chiefs[‡]

TRAVEL
A Romantic's Guide to the Country Inns of Britain and Ireland (1979)

MEMOIR
Blue Water, Green Skipper (1977)

[*]A Holly Barker Novel   [†]A Stone Barrington Novel
[‡]A Will Lee Novel   [§]An Ed Eagle Novel

SON OF
STONE

A STONE BARRINGTON NOVEL

Stuart Woods

DOUBLEDAY LARGE PRINT HOME LIBRARY EDITION

G. P. PUTNAM'S SONS   NEW YORK

This Large Print Edition, prepared especially for Doubleday Large Print Home Library, contains the complete, unabridged text of the original Publisher's Edition.

PUTNAM

G. P. PUTNAM'S SONS
Publishers Since 1838
Published by the Penguin Group
Penguin Group (USA) Inc., 375 Hudson Street, New York, New York 10014, USA

ISBN 978-1-61129-979-3

Printed in the United States of America

This is a work of fiction. Names, characters, places, and incidents either are the product of the author's imagination or are used fictitiously, and any resemblance to actual persons, living or dead, businesses, companies, events, or locales is entirely coincidental.

While the author has made every effort to provide accurate telephone numbers and Internet addresses at the time of publication, neither the publisher nor the author assumes any responsibility for errors, or for changes that occur after publication. Further, the publisher does not have any control over and does not assume any responsibility for author or third-party websites or their content.

This book is for Sandy Gotham Meehan

This Large Print Book carries the
Seal of Approval of N.A.V.H.

SON OF
STONE

1

Elaine's, late.

Stone Barrington and Dino Bacchetti sat, sipping what each of them usually sipped, gazing desultorily at the menu. Elaine came and sat down.

"Having problems deciding?" she asked.

"Always," Dino said.

"Are you being a smart-ass?" she asked.

"I'm torn between the pasta special and the osso buco," Dino said.

"Yeah," Stone said, "Dino is always torn."

"Are you being a smart-ass?" Dino asked.

"I'm just backing you up, pal," Stone said.

"Oh."

"Have the pasta," Elaine said. "It's terrific."

"How can I pass that up?" Dino asked, closing his menu.

"Dino," Stone said, "you're veering toward the ironic again. Watch yourself."

Elaine looked at Dino. "You're lucky there isn't a steak knife on the table." She flagged down a passing waiter. "Two pasta specials," she said, her finger wagging between Stone and Dino.

"I'll have the osso buco," Stone said.

"I just sold the last one," the waiter replied.

"Tell you what," Stone said, "I'll have the pasta special, with a chopped spinach salad to start."

"Me, too, on the salad," Dino said.

"And a bottle of the Mondavi Napa Cabernet," Stone added.

"Good," Elaine said, then she got up

and wandered a couple of tables away and sat down there.

"That was close," Stone said. "You could have gotten a fork in the chest."

"I didn't want the pasta," Dino replied.

"Then why didn't you order the osso buco to begin with?"

"They were out."

"You didn't know that."

"Does it matter? They wouldn't have had it anyway."

They sat in silence for a moment, Stone sipping his Knob Creek, Dino sipping his Johnnie Walker Black.

"When does Ben get home for the holidays?" Stone asked. Benito was Dino's teenaged son.

"Tomorrow," Dino replied. "I get him first. Mary Ann will have him for Christmas dinner at her father's."

"Could you bring him to dinner tomorrow night?"

Dino looked at him oddly. "Since when did you especially want to have dinner with Benito?"

"Since Arrington decided to come to New York for Christmas and bring Peter."

"You didn't tell me."

"I didn't know until tonight. I was just leaving the house when she called. They're due in early tomorrow afternoon." Stone showed Dino the photo of the boy that Arrington had given him. "This was over a year ago," he said. "I guess he's bigger now."

Dino gazed at the photograph. "Amazingly like your father," he said.

"How would you know? You never met my father."

"I've met the photograph of him in your study about a thousand times," Dino replied.

"Oh, yeah."

"Does he know?"

"Who?"

"Peter."

"Don't start that again," Stone said.

"I didn't start it, you did; some years back."

Stone's shoulders sagged. "All right, all right."

"When exactly was it? I know you know."

Stone cast his thoughts back. "Right before we were going to the islands for the holidays, to St. Marks. The night before, actually. I had bought her a ring."

"You never told me that. You were really going to ask her?"

"Yes, I was. That morning it started snowing. I got to the airport and got a call from her saying that she was stuck in a meeting at the *New Yorker*. She had written a piece for them, and she was working with the editor. She said she'd get the same flight the next day. I was pissed off, but my bags were already on the airplane, and I didn't want to go through *that* a day later, so I left. As it turned out, while she was at the *New Yorker* they assigned her to write a profile of Vance Calder."

"Uh-oh."

"Exactly. Turns out I got the last flight out of the airport before they closed it because of the snowstorm. She was stuck in the city for another day. Then Vance arrived in town and they had dinner. I met the flight the following day, and she wasn't on it, and I couldn't get her on the phone. Finally, a few days later, I got a fax at my hotel."

"A Dear Stone letter?"

"Right. She was marrying Vance."

"And when did she find out she was pregnant?"

"I'm not sure. I was out in L.A. four or five months later, and . . ."

"I was there, too, remember?"

"Yes, I remember. And when I saw her there she was obviously pregnant."

"Did she say whose it was?"

"No, because she didn't know."

"The two . . . events were too close together, huh?"

"Right."

"When did she know?"

"Not until after Vance's death, I think."

They were quiet again. "Had she seen the photograph of your father?"

"Sure, she was in the house a lot when we first met."

"So she knew sooner than Vance's death?"

"I don't know; she may have been in denial."

"Did Vance know?"

Stone shook his head. "She told me the subject never came up."

"When did she finally admit it to you?"

"When we were in Maine a few years

back, remember? Then, when you and I were staying at her house in Bel-Air last year, we had a frank talk about it. She said she had had a brush with ovarian cancer and had surgery, and that seemed to get her thinking about Peter's future. She wanted me to spend some time with Peter, but it hasn't happened until now. He's been in boarding school in Virginia for more than a year."

"So, we're looking at a family reunion, huh?"

Stone grinned ruefully. "I never thought of it that way. Arrington and I have spent so little time together over the years."

"So, how are you feeling about this?" Dino asked.

"Scared stiff," Stone said.

2

Arrington Calder awoke in her rented house in Virginia and immediately smelled the man lying next to her. It was odd how he had this consistent personal odor—not unpleasant, but certainly distinctive. He even had it immediately after showering. It was strange.

She carefully lifted his arm from across her body, because she didn't want to wake him yet. Today, she had to have a conversation with him that she didn't want to have and that he wouldn't want to hear, and she was putting it off until the last minute. He was extraordinarily jealous, something she had found a little attractive when she had first started seeing, then sleeping with, him, after she had hired him to design her new house. He was prominent among Virginia architects and was a professor of architecture at the University of Virginia in nearby Charlottesville. His name was Timothy Rutledge.

She managed to slip out of bed without waking him and tiptoed across the bedroom, through the dressing room, where her packed bags, still open, awaited her departure, then into the bathroom, where she closed the door to shut out the sound of the shower. She washed her face, having not had time to do that the night before, because of his persistence.

She got into the shower and began to feel better. In a couple of hours she would be away from here for a while, and that would give him time for his ardor to cool.

She was washing her hair, her eyes closed against the shampoo, when he let himself into the shower. She tried to drive her elbow into his belly, but his arms were around her from behind, pinning hers to her body. He fumbled around, trying to enter her from behind, but she struggled free. "Get out!" she said, pushing him out the swinging glass door.

He stood on the bath mat, fuming. "What's the matter with you?" he demanded.

"Go down and start breakfast," she said. "I'll be there in half an hour."

"Why are your bags packed?" he asked.

"I'll talk to you downstairs. Now go!"

Reluctantly, he went.

She rinsed her hair thoroughly, then shut off the water and felt for the bath sheet on the hook outside the door. She dried herself, then picked up the hair dryer and dried her blond hair, helping it into place with a brush. That done, she applied her makeup, then got into her traveling clothes, a pants suit. She picked up the phone in her dressing room and pressed a button for her son's room. "Peter," she said, "time to get up."

He picked up the phone. "I'm way ahead of you," he said. "I'm packing."

"Good boy." She hung up and went downstairs. Tim had prepared eggs, bacon, and toast, and she sat down and began to eat.

"Where are you going?" Tim asked. He seemed calmer now.

"To New York."

"Why?"

"Family business."

"You don't want to tell me?"

"Not really. It's none of your business. Eat your breakfast; I want you gone before Peter comes down."

He made a stab at the food. "How long will you be gone?"

"Through Christmas," she said.

"We'll have to talk about the finishing touches on the house."

"You can reach me on my cell phone," she said.

"I had hoped we could spend Christmas together," he said. "The three of us."

"Tim, there isn't going to be any three of us. Peter is visiting his father in New York."

"I thought his father was dead."

"That was his stepfather."

He looked puzzled. "Vance Calder wasn't Peter's father?"

"He was not."

"Then who is?"

"Please don't concern yourself with my private life," Arrington said. She stood up and put her dishes in the sink. "I have to finish packing now. We'll be leaving soon." She heard Peter coming down the stairs.

"Please leave quickly by the back door," she said, taking his half-eaten breakfast and scraping it into the garbage disposal.

"We'll talk tomorrow," he said, getting into his coat.

"Not unless it's something about the house," she replied.

He gave her an angry look, then he walked out the kitchen door.

Peter came into the kitchen. "What's for breakfast?" he asked. He was fifteen now, big and mature for his age.

"What would you like?"

"Oh, I'll just toast myself a muffin," he said, opening the fridge.

"Will you be ready to go in half an hour?" she asked.

"I'm ready to go now, but my muffin isn't."

"The crew has the airplane ready. Thirty minutes."

"I'm with you," he said.

"Peter, I'm sending you ahead alone," she said. "I have an appointment in Charlottesville, and it's going to take the whole day. The airplane will come back for me."

Peter shrugged. "Okay, I guess."

Arrington went back upstairs to close her cases. Everything was so good right now, except for this thing with Tim Rutledge. She would put an end to that over Christmas.

3

Stone spent the morning actually working. Since his elevation to full partnership at Woodman & Weld, and since his appointment to the boards of Strategic Services and Centurion Studios, he had been required to read—and even understand—every bit of financial paper sent to him by the law firm and by both companies, so that he could intelligently discuss them at meetings. Today, he and Mike Freeman, chairman and CEO of Strategic Services, who also served on the Centurion board, would be meeting Leo Goldman, Jr., the CEO of the studio appointed a year before, when Rick Barron, longtime head of the studio, retired and became merely chairman.

Stone had taken only one accounting course in college, and he thanked God that he had not slept through it. Soon he could read a balance sheet with the best of them.

He had a sandwich at his desk, anticipating the arrival of Arrington Calder and her son, Peter. He buzzed his secretary, Joan Robertson.

"Yes, master?"

"I'm going to have this little boy on my hands for the better part of two weeks," Stone said. "What the hell am I going to do with him? Children's theater? Museum of Natural History? Boats on the pond in Central Park?"

"How old is the boy?" she asked.

"Twelve, I think."

"Well, that lets out girls; he'll still hate them. How about South Street Seaport? Boys love sailing vessels."

"Good one," Stone said, making a note. "More."

"Ummm . . . Central Park Zoo?"

"Another good one. More."

"The Lion King?"

"Oh, God, I've been avoiding that for years."

"You'll love it, believe me. And that's enough for three or four days. I'll do some research. What are you doing for dinner tonight? Not Elaine's, I hope."

"Why not Elaine's? He might see a movie star, or something. Anyway, Dino is bringing Ben, who's just home from school for Christmas."

"Well, I wouldn't worry too much about what to do with him. After all, Arrington will be here, too, and she, at least, is accustomed to acting as a parent."

"Don't say 'parent,'" he said. "Hearing it gives me the willies. I'll be his host."

"You'll survive," she said, then hung up.

Stone finished his sandwich, frequently checking his watch. Arrington's Gulfstream III was due into Teterboro at noon, or so, and he had hired a driver and sent his car to meet them. So, he reckoned, they should be here about . . .

the upstairs doorbell rang . . . now. He took a deep breath, got into his jacket, and ran up the stairs to the front hall. One more deep breath, a big smile slapped on his face, and he opened the door.

A handsome young man stood there, wearing a tweed jacket and a necktie and holding a briefcase, the driver behind him with two more cases. What the hell?

"Uncle Stone?" the young man said.

"Peter? I wouldn't have recognized you! Come in! Is your mother still in the car?"

Peter stepped in and shucked off his overcoat. "No, sir," he said.

"Just put the cases on the elevator," Stone said to the driver. "Then put the car in the garage, and you're done." He pressed a fifty into the man's hand and closed the door.

"Now," he said to Peter. "What did you just say?"

Peter handed him a sealed envelope, the back of which was emblazoned with the words "Calder Hall."

"Come in, come in," Stone said to the boy. "Have a seat while I read this." He took a chair himself and tore open the envelope.

Stone, I'm sorry to tell you this at the last minute, but I had a bad day yesterday, and my doctor has put me into the hospital, where they're running some tests. I hope this is not a recurrence of the cancer, but I'll know soon. In the meantime, take good care of our boy, and remember, don't tell him anything. I'll be in touch.

**Fondly,
Arrington**

"I think mostly she's just tired, Uncle Stone," Peter said. "She said she'd call tomorrow."

Stone stuffed the envelope back into his pocket. "Well, I guess it's just you and me, then, Peter. And by the way, just call me Stone, okay? I'm not your uncle anyway."

Peter managed a smile. "All right, Stone."

"How old are you now?"

"Fifteen," Peter said.

"My God, I somehow thought you were twelve." He handed the boy the photograph of him.

"I was twelve when this was taken," he said.

"When did you turn fifteen?"

"Nearly a year ago. I'll be sixteen next month."

"Sixteen!" *My God*, he thought. *Has it been that long*?

"Yes, sir."

"And don't call me sir, either. Let's just be friends. How tall are you?"

"Five feet eleven and a half inches, si—Stone."

"That's tall for fifteen—er, sixteen—isn't it?"

"I think so. The doctor told me I'll be well over six feet."

"I expect you will. And your voice has already changed; you're a baritone."

"It happens, I guess. I sounded pretty funny for a while there."

"I expect you did. Did your mother

tell you I have a friend who's a policeman, Dino Bacchetti?"

"Yes."

"Well, Dino has a son who's . . . about
your age, and we're having dinner with
them tonight."

"At Elaine's?"

"Your mother told you about Elaine's?"

"She told me a *lot* about it. She said
it was her favorite place in New York."

"Is this your first visit to New York?"

"Yes, it is. My folks always left me at
home when they came here."

"I think you're going to like it," Stone
said. "Come on, let's go find your room."

They got onto the elevator, rode up
two floors, and entered the smallest
guest room, adjacent to Stone's master
suite. He hadn't wanted the boy to feel
lost in one of the bigger rooms.

"Have you had lunch?"

"Yes, they fed me on the airplane,"
he replied.

"What do you think of your mother's
new Gulfstream?"

"Wow!" Peter said.

"Exactly. Now, I have to go to a meeting with the new head of Centurion Stu-

dios in a few minutes. Why don't you get unpacked and watch some TV?"

"You're seeing Mr. Goldman? Stone, I'd like very much to meet him. May I come with you? I'm a film student."

Stone was taken aback, but what the hell? Goldman couldn't object to meeting the son of Vance Calder, his studio's greatest star. "Of course, Peter. I'll be glad to have you come along. Go ahead and get settled, then come down to my office, on the bottom floor. We're due at Centurion's New York office in forty-five minutes."

"I'll be down in fifteen," Peter said, unsnapping a suitcase and starting to hang up jackets and suits.

Stone went back to his office, shaking his head. What a shock! The kid was nearly a man in both appearance and manner!

4

Stone and Peter arrived at Centurion's Fifth Avenue offices on time. Peter was carrying a slim leather envelope-style briefcase, and Stone wondered what was in it. They were asked to wait for a moment while Leo Goldman finished a conference call to the coast.

"You're a film student?" Stone asked Peter. "In high school?"

"We have only one film class at school, so perhaps I should have said, 'student of film.'"

"I see. What part of film most interests you?"

"I want to direct," Peter replied.

Of course, Stone thought. Everybody wants to direct. "Good," he said.

"Mr. Goldman will see you now," the secretary said, just as Mike Freeman walked in.

"Sorry I'm late," he said, shaking hands with Stone.

"We had a short wait anyway," Stone replied. "Mike, this is Peter, Arrington's son."

"Of course," Mike said, shaking the boy's hand. "I heard a lot about you from your mother on a flight across the country in her new airplane."

"Yes, she told me you helped her find and buy it," Peter said.

They walked into a large square room, which was decorated with abstract paintings. Leo Goldman, Jr., rose from his chair and pumped everybody's hand. He was short, stocky, and balding, and he waved an unlit cigar when he talked.

"And this is my friend Peter," Stone said. For some reason, he didn't mention Peter's last name. He wasn't sure why.

"Good to see you, Stone, Mike. And Peter, I'm very glad to know you."

Peter nodded and managed a shy smile.

"Peter is a student of film," Stone said, "and he wanted to meet you."

"Yes, Mr. Goldman," Peter said, "I'm an admirer of your work as a producer, particularly *Chain Letter*."

Goldman looked surprised. "Well, Peter, you have an eye for quality, but perhaps not for commercial success. That one was my worst turkey."

"Oh, I liked *Blast*, too," Peter said. "And I liked your father's work when he was running Centurion."

Goldman roared. "That's more like it. Let's sit." He waved them to a round conference table in a corner, and after a few pleasantries, Goldman launched into a description of his first year at the helm, covering grosses and expenses along the way. He talked nonstop for forty minutes, also covering his production plans for the coming year and a number of TV pilots that were currently in production. "Any questions?" he asked when he was done.

"Not from me," Stone said. "I think you've covered everything I could have asked."

"That goes for me, too," Mike Freeman replied.

"May I ask a question?" Peter said, half raising his hand.

The three men stared at him.

"Of course, Peter," Goldman said.

"I noticed that three of the new productions that you've mentioned are budgeted at between seventy and eighty million dollars, whereas in the past Centurion has always kept its budgets in the fifty-million-dollar range. Why the increase?"

Goldman blinked. "You've been reading the annual reports, haven't you?"

"I read everything about Centurion," Peter said. "It interests me."

"Well, there are three things that have increased these budgets: creeping rises in general costs, which are inevitable; increased salaries for the stars of those films, who are all hot young actors; and the fact that all three of those pictures are action-based and shot on location,

instead of just ordinary in-studio productions."

"Do you think the grosses will justify
the increases in budgets?" Peter asked.

"I think the grosses will *more* than
justify the increases," Goldman said,
"and if I'm wrong, I'll be answering to
Stone, Mike, and the other directors this
time next year."

"Thank you," Peter said.

"Anything else, gentlemen? Peter?"

All three shook their heads. "We'll let
you get back to work, Leo," Stone said,
rising.

As they took their leave, pausing at
the office door to shake hands, Peter
spoke up again. "Mr. Goldman, I hope
this isn't an imposition, but I wonder if I
could ask your opinion about something
I'm working on."

"Sure, Peter. What are you working
on?"

Peter opened his leather envelope
and handed Goldman a bound sheaf of
papers and a DVD. "I'm making a film
at school, and this is the script and a
recording of the seventy minutes I've

already shot. I'd appreciate it very much if you could find time to take a look at it and let me know what you think. I could use some expert advice."

Goldman received the script and the disc. "Where can I get in touch with you?"

"At Stone's, for the next two weeks," Peter replied.

"I'll be in touch," Goldman said.

The three left the building, and Peter did some window-shopping while Stone and Mike talked.

"How old is that kid?" Mike asked.

"Fifteen, going on sixteen."

"Going on forty," Mike said. "He certainly knows how to take advantage of an opportunity, and he has charm, too. Have you looked at his script or the recording?"

Stone shook his head. "I knew nothing about it. He asked if he could come to our meeting, said he was a student of film, but no more than that."

Mike shook his head and laughed. "He's got enough chutzpah for the film business."

"He certainly does," Stone said. "And I'm still getting over the fact that he's not the twelve-year-old I was expecting."

"He took in every word of Leo's briefing, too, and asked good questions that neither you nor I thought of."

"Embarrassing, wasn't it?" They both laughed, then said good-bye and departed in opposite directions.

Stone and Peter strolled down Fifth Avenue together through the throngs of shoppers. They passed the Christmas tree in Rockefeller Plaza.

"That's nice," Peter said. "I've seen it on TV."

"Yes, it is."

"I hope I didn't speak out of turn at the meeting," Peter said.

"Not at all, Peter. Mike and I were impressed with your understanding of what Leo was saying. We both completely missed the budget increases, which I'm sure is what Leo intended."

Peter laughed aloud. "I'll bet he did, too."

"What grade are you in now?"

"Well," Peter said, "that's kind of problematical."

"Oh? You aren't about to get booted out, are you?"

"Oh, no!" Peter said, looking shocked.

"Only joking," Stone said.

Peter looked relieved. "It's just that I've been on sort of a special program of courses," he said. "And it looks like I'll be graduating in June."

Stone blinked. "At fifteen?"

"I'll be sixteen. I know it's unusual, but the school said they thought the accelerated program was the best way to keep me interested."

"Were they right?"

"Oh, yes; it's been great!"

Stone wondered how he was going to keep this kid interested for two weeks.

When they arrived back at the house Stone took Peter in through the office entrance and introduced him to Joan.

"I'm very glad to meet you, Peter," she said. "Funny, I was expecting someone younger." She shot a glance at Stone, who rolled his eyes.

"Stone, your client Herbert Fisher is waiting to see you," she said.

Stone sighed. "Come on, Peter," he said. "I'll introduce you to a New York character." He led the way to his office.

5

Stone introduced Peter to Herbie Fisher. "Peter, I have some business to discuss with Herbie. Why don't you go upstairs and get unpacked? We'll leave for dinner at eight-fifteen."

"All right," Peter said, and ran up the stairs.

Stone turned and looked at Herbie. "What's going on, Herbie?" he asked. "You look kind of soggy."

"That's because I went for a swim in New York Harbor."

"In December?"

"It wasn't exactly my choice."

Stone went into the little bathroom off his office, got a towel, returned and handed it to Herbie. "Have a seat and tell me about it."

Herbie took off his sodden overcoat, draped it over a chair, and sat down, running the towel over his hair. "Well, I went on a singles lunchtime cruise," he said.

"They do cruises in December?"

"Singles don't care if it's cold; it's warm inside the yacht."

"Yacht?"

"These are expensive cruises. They use a seventy-foot yacht, and they serve a good lunch and wine. It's two hundred fifty a head."

"Sounds profitable. Any likely women?"

"Yes, a number."

"So why did you decide to get off before the yacht reached the dock?"

"There was an altercation," Herbie said.

"What started it?"

"There were these two guys, dressed well, but kind of beefy. They had knives."

"For this they charge two-fifty a head?" Stone asked.

"I don't know what they were doing there. Well, no, that's wrong; I have a very good idea what they were doing there."

"Which was?"

"Stephanie."

Stephanie was Herbie's sort of ex-wife. She and her brother had, according to news reports, stolen nearly a billion dollars from their father's asset management firm and skipped to a Pacific island nation with no extradition treaty.

"She sent me some divorce papers a couple of times, but I just threw them away," Herbie said.

"Never a good idea to throw away legal documents," Stone pointed out. "Then what?"

"I was standing near the rear of the yacht's saloon, talking to a girl, and these two guys appeared and said they needed to talk to me. They shoved me out on the afterdeck, and one of them said, 'You should have signed the papers.' Then both of them produced switchblades."

"And how did you handle that?" Stone asked, fascinated now.

"I thought about it for about a nano-second," Herbie said, "and then I decided that there was no way to handle it that didn't involve a lot of spilled blood, and it was my blood in question, so I ran for the rail. I jumped on a rear cockpit seat running, then just took a long leap."

"And where was the yacht at this time?"

"Out near the Statue of Liberty," Herbie replied.

"I suppose the two guys didn't follow you into the water?"

"No, it was really, really cold. I made for Lady Liberty."

"Wearing an overcoat?"

"I thought it would get even colder if I took it off. I swam like hell, and I was beginning to get pretty tired when my feet touched bottom. I waded the rest of the way. There was a dock with a ladder, so I climbed up that. I found a men's room and turned on the heated hand-dryer thing, you know?"

"Yes, I've met many of them."

"I dried my clothes a little and got warm, then I went back outside and mingled with the tourists, who were boarding the ferry for the return trip. Nobody asked me for a ticket."

"I guess they're unaccustomed to selling tickets to patrons who arrived at the statue under their own steam."

"Yeah. When I got ashore I took a cab here."

"Why, Herbie? What would you like me to do?"

"I would like to be divorced," Herbie replied. "Will you handle that for me?"

Herbie had won the lottery a couple of years before, and he had paid Stone a million-dollar retainer to handle all his legal affairs, and not a few of his personal problems.

"Of course," Stone said. "Maybe the best way to start would be to send me the papers Stephanie asked you to sign. Do you still have them?"

"Yeah, they're somewhere in my apartment."

"Well, grab a cab, go home, get out of those clothes, take a nice hot bath with a glass of brandy floating in it, and when the brandy is all gone, get out of the tub and fax me the papers."

"That's the best advice I've had all day," Herbie said. With some difficulty he got into the sodden overcoat, and Stone walked him to the door.

"And, Herbie," Stone said, "don't let anybody you don't know into your apartment. Tell the doorman to be on the lookout for strangers who want to see you, and don't hesitate to call the police if the two guys show up."

Herbie nodded and ran for a cab.

Stone stepped into Joan's office. "Herbie just took a dip in New York Harbor," he said.

"He told me."

"How much of Herbie's retainer is left?"

"About half a million dollars," she said.

"I don't suppose we can just write him a check."

"Yeah, sure."

"He's faxing over some divorce papers from Stephanie."

"I'll bring them to you when they come."

Stone nodded and went to his desk. He returned some phone calls, and then Joan buzzed him.

"Herbie's on the phone," she said. "I'll bring in the papers."

Stone picked up the phone. "The fax just arrived, Herbie."

"I know, I just sent it."

Stone took the papers from Joan. "Hang on while I take a quick look through them." He did so. "Okay, they're pretty standard. She wants you to admit to adultery and agree to a divorce."

"Adultery? I didn't do any adultery."

"It doesn't matter. New York is the last state with no-fault divorce; it has to be for cause, the usual choices being adultery, cruelty, or mental cruelty. There's a move afoot in the state legislature to change that, but it hasn't happened yet."

"How about stealing a billion dollars and running?" Herbie asked. "Is that a good enough cause?"

Stone thought about it. "Well, it wasn't your billion dollars, was it? I'm not sure if stealing somebody else's billion dollars is grounds for divorce."

"It's gotta be," Herbie said. "I mean, if she had stuck up a liquor store and had gone to prison for it, wouldn't that be grounds?"

"Yes, I suppose so, but, Herbie, if you want the quick way out of this, it's to just sign the papers, and it will soon be over."

"I'm not having it said in the papers that I committed adultery."

"All right, how about this? I'll draw up a petition for divorce claiming that she's the adulterer. You can sue her, instead of the other way around."

"I like that better," Herbie said.

"Wait a minute, she's still on the Pacific island, isn't she?"

"As far as I know."

"Then it would be very difficult to serve her with the papers. Let me call her lawyer and see if we can work out something."

"Stone, what about the division of property?"

"Well, you're both entitled to equitable division of your assets, but you were only married for a couple of months before she left, the property you each owned before the marriage is exempt, and neither of you would have had time to accumulate much in the way of assets during the marriage."

"How about the billion dollars she stole? That was accumulated during the marriage, so isn't it a marital asset?"

"Well, now I'm stumped, Herbie. I think there would be a lot of problems with that. First of all, she's obviously put the money out of reach of the government or anybody else, so even if we won the case, you'd never be able to seize the assets."

"Maybe not, but it would be fun to win it."

"It would be an expensive process, Herbie."

"I still have a big credit with you, don't I?"

"It would be throwing good money after bad."

"But satisfying."

"Herbie, let me talk to her attorney and see what we can work out. I'll get back to you after Christmas."

"Why after Christmas? How long could it take?"

"People have a way of disappearing from their offices around the holidays, and I've got houseguests on my hands. You met one of them this morning."

"Well, okay."

"I'll speak to you after New Year's."

"Wait a minute, you said after Christmas."

"Nobody's back in the office until after New Year's. It's just a fact of life, Herbie. Bye-bye and Merry Christmas," Stone said cheerfully, then hung up before he got a response.

Joan was leaning against the doorjamb, laughing.

"Oh, shut up," Stone said.

"And Merry Christmas to you, too!" she said, and went back to her office.

6

Stone and Peter arrived at Elaine's slightly before Dino and Ben, so they had a good view of the boys as they entered. Ben was dressed in black leather jeans and a jacket and a black T-shirt. What appeared to Stone to be some sort of satanic symbol hung from a chain around the boy's neck. Like his father, Ben was of slight stature, but wiry. Introductions were made, and the boys shook hands solemnly, if not warily. They all sat down.

Ben gazed across the table at Peter's tweed jacket and necktie. "You always dress like that?" he asked. "Or just when trying to impress adults?"

"Most of the time," Peter replied, glancing at a menu. "The girls seem to like it."

Stone and Dino exchanged a glance and rolled their eyes.

"I'm staying out of this," Dino said.

"As am I," Stone replied.

Peter nodded at the metallic object on the chain around Ben's neck. "Isn't that the Egyptian symbol for sexual impotence? Why are you advertising?"

Ben laughed in spite of himself. "He's cool," he said to Stone.

Stone and Dino stopped laughing long enough to order booze for themselves and sodas for the boys. Ben and Peter launched into a comparison of their schools and the girls available at each. They agreed that there was a dearth of such companionship, just as their respective headmasters had intended.

"I'm getting out in June," Ben said.

"So am I," Peter replied.

"What are your plans, college?"

"Not yet," Peter said. "I have a plan, though."

"Something you don't want them to know about?" Ben asked, nodding at Stone and Dino.

"Pretty much."

"Come with me," Ben said. He got up and went to the bar, carrying his soda, and Peter followed. They entered into an intense conversation.

"Maybe this was a good idea," Dino said.

"I think it was," Stone said. He told Dino about their afternoon and the meeting with Leo Goldman, Jr.

"So the kid's graduating from high school at sixteen? And I thought Ben's getting out at eighteen was pretty good."

"It is, Dino."

"Trouble is, I don't know if he's mature enough to handle college. I'd like him to do something else for a year, but he's not ready to be shipped off to Europe, either. What's Peter going to do?"

"I haven't the faintest idea," Stone said, "but I think he's telling Ben right now. Maybe he'll get around to telling me later."

"Where's Arrington?"

"In the hospital."

"Not the cancer thing again, I hope."

"She doesn't seem to be sure; they're running tests. She's supposed to call me tomorrow."

"She looked fine a year ago in L.A."

"She sure did. Peter thinks she's just tired. She's been building her new house in Virginia, and that's hard work, even if you're not wielding a hammer."

"I guess."

The two boys returned to the table and looked at the menu. "What's osso buco?" Peter asked.

"Try it; you won't be sorry."

"Whatever you say, Stone."

Ben spoke up. "It's an animal leg with sauce. I'll have it, too, Pop."

"How many times I have to tell you," Dino said, "don't call me 'Pop.'"

"What's the matter with that?" Stone asked.

"It's what I called my old man."

"Oh, okay." He looked at Ben and shrugged.

Their food arrived and dinner continued with two different conversations going on: one between Stone and Dino, the other between the two boys, who seemed to be speaking in code.

"You want a date tomorrow night?" Ben asked Peter, suddenly breaking into English. "My girl's got a hot friend."

"Sure," Peter said.

"We'd better wait until we hear from your mother tomorrow," Stone said. "She may have plans for us."

"Okay," Peter said. "Can I call you tomorrow, Ben?"

"Yeah, sure. I'm staying at the old man's."

"Don't call me 'the old man' either," Dino said.

"I'm running out of names," Ben said. "How about Pater?"

"Not unless you want a fat lip."

"How about 'hey you'?"

"That's better than Pater, but still not good enough for you to get money out of me for a date tomorrow night."

"Gee, Dad, thanks! I didn't know you knew I was broke."

"You're always broke," Dino said.

"Can I have the car?"

"Take the subway; you can't afford to park, and I'm not having my car towed."

"Awright, awright, Dad."

Stone spoke up. "And you might remember that neither of you is of drinking age."

On the way home in the cab Peter talked excitedly about Ben. "He's really a great guy, in spite of the bluster."

"I'm glad to hear it. Actually, he's a lot like Dino."

"I guess he would be, wouldn't he?"

They arrived at the house, and Stone went to his study to check the answering machine for messages, while Peter wandered around the room, looking at books and objects. Stone was writing down a message when he looked up and saw Peter holding a framed photograph of Stone's father, staring at it intently. He put the phone down.

"Who's this?" Peter asked.

"That's my father," Stone said.

"Funny," Peter replied, "he looks very familiar." He sank into a wing chair across from Stone.

Stone steeled himself; he knew the question that was coming, and he didn't want to answer it. "So what's this plan of yours for after you graduate?"

"It's like this," Peter said. "I know I can handle the courses in college, but at sixteen, I'm not ready to be in a freshman class where everybody is two or three years older than I am." He paused. "For one thing, no attractive girl is going to give me the time of day."

"That's an interesting observation," Stone replied. "Have you considered an alternative?"

"Yes. There's a prep school on the Upper East Side of Manhattan called Knickerbocker Hall."

"I've heard of it, of course," Stone said. "What attracts you to it?"

"It's performing-arts oriented, and they have a good film school," Peter said. "I could study film, then, in two years, I could enter a good university as a junior."

"You'll still be only eighteen," Stone pointed out.

"Yes, but I'll look older. I'll have

achieved my full height by then and filled out some, and I'm already shaving. I'll lie about my age to the kids at Knickerbocker, though the administration will know my age, of course, and I'll continue to do that in college."

"Have you given any thought to where you want to go to college?"

"I think I'll want to go to the Yale Drama School."

"Are you interested in acting?"

"No, but I'm interested in actors, because that's who I want to work with. And they have a director's program. I already know a lot about film, but I want to learn about the theater, too."

"That sounds like a very good plan to me. Do you think your mother will let you go to a boarding school in New York?"

"Knickerbocker isn't a boarding school," Peter replied, then sat silently while he let that sink in.

Stone got it almost at once. "Well," he said, "I've got plenty of room here."

"Thank you," Peter said. "I was hoping you'd say that."

"You knew I would, didn't you?"

"Not until just a moment ago," Peter replied. He held up the photograph of Stone's father. "When I saw this."

Stone took a deep breath. "Do you have any questions, Peter?"

"All my questions have been answered," Peter said, "some of which I've been asking myself for a long time."

"Has your mother talked to you about this?"

"No, and if I got too close to the question, she adroitly changed the subject. Did she make you promise not to tell me?"

"Yes."

"Well, you haven't," Peter said. "I suppose you could say my grandfather told me." He looked at the photograph again. "I wish I had known him."

"So do I," Stone said. "You two would have gotten along famously. You'd have liked your grandmother, too. She was a painter; I expect you got your artistic bent from her."

"There's something else," Peter said.

"What's that?"

"I want to legally change my name to Barrington, for a number of reasons."

Stone blinked. "What are your reasons?"

"We've just talked about the first one, but from the time I entered boarding school I've been very uncomfortable with the name Calder. I've learned not to like being the son of so famous a movie star. When they know that, it colors every conversation, warps every friendship. I don't want to go through my life that way, especially in film school or in the film business."

"Your reasons are sound," Stone said, "but you're going to have to talk with your mother about all this."

"Will you help me out with that?"

"No, I'm new in your life, but you have a close relationship with your mother. I'll sit silently and listen, if moral support will help."

"I'll figure it out when she gets here," Peter said. "One other thing: I'm not comfortable with either Pop or Pater, so it will have to be Dad."

Stone laughed. "I can live with that."

Stone walked Peter up to his room,

and they hugged briefly, then parted for the night.

Stone lay in bed feeling, suddenly, like a different person.

7

Stone was still in bed, having breakfast and reading the *Times*, when Peter knocked and came into his room.

"Good morning," Stone said. "I thought you'd be sleeping late."

"I rarely sleep late," Peter said. "I've already edited a scene of my film on my laptop."

"That's industrious. Would you like some breakfast?"

"I found the kitchen, and Helene made me some scrambled eggs." Peter looked at the four paintings of New York scenes on Stone's bedroom wall. "I like these pictures," he said.

"They were painted by your grand-mother," Stone replied. "She has work in the Metropolitan Museum, too, in the American Collection."

"I'm impressed," Peter said, looking at them more closely.

"What would you like to do today?"

"I just talked to Ben. There's a heist-film festival at some place called the Film Forum—*The Killers, The Asphalt Jungle,* like that. I thought we'd get in two or three this afternoon. Ben has never seen anything older than *Finding Nemo.*"

Stone laughed. "You can educate him."

"Don't worry," Peter said, "he'll love it. He'll end up watching them on his cell phone. Mom won't let me have a cell phone; she says I'd be talking on it all the time, instead of working or study-ing."

"Mothers are like that," Stone said.

"I'd better get back to work," the boy said, then left.

Stone picked up the phone and buzzed Joan.

"Yes, boss?"

"Will you go up to the Apple Store on Fifth at Fifty-ninth Street and buy an iPhone and an iPad, the high-end models?"

"But you already have those things," Joan said.

"Yeah, but Peter doesn't, and it's his birthday soon."

"Oh, sure."

"Sign him up in the name of Peter Barrington, and make his age eighteen on the application, so there won't be any problem. Use this house for his address and put it all on my Amex card."

"Will do."

"And get him some accessories, too; you know the sort of thing, and get it all gift wrapped."

"I'm on it. Hang on, the phone's ringing." She put him on hold and then came back. "It's Seth Keener, Stephanie Fisher's attorney."

"Got it," Stone said. (He picked up the other line.) "Mr. Keener? Stone Barrington. I'm attorney to Herbert Fisher."

"Oh, good," Keener said. "Has he signed the papers?"

"No, and he's not going to."

"He wants to stay married to Stephanie?"

"He doesn't want that, either, but he's not going on record as an adulterer."

"Name his poison: Cruelty? Mental cruelty?"

"Mr. Fisher will be the complainant and the cause will be abandonment—on her part. I don't think she can argue with that."

Keener sighed. "I'll put it to her."

"Are you in immediate touch with her?"

"I can't comment on that—attorney-client privilege."

"I suppose that applies, especially if she's a fugitive from justice."

"I'll ignore that. Send me the paperwork, and I'll have a go. See you."

"Just a minute, we're not finished," Stone said. "There's the issue of a financial settlement."

"Oh? What's Mr. Fisher offering?"

"He's offering nothing," Stone replied. "What will Mrs. Fisher offer?"

"Are you kidding?"

"Certainly not. I believe we're both aware that Mrs. Fisher acquired substantial assets during the marriage. Whereas Mr. Fisher did not."

"If you're talking about those nasty press reports of her looting the family firm, that's all nonsense."

"Then why is she on the FBI's most-wanted list, along with her brother?"

"You know I can't discuss that."

Stone suddenly had an idea. "We can avoid discussing that in court if Mrs. Fisher would be amenable to sharing some of her premarital assets instead."

"What did you have in mind, exactly?" Keener asked warily.

"Well, I'm informed that Mrs. Fisher had a substantial account at her father's firm. She won't be needing that."

"That's outrageous!" Keener said.

"So is running off with the piggy bank," Stone replied. "If you give it some thought, I think you'll see that this is an easy way out for her."

"Send me the papers," Keener said.

"There is the problem of service,"

Stone said. "Can you accept service on her behalf?"

"Yes."

"It will be done." Both men hung up, and Stone buzzed Joan. "Print out a boilerplate divorce document with Herbie as the complainant and the cause as abandonment by Stephanie, contingent on an agreed settlement, then messenger it over to Keener."

"Will do."

Stone went back to his crossword, but almost immediately, Joan buzzed him again.

"Arrington on line one."

Stone picked it up. "Good morning. How are you feeling?"

"Much better," she said. "It was just an infection, not a recurrence, so an antibiotic fixed everything. I'll be arriving late this afternoon. Can you have your car meet me?"

"Of course. What time?"

"Five o'clock?"

"You can avoid rush hour if you land at three."

"Good point. I guess I can do that. How are you and Peter getting along?"

"Famously." Stone told her about the meeting at Centurion.

"The little devil!"

"Not so little; you should have warned me."

"You didn't tell him anything, did you?"

"Not a word," Stone said. "He told me."

"What!"

"He picked up the photograph of my father in my study, and it was all over. I answered a few questions, but he's still going to want to hear from you."

"Oh, God," she said. "I've dreaded this."

"Everybody's very impressed with him, especially his maturity," Stone said.

"I know, I know. He taught himself to read at three, and by four he was speaking like an adult, in complete paragraphs. He was just astonishing; he still is."

"I'll go along with that."

"You have to remember, Stone, that although he speaks like an adult, he's still only sixteen years old, next month, and in many ways, that's his emotional age."

"I haven't seen a single sign of that," Stone said.

"It will come up, believe me."

"You didn't tell me he was about to have a birthday."

"I apologize; that was a lapse on my part. Do you want to know what to get him for a present?"

"That's already taken care of."

"Oh, good. All right, I'll see you late this afternoon."

"Where would you like to have dinner?"

"Did you and Peter dine at Elaine's last night?"

"Yes, with Dino and Ben. He and Peter are going to the movies this afternoon."

"Then let's go to the Four Seasons."

"I'll have Joan book it. Eight o'clock?"

"All right. Bye-bye." She hung up.

Stone gave Joan her instructions.

"All right, I'll get the i-stuff on my lunch hour."

"You can still take a lunch hour," Stone said. "Tell the Woodman & Weld

operator to pick up." They had a telephone arrangement with the law firm so
that Stone could be called there, and
the caller patched through to his home
office or a message taken.

Stone hung up and started on the
crossword.

8

Stone was at his desk at mid-afternoon when Joan buzzed.

"Seth Keener on one."

Stone picked up. "Yes, Seth?"

"My client has agreed to accept Mr. Fisher's terms."

"Good. When can I expect the paperwork back for his signature?"

"Will you accept a fax?"

"Does she have access to a color fax?"

"Possibly."

"Have her sign in blue ink and fax without a heading, then FedEx the orig-

inals. What is her proposal for a settlement?"

"She has a little over three million in
her account at the family firm."

"I think he might accept that."

"She's willing, but the account is frozen. He'll have to wait until the feds un-
freeze it."

"And that will be about the same day
as Antarctica unfreezes."

"If you say so. She has no other assets available. I'm sure Mr. Fisher
wouldn't want . . . questionable assets."
He paused. "There is another possibility, but we'll have to go off the record."

Stone pressed the record button on
his phone. "What is her proposal?"

"She's willing to backdate a transfer
of her assets to a date before her departure of the country."

"That would be felonious. Let's go
back on the record."

"All right."

"What is the family firm's position? I
would be surprised if they or their insurance company haven't made a pass at
that account."

"I'm looking at a printout from online,"

Keener said. "There's no notation to that effect. I'll e-mail you the user name and password when we receive Mr. Fisher's signed documents."

"Is there a notation from the feds?"

"Yes, from the U.S. Attorney for the Southern District of New York."

"I'm willing to recommend to my client that he accept the account as full settlement in the divorce."

"With a notation mentioning the federal freeze order, of course."

"Yes."

"All right, send me an addendum to the divorce complaint and I'll get it taken care of."

"Right," Stone said, and hung up. He buzzed Joan and dictated the addendum. "And get me Herbie," he said.

Herbie came on the line. "Yes, Stone?"

"I hope you didn't catch cold."

"No, your suggestion of the hot bath and the brandy worked very well."

"I have a proposal from Stephanie's attorney."

"Shoot."

"She'll agree to the divorce with her abandonment as the cause, and she'll sign over to you her account at the family firm, which amounts to three million dollars."

"Really?"

"There's a catch: the feds have frozen the account."

"Any chance it will ever be unfrozen?"

"Slim and none, but I can have a go, and the best part is, you win. That will look just fine in the papers, if it makes the papers."

"I like that," Herbie said. "Send me the documents."

"Will do." Stone hung up and buzzed Joan. "Have you noticed Herbie becoming more sane?" he asked.

"Maybe it's a prolonged lucid interval," she replied. "He does seem more together."

"Do you have any idea why?"

"I don't think I'm supposed to tell you this, but he's been going to law school for the past three years."

Stone was astonished. "But he already has that bogus Internet law degree, and he ostensibly passed the bar exam."

"I think he feels guilty about that, and

after all, what else would he do with his days? It's not like he works for a living."

"You have a point." The doorbell rang. Stone hung up and ran upstairs and opened the door. Arrington stood there, looking sharp in a Chanel suit with a gorgeous sable coat over her shoulders. They embraced and Stone sent her luggage up to the master suite.

"You look wonderful," he said, helping her out of her coat and hanging it in the hall closet.

"I don't know about the master suite," she said. "Maybe I should sleep in a guest room."

Stone thought about that. "It's up to you," he said, "but I wouldn't enjoy sneaking around."

"All right, since Peter knows, anyway."

"Good." He took her upstairs and got out a couple of luggage racks for her bags.

"I'd like a nap," she said. "Alone."

"Of course. Get unpacked and relax; I have work to do anyway." He kissed her and left her alone.

Joan was buzzing him as he got back to his office. "Leo Goldman on one."

Stone picked up. "Hello, Leo. Are you back in L.A.?"

"I'm on the Centurion jet," Leo replied. "Listen, how old is Arrington's kid?"

Stone thought for a fraction of a second. "He just turned eighteen."

"Good," Leo said.

"Why?"

"If he's eighteen, he can sign a contract."

"A contract for what?"

"I want to buy his movie."

Stone had forgotten about Peter's submission. "Why?"

"Because it's better than anything indie I saw at the Sundance Film Festival last year."

"Leo, is Peter's name written anywhere on the material he gave you?"

"Ah, no; there's no title page."

"Leo, this is what I want you to do: the moment you're back in L.A. I want you to FedEx that script and the DVD back to me, and I want you never to mention it to *anybody* until I give you the okay."

"But, Stone, it's *good*! One might even say brilliant—at least one would if one knew it was written and directed by an eighteen-year-old."

"It's complicated, Leo, and believe me, you don't want to piss off his mother. She is, after all, Centurion's largest stockholder. I want your word."

"As long as I have your word to see the finished product before anyone else in the business."

"You have it," Stone replied.

"Done. You'll have it back tomorrow."

"And you won't keep a copy, Leo."

"I give you my word on that, too."

"Thanks, Leo. I'll look forward to receiving it tomorrow."

"Bye, Stone." Leo sounded very disappointed.

Stone tried not to think what would happen if word got around L.A. that a sixteen-year-old boy, ostensibly the son of a huge movie star, had written and directed a feature film. The thought of the aftermath made sweat pop out on his brow.

9

Stone woke Arrington with a light kiss on the lips.

"What time is it?"

"You have an hour and a half until dinner," Stone said. "Peter just got home from the movies, and he's showering."

She sat up. "I think I'd better do that, too. It will wake me up."

"Are you sure you're feeling all right?"

"Oh, yes, I was just tired from the trip. I'm feeling much better after my nap." She got up and began unpacking her bags and putting her clothes in the second dressing room. "Is there anything I should know about your conversations with Peter before we sit down to dinner?"

"Yes. I got him an iPhone for his birthday, which I know is against your wishes, but there will be a condition that he leave it with you when he returns to school in January. I'd like him to have it while he's in New York."

"I suppose that's a good idea. Is there anything else I should know?"

"Peter has some ideas about his future, but I think you should hear them from him."

"Anything that will give me a heart attack?"

Stone laughed. "I doubt it, and I think you should hear him out."

"Peter can be very persuasive," Arrington said, slipping out of her suit and hanging it up.

"You've lost some weight," he commented.

"Yes, I've been trying."

"You look very elegant."

She slipped off her underwear and tossed it into the hamper, then came and put her arms around him. "I hope I haven't lost anything you liked."

He caressed her ass and her breasts. "Nope, it's all still there."

She kissed him. "You can explore later," she said, then went into her bathroom to run a tub.

They walked up the stairs into the Four Seasons restaurant and checked in at the desk.

"Is this the power lunch place?" Peter asked, looking around.

Stone thought he looked very handsome in his blue suit. "Yes, right over there, in the Grill Room. We're dining in the Pool Room."

"They play pool here?"

"No, they *have* a pool." They were led to a table at poolside. Stone ordered champagne for Arrington and himself and Peter asked for fizzy water and was brought San Pellegrino.

When the champagne came, Stone raised his glass. "Happy birthday, Peter." He nodded to the captain, who brought over two gift-wrapped boxes. "The smaller one is from your mother."

"But she already gave me my laptop," Peter said.

"It's a second gift," Arrington said, "and it has strings attached."

Peter ripped off the paper. "Wow!" he said. "You're letting me have a phone?"

"The strings are: you leave it with me when you return to school."

"Oh," he said, looking disappointed. He opened the other box. "An iPad! Wonderful." He switched it on.

"It will need charging," Stone said. "Leave it until later."

Peter put the gifts back into their boxes, and a waiter took away the tattered wrappings. Peter looked at them both. "Thank you so much," he said. "I think you two should get married," he added.

Arrington put her face in her hands. "Oh, God!"

"You need to edit your thoughts before speaking, Peter," Stone said.

Arrington took her hands away. "You certainly do, young man. My marital status is not at your disposal; in fact it's none of your business."

"Yes, it is," Peter replied. "It will make me happy."

"You're already happy," she said. "Stone and I will make any decisions about our personal lives without your further input. Is that clear?"

"Yes, ma'am," he said, but not sheepishly. "Oh, and I want to change my name."

Arrington looked at him, baffled. "What's wrong with Peter? It's a very nice name."

"No, I want to change Calder to Barrington."

She stared at him, speechless.

"You don't know what I've had to go through at school for having a movie star for a father. I don't want to hear that at my next school."

Arrington's face became sympathetic. "Oh, I'm sorry, Peter, I didn't know."

"It wasn't so bad in L.A., because lots of kids had movie people for parents, but in Virginia it's very, very different."

Arrington thought about it for a moment, then turned toward Stone. "What do you think about this?"

"I wouldn't be in the least displeased," Stone replied.

"Do you think he's old enough to make that decision?"

"It's your decision, really," Stone said, "but it needs to be decided, one way or the other, before he gets any older."

"What would we tell them at the school?" Arrington asked Peter.

"That we're changing my name from my stepfather's to my father's."

"I suppose that's accurate," she said.

"I would be a lot more comfortable in myself," Peter said.

She looked at her son, then at Stone. "How can I object?"

"Welcome to the Barrington family, Peter," Stone said, "such as it is. You and I are the only living members."

"Thank you, Dad," Peter said.

"He never called Vance that," Arrington said.

"He asked me to call him Vance," Peter said.

"Yes, he did," she admitted. "I wondered why he did that."

"Because he knew something I didn't," Peter said.

The captain came with menus, and the subject was put aside while they ordered. Then, when the menus had been taken away, Peter said, "Next subject: my new school."

"Oh?" Arrington said. "What about it?"

"I want it to be Knickerbocker Hall."

"That has a familiar ring," she said. "Where is it?"

"Right here, in New York," Peter said. "On the Upper East Side."

"A boarding school on the Upper East Side?"

"It's not a boarding school," Peter pointed out.

Stone intervened. "Peter now has a home in New York," he said.

Arrington was looking back and forth between them, her brow furrowed.

"It has a performing arts program, including a film school. I want to do college-level work there and then go to Yale Drama School."

"Was this your idea?" she asked Stone.

"Only the part about his living with me while he's in school. The rest is entirely his; I didn't know about Knickerbocker."

"Let me think about it," Arrington said.

"And I want to be eighteen," Peter said.

"You will be, in two years," his mother pointed out.

"I mean, when I go to Knickerbocker, I want them to think I'm eighteen. I don't want to be the only sixteen-year-old among a bunch of eighteen-year-olds."

Arrington looked at Stone questioningly.

"I think he can pull it off," Stone said. "Look at him; listen to him. I don't know any eighteen-year-olds that grown up."

"But I would miss sixteen and seventeen," Arrington said, plaintively.

"I wouldn't miss them," Peter said.

They put all this aside and dined well. When they had finished their entrees and ordered dessert, Arrington sighed deeply. "All right, I agree," she said.

"Agree to which things?" Peter asked.

"All of them. You're Peter Barrington,

you're eighteen, and you can go to Knickerbocker what's-its-name."

"Hall," Peter said.

"And to Yale, too. That's assuming you can get into these places."

"I can," Peter said.

"He never lacked confidence," she said to Stone.

"Sometimes confidence is justified," Stone said.

They had a birthday cake for dessert. It had eighteen candles.

10

Stone woke the following morning with someone fondling his crotch. "Is that you?" he asked.

"It had better be," Arrington replied. "And it seems to be working."

"I can vouch for that," he said.

She climbed onto him and took him inside her.

"You're all wet," he said.

"Normally, I would take that statement amiss, but on this occasion, you're perfectly correct." She moved gently up and down. "I liked the way things went last evening," she said.

"So did I, and I like the way things are going now."

She laughed, and the contraction was instantly transmitted to Stone. "Keep laughing," he said. "It feels good."

And she did.

Joan came into Stone's office. "I booked Arrington and Peter at Radio City Music Hall for the matinee," she said.

"Why not me?"

"You have to work for a living these days, and your first client of the day is outside, waiting."

"Anybody I know?"

There was a rap at the door, and Herbert Fisher stuck his head in. "Good morning. Got time for me?"

"Always," Stone said, without the usual irony.

Herbie came in and sat down. "You wanted me to sign the documents?"

Stone handed him the stack, with the signature pages flagged, and a blue-ink pen. "You'll note that Stephanie has already signed them."

Herbie looked at her signature. "Don't tell me she's in New York."

"Color fax." Stone said. "Her attorney accepted service."

"What are the chances we'll get the feds to let go of the three million?"

"I told you before: two chances, slim and none."

"I like slim better," Herbie said, shoving back the signed documents.

He buzzed Joan. "Documents ready for delivery to the court and to Seth Keener." She came and got them.

"How long before I'm a free man?" Herbie asked.

"You're a free man now," Stone said. "The rest is red tape. A couple of months of that, probably."

"I've met a nice girl."

"Slow down, Herbie; you always move too fast. Employ a little skepticism this time, and you'll save on legal fees later."

"I've been going to law school at NYU," Herbie said.

"No kidding?" Stone said, playing straight man. "How come?"

"I was not entirely satisfied with the

quality of my Internet legal education,"
Herbie said.

"I see."

"I'm going to pass the bar again, too."

"Congratulations in advance."

"Then I thought I might take you as a
partner," Herbie said confidently, leaning back in his chair. "I'll front the money
for expanding the practice."

"I'm deeply flattered, Herbie, but you
may not have heard that, for a year now,
I've been a partner at Woodman &
Weld."

"I saw the announcement in the
Times," Herbie said.

"You're reading something besides
the *Post* these days?"

"The *Wall Street Journal,* too."

"Well, you're a man of means; that's
appropriate reading."

"I managed to increase my net worth
this year, too," Herbie said. "A first."

Stone laughed. "I believe you. How
did you do that in the middle of a recession?"

"I bought a small office building on
Lexington Avenue, and I did okay in the
market, too."

"Wow. Who closed on the real estate for you?"

Herbie handed him an envelope. "You. Here's the sales contract."

Stone opened the envelope and looked at the document. "That sounds like a very good price. Do you have tenants?"

"I bought it fully rented."

"Are you going to be the new Donald?"

"Hardly, but it's a good investment."

"I don't doubt it."

"I saw the two thugs again," Herbie said.

"The ones responsible for your dip in the harbor?"

"The very ones. They were across the street from my building when I came downstairs this morning. Stone, can you get me a carry permit for a handgun?"

"Herbie, that's the hardest document to get that the city issues. I could get you a building permit at Ground Zero more easily."

"What are the requirements for a carry license?"

"Essentially, you have to prove that you regularly carry large amounts of cash, like a payroll, or quantities of diamonds or other jewelry on a regular basis."

"How about having my life threatened? Does that count?"

"I'm afraid the NYPD—the issuing authority—places more value on property than life."

"I thought the Supreme Court decision on the D.C. case changed everything."

"Everything but the NYPD and the mayor. It could happen, eventually, but they'll have to be dragged kicking and screaming into the new era. If you want something to do, you could get a couple of your classmates together and sue the city."

"Not a bad idea," Herbie said. "And in the meantime I have to fend off hired killers with my bare hands?"

Stone raised a finger and picked up the phone. "Get me Seth Keener," he said to Joan.

"Keener," the voice said.

"Seth, it's Stone Barrington. My client

Herbert Fisher is in my office to sign the divorce papers, but he insists on one further condition."

"I thought we had a deal," Keener said.

"This is an easy one: Mr. Fisher insists that his soon-to-be-former wife stop trying to have him killed."

"What are you talking about?"

"Mr. Fisher has already experienced an encounter on a yacht in New York Harbor that required him to choose between being knifed by two thugs or taking a swim in December. The thugs are still following him."

"I have no knowledge of anything like that," Keener said.

"That's what I would say, too, in the circumstances. Would you be kind enough to mention the situation to Mrs. Fisher?"

"If you insist, but I still maintain she has nothing to do with thugs following Mr. Fisher."

"Let me know what she says, will you?"

"Sure, I will."

Stone hung up. "I'm afraid that's all

we can do to put an end to it. In the meantime, may I suggest that you carry a roll of quarters in each coat pocket?"

"You think I can buy them off with quarters, Stone?"

"No, but holding them will more than double the weight of your fists and greatly enhance the effects of a punch in the nose. And if the cops ask, you can say you carry the coins for the parking meters."

Herbie got up and with a little wave departed Stone's office. "For this I pay five hundred bucks an hour?" he called out from down the hallway.

11

Stone attended a partners' meeting at Woodman & Weld in the afternoon, and afterward he asked for a few minutes with his old friend and law-school class-mate Bill Eggers, the firm's managing partner.

"What's up, Stone? You look like a man with a problem."

"Nothing life-threatening," Stone replied, "just a little thorny. But I think that addressing some issues now will greatly smooth things for the future."

"Tell me about it."

"For a start, you correctly assessed

the resemblance between the photograph of my father and Arrington's son,
Peter."

"Ahhh," Eggers said. "So you're finally willing to cop to that?"

"I've always been willing, but Arrington was slow to come to that point.
Recent events have changed things."

"Changed them how?"

"Well, Peter arrived in town a couple
of days ago, a day ahead of his mother,
who was under the weather. She arrived
yesterday. Peter saw the photograph of
my father and, apparently, considering
some past suspicions, put the whole
thing together in a flash. The boy is extraordinarily bright."

"Every father thinks that, Stone, trust
me."

"Not every father has a son who is
graduating from high school at sixteen
and is already writing and directing his
first feature film."

"Oh, *that* kind of bright."

"Yes. He's big for his age, mature as
most people get in their mid-thirties,
and very well-spoken and well-man-
nered."

STUART WOODS 87

"I'd like to meet him."

"You will, in due course," Stone said. "But now some steps have to be taken to regularize his life."

"Regularize?"

"He's been in a prep school in Virginia for a few months, and is now way ahead of not just his peers, but the seniors. He's also saddled with Vance Calder's name, and he doesn't like the treatment he receives because of it."

"And what's your solution for handling it?"

"Not my solution, entirely, but Peter's, and his mother has fully bought into it."

"Go on."

"Peter wants to attend a performing-arts prep school on the Upper East Side called Knickerbocker Hall, doing college-level work and attending their film school."

"Sounds good."

"And he wants to change his name to Barrington before he applies."

"I see."

"And he wants them to think he's eighteen."

Eggers blinked. "And how does he plan to do that?"

"Just by telling the school that he's eighteen. When you've met him you'll see that nobody will doubt him."

"He's currently a resident of Virginia?"

"Yes."

"Then I'll have an associated firm in Virginia do a straightforward change of name in the courts down there. They can also notify his school of the change and request that all his records there be changed to Barrington."

"This has to be done in such a way that no one in the media catches it."

"Legally, it will have to be advertised locally, but there are always obscure publications that can satisfy that requirement. We have to have a reason stated for the change of name in the petition to the court. What do you want to say?"

Stone thought about it. "Damned if I know."

"How about: 'Petitioner wishes his surname to be that of his natural father'?"

"He's too young to be a petitioner; I

suppose Arrington will have to fill that role."

"I thought he was going to be eighteen."

"Well, to all intents and purposes—except for legal ones, of course."

Eggers tilted back in his chair, rested his feet on his desk, and pressed his fingertips together in a thoughtful pose. "Where was he born?"

"In Los Angeles."

"How about we get his birth certificate reissued and his old one removed? That should solve the problem."

"How the hell are you going to do that? You can't just hire some clerk to steal a public record and replace it with a forgery."

"Well, I suppose you could, but that's messy. All we need is a judge to order a reissuing of the certificate, for the same reason as we give in Virginia, and along the way, to correct a typographical error with regard to birth date. We should still do the name change in Virginia, because of his school."

"And what kind of judge are you going to get to do that?"

"One that you and I went to law school with. Remember Carling Steadman?"

"Steadman is a judge in L.A.? I didn't know that."

"Then you must not read the alumni journal."

"I guess not."

"The firm has had some dealings with him the past few years; he's always ruled in our favor. And I had dinner with him and his wife when I was in L.A. a few weeks ago. Carling has started a foundation dedicated to the defense of indigents in L.A. County. He doesn't know it, but I'm going to make a twenty-five-thousand-dollar donation at a fund-raising dinner they're having next week."

"The media are going to be a bigger problem in L.A. than they would in Virginia," Stone pointed out.

"We'll petition that the boy's old birth certificate be permanently sealed. No reporter is going to be looking for one belonging to a Peter Barrington."

"Good point."

"Leave it with me. How do you want the name to appear on the certificate? You don't want Calder there, do you?"

"No." Stone thought for a minute. "Make it Malon Peter Barrington."

"Your father's name, as I recall. A happy coincidence."

"Correct. Better make it Malon Peter Barrington the Second."

Eggers wrote it down, along with Peter's new birth date. "I'll get on it," he said. "Will Peter need any help with getting into the school? I'll see if anybody here has a connection."

"Thank you, yes. I can get Leo Goldman to write a recommendation, too, based on what he's seen of a film Peter is working on."

"At a film school, that couldn't hurt."

"And he wants to go to Yale Drama School after Knickerbocker."

"I can get half a dozen letters to back him there. Just tell him to make outstanding grades, join some school organizations, and do some charity work."

"I don't think that will be a problem."

"I'll call you when I have a grip on this," Eggers said. The two men shook hands and Stone headed for home, a ten-minute walk.

As Stone walked into his office Joan
called out, "Bill Eggers on line one."

Stone went to his desk and picked
up the phone. "Did I forget something?"

"No. I spoke to Carling Steadman.
His order will be issued tomorrow, and
you'll have a dozen certified copies of
the new birth certificate by FedEx on
Monday. Peter will need them for school
applications, et cetera. A couple of other
things: we've got a partner here, Willard
Powers, who is an alumnus of Peter's
school in Virginia and who is a trustee.
He's going to speak with the headmaster about changing the name on Peter's
records. He knows of another case
where this was done, so he doesn't
think it will be a problem."

"That's wonderful."

"And do you know of a grand dame
actress named Letitia Covington?"

"The new Helen Hayes? Of course."

"She's the mother of a client of ours,
and she was a founding board member
of the performing arts program at Knickerbocker Hall. Peter has an appoint-

ment to meet her on Monday afternoon at three o'clock. Tell Peter to bring some sort of example of his film work." Eggers gave Stone the address.

"Wow, Bill," Stone said, "I don't know how to thank you."

"All part of being a partner of the firm," Eggers said. "This won't be the last time the relationship will work for you."

Stone hung up. Joan came in and handed him a FedEx package from Leo Goldman. "This just arrived," she said.

12

Later in the afternoon, Herbie Fisher called.

"Yes, Herbie?"

"Stone, the two guys are still outside. I can see them from my terrace. If I can't get a carry license, I'm going to have to carry anyway."

"Herbie, if you have ambitions to practice law, then you do not want a felony weapons charge on your record. You can understand that, can't you? It would mean *no law license*, and the one you illegally obtained would be shredded."

"Oh."

"Exactly."

"Then what can I do?"

"We can call your uncle Bob and get a couple of his guys put on the job. They can watch your back." Herbie's uncle Bob was Bob Berman, a retired police officer who often did technical and security work for Stone.

"I don't want to bring Uncle Bob into this," Herbie said. "He's getting used to my being a straight character, and I want nothing to change his mind."

"Very well, I'm on the board of a very large, very able security company called Strategic Services. I can arrange for them to supply you with anything from a bodyguard to a fleet of black helicopters, bristling with air-to-ground missiles."

"Sounds good. Let's talk to them about something at the low end of that range."

"I'll get right on it," Stone said, then hung up and dialed Mike Freeman.

"Yes, Stone?"

"Mike, I have a small security job for you."

"How small?"

"Two armed men, round the clock?"

"Tell me about it."

"A client of mine, a wealthy young man named Herbert Fisher, a law student, is attempting to disentangle himself from a poor decision called marriage. Although his wife has agreed to the terms of the divorce, she appears to be having him followed by two men who, on one occasion, have driven him off a yacht at knifepoint into New York Harbor. They're still on him."

"Is Mr. Fisher presently operating as a single man?"

"Yes, he likes women."

"Then I have an idea," Mike said, and told him about it.

"I think he would be very pleased," Stone said.

"Eight o'clock tonight be a good starting time?"

"Yes, and I think it might be useful if your two men at some point had a conversation with the two sinister men regarding their intentions."

"Of course. Tell Mr. Fisher to expect three operatives at eight o'clock this evening. They will identify themselves properly."

"Thank you so much, Mike." Stone hung up and called Herbie. "What are your plans for the evening, Herbie?"

"I was going to go to Elaine's for dinner, but I don't want to leave the house, so I'm just going to order in."

"Reschedule," Stone said, "and don't bother getting a date, just be ready at eight." Stone hung up.

Arrington and Peter bustled in from Radio City, shaking snow off their coats and rubbing their red cheeks. "I need a drink," Arrington said.

"Right this way," Stone replied, leading them to his study. He poured Knob Creeks for them, then made a hot cup of tea and honey for Peter. They all sat down.

"How was the show?" Stone asked.

"Spectacular!" Peter replied. "They even had three-D! And the Rockettes, wow!"

"There's an old Jack Douglas story," Stone said, "—he was a comedy writer for *The Tonight Show*—about a young couple who went to Radio City Music Hall on their honeymoon, and during the stage show, the young man got up to go to the men's room, took a wrong turn, and was kicked to death by the Rockettes."

Peter collapsed in laughter; it took Arrington a moment to get it, then she laughed, too.

"I'm going to tell all my friends that happened when we were there," Peter said.

"Always attribute," Stone replied. "It's good manners."

"Will you take us to Elaine's tonight?" Arrington asked. "Peter is dying to go."

"Of course." Stone picked up the phone and made the reservation.

"We have some news," Arrington said, glancing at Peter, who smiled broadly.

"What is it?" Stone asked, puzzled.

"You are looking at the most recent high school graduate of Peter's school," she said, pointing at her son.

"I don't understand."

"I had a call this afternoon from his

headmaster. Peter neglected to tell me that he had a major oral examination just before the holidays."

"It was more like a conversation with half a dozen faculty members," Peter said, looking sheepish.

"I think that's how they meant it to seem," Arrington said. "Apparently, there was some concern among the faculty about Peter's advanced state in all his courses, so they decided to test in depth his knowledge and comprehension of the high school curriculum. Long story short, he knocked the oral out of the park, and as a result they agreed, after he left, that the school had nothing further to offer him of any value. So, they have issued him a high school diploma, with honors, and recommended that he either be privately tutored or attend a good university with a program for exceptional students."

"Congratulations, Peter," Stone said, clapping him on the back.

"Well, it would have been boring to spend the rest of the academic year there, except for my film, of course, but I can work on that anywhere. All the footage is shot; I just have to edit and score it."

"And," Arrington said, "it looks as though Peter himself has already scoped out his next few years of education."

"That, I have," Peter said.

"Well, I have news, too," Stone said. "Woodman & Weld are arranging for a petition for Peter's name change to be lodged with a Virginia court, and also— this surprised me greatly—a Los Angeles judge is directing that Peter's original birth certificate be reissued with his new name . . . and age."

Peter was jumping up and down, now. "Yes, yes, yes," he kept shouting.

"If you approve," Stone said, "you will be named after your grandfather: Malon Peter Barrington the Second."

"I love it!" Peter shouted.

They finally managed to calm him down. "Now, Peter," Stone said, "does the name Letitia Covington mean anything to you?"

"Sure," Peter said, "she's the great old actress. Mom and I saw her in a big production at the Kennedy Center in Washington last year."

"Well, Ms. Covington is a founder of the performing arts program at Knickerbocker Hall, and you have an interview with her on Monday afternoon at three."

Peter's jaw dropped. "How did you do this?"

"The lady is the mother of one of Woodman & Weld's clients, and a phone call was made on your behalf. She wants you to bring with you what you have of your screenplay and film."

Peter fell back onto the sofa, clutching his chest. "I'm having a heart attack!"

"Relax, and drink your tea," Stone said.

"Oh, listen, I'd like to get my driver's license," Peter said.

"Peter!" his mother interjected. "You're only sixteen!"

Peter smiled. "Not anymore," he said.

"Oh, God," Arrington moaned, "we've created a monster!"

13

Arrington was stretched out on the bed in her slip. She took a deep breath and let it out. "There's something I have to tell you," she said.

Stone sat down on the bed. He didn't like the sound of this. "All right."

"I've been seeing someone for the past year. Back in Virginia."

Stone allowed himself to think about all the women he'd been out with during that time. "All right," he said.

"You're not jealous?" she said with mock concern.

"Well, of course, but you're a free

woman. Are you having some sort of problem with him?"

"He's the architect for the new house," she said, seeming to evade his question. "The relationship began to sour a few weeks ago, but I didn't want to cut him off at the knees while he was still working on the house."

"That's a reasonable decision to make," Stone said. "I assume you will eventually get around to answering my question."

"What question was that?" she asked, innocently.

"Is he giving you trouble?"

"Sort of."

"Sort of how?"

"He's becoming jealous of you."

"Why has he even heard of me?" Stone asked.

"I've mentioned you a few times as being an old friend. He latched onto your name immediately, and began making little digs about you."

"I can handle little digs," Stone said.

"He turned up at the hospital in Charlottesville yesterday and intimated to the nurse at the desk that he was some sort of intimate of mine, and they let him into my room. An argument ensued, not our first."

"Was his behavior an escalation over what you've seen in the past?"

"Yes. He very nearly became violent, but a doctor walked into the room at just the right moment."

"What do you think he would have done?"

"I'm not sure, but recently I heard that he had beaten up a woman he'd been seeing last year, and that he was just off probation for that incident. Then, when he had gone a nurse came into my room when I was alone and warned me about him."

"Warned you how?"

"She told me that he had been seeing her older sister earlier this year, while he was still on probation, and he had been violent with her, had broken her nose. The nurse called him and said if he saw her sister again, she'd report him and he'd be sent to prison for breaking his probation. He responded that, if she did that, he would kill both her sister and her."

"This is not good," Stone said.

"No, it's not. I felt lucky to have gotten out of the state without further trouble from him."

"I think it might be best if I speak to him," Stone said.

"Oh, no, Stone! That might just roil the waters."

"Don't worry, I've handled this sort of thing before for clients, and you're my client. He just needs to be reminded of what he has to lose. He's a professor at UVA; he's a respected architect, well known in the community. If he behaves badly, that could all go away. Requesting a protective order from the court could make that happen, once the locals heard about it."

"If you think that's the way to go, then fine, but I'm just afraid that he's become more irrational the past few months, and I don't want you to push him over the edge."

"Don't worry, I'll be very lawyerly," Stone said. "I won't yell at him or make overt threats."

Arrington took his hand. "Then I'll trust you to handle him," she said.

14

Stone called Dino and invited him and Ben to join them for dinner, and by eight-thirty they were about to be seated at Elaine's.

Peter tugged at Stone's sleeve. "Dad, may Ben and I have our own table?"

Stone looked at Arrington and she nodded. Stone arranged it, two tables down, then the three adults took their seats.

"I'm glad they're getting along," Dino said. "Ben doesn't warm to a whole lot of people."

"I'm glad, too, Dino," Arrington said.

"Before I forget," Dino said, "I've been asked to deliver an invitation. Eduardo Bianchi has invited the three of you to join his family for Christmas dinner. Strangely enough, I'm invited, too." Eduardo was Dino's former father-in-law.

"Arrington?" Stone asked.

"Yes, of course; we don't have other plans, do we?"

"The choices are dinner at a hotel or a Chinese restaurant."

"We'd love to, Dino," Arrington said.

"Eduardo is very interested to meet Peter," Dino said. "He's been hearing about him from Ben."

"I wonder if the boys will insist on their own table," Stone said, glancing down to where they sat, talking rapidly and gesticulating.

"Stone," Dino said, "Ben seems to think that Peter is eighteen. Why is that?"

"I'd better bring you up to date," Stone said, then he told him about all the arrangements that had been made. "It's better this way, we think."

"I think it's better for Ben, too; I won't tell him."

Stone looked up to see Herbie Fisher enter the restaurant in the company of a petite, dark-haired beauty. Herbie brought her to the table. "Good evening, Stone, Dino. I'd like you to meet Gina Carlo."

Stone and Dino stood and shook hands. "And, Herbie," Stone said, "you haven't met my friend Arrington. Arrington, this is my client Herbert Fisher."

"I've heard good things about you," Herbie said. "Mostly from Joan, Stone's secretary."

"I'm glad she has a good opinion of me," Arrington replied, smiling.

Herbie excused himself, and they were shown to a table at the rear of the restaurant. A moment later, two large men came in and were given a table in Siberia, where the tourists were sent. Then, after another moment, two other large men came in and took seats at their table. Some hard looks were exchanged, and one of the second pair spoke, uninterrupted, for about a minute. The first two men looked at each other, shrugged, and then left the restaurant.

"What was that all about?" Dino asked.

"Herbie," Stone said, "for reasons too complicated to go into, is now in the care of Strategic Services. The young woman, Gina Carlo, is one of Mike Freeman's operatives, as are the second pair of men who followed them in. The first two men have been causing Herbie some concern, and, after having been spoken to, they have obviously decided that discretion is the better part of valor."

"Okay," Dino said.

"Whatever you say," Arrington said.

They ordered drinks and looked at the menu.

"Funny thing," Dino said, "after a trip to Film Forum with Peter, Ben has suddenly acquired an interest in old movies. He can't stop talking about them."

"I'm glad to hear it," Stone said. "Peter is obsessed, and it's good for him to have a friend who shares his excitement."

"That's probably what they're talking about now," Arrington said.

Dino glanced at the two boys. "I certainly hope so," he said. "I wouldn't want Ben to lead Peter astray."

"Astray how?" Arrington asked.

Dino looked uncomfortable. "Ben has a tendency, when he comes home from school, to be interested in things beyond his years."

"Like what?" Stone asked.

"Like downtown clubs," Dino explained. "Once a cop brought him home, after some sort of ruckus in SoHo."

"Dino," Arrington said, "you're not raising some sort of juvenile delinquent, are you?"

"First of all, I'm not raising him; he's at that school in Connecticut, and his mother and grandfather have a lot more to say about his upbringing than I do. Second, he's not a juvenile delinquent; he just wants to be twenty-five, at a time when most kids are looking forward to nineteen. For what it's worth, I think Peter just might be a steadying hand."

"What's Ben doing about college?" Arrington asked.

"He's got an early acceptance from Columbia," Dino replied, "with the help

of his grandfather, who is a major con-
tributor. Of course, he's always made
good grades, with little apparent effort,
so he's not exactly being foisted on the
school."

"That's wonderful!" Arrington en-
thused. "An Ivy Leaguer in the family!"

"How about that?" Dino said.

Later, when they had all dined and were
leaving, Stone noted that Herbie and
Gina were deep in conversation at their
table. He had a feeling they weren't discussing personal security.

The two bodyguards looked sleepy.

They arrived home and good nights
were said. Back in the master suite, Arrington got into bed next to Stone.
"Have you noticed," she said, "that Peter's clothes have gotten a little too
snug?"

"Yes, I have," Stone said. "I'll deal
with that tomorrow."

"Thank you," she sighed. "He hates it
when I buy clothes for him."

The following morning Stone took Peter up to Madison and Seventy-second to the Ralph Lauren men's store. He found the right department and bought Peter a blue blazer, a couple of tweed jackets, a blue suit, and some odd trousers, making sure there was room for growth in all of them. Peter picked out a handsome topcoat, some shirts and shoes. Everything would be delivered in a couple of days.

Stone went home feeling very fatherly, a condition he was becoming accustomed to.

15

Mid-Monday morning, two FedEx packages arrived—one containing a dozen certified copies of Peter's new California birth certificate, with a covering letter from the court stating that his former certificate had been sealed by court order. The second envelope contained Peter's high school diploma, with the notation "With Honors," a copy of the transcript of his academic record, and a "To Whom It May Concern" letter from the headmaster describing Peter as a true scholar and a perfect gentleman. All these materials were in the name of

Malon Peter Barrington II. Only the Virginia name-change order remained to be received.

Stone buzzed Peter in his room and asked him to come down to his office for a chat. They sat on the leather sofa, and Stone gave Peter the documents he had received. "This is all official, now," he said. "Joan has made copies of your transcript, of which this is one, and she has put the other eleven certified copies of your birth certificate in my office safe, where they will be secure. You'll need them at various times."

"Thank you, Dad," Peter said, tucking the documents back into the envelope.

"When you see Letitia Covington this afternoon, you might take those documents along, just in case they're needed, and don't forget a copy of your screenplay and the DVD of your edited footage."

"I won't."

"By the way, I had a call from Leo Goldman, who was very impressed with the work you've done on your film—so impressed that he immediately wanted to buy it for Centurion."

"You mean it's going to be released?"

"Not yet, and probably not for some time."

"What's the delay?"

"I swore Leo to secrecy about you and the screenplay. If he released it, say, at Sundance, as the work of a six-teen-year-old, a sensation would ensue, and a number of things would happen: first, you would become famous way before your time, which could wreck your desire for some anonymity and a good education. Fame can be a good thing, but not in this case. You would forever be known as a boy wonder, and it would be very difficult for you to out-grow that."

"Like Orson Welles?"

"Something like that. Of course, Welles was twenty-four when he made *Citizen Kane*, but that was still very young, and in spite of his brilliance he was ill-equipped to deal with the stu-dios and the smart, ruthless men who ran them, and his career suffered for the rest of his life."

"I read a good biography of Welles," Peter said, "and he's one of my heroes, along with Elia Kazan, but you're right about how the studios treated him."

"Welles was a genius," Stone said, "but Kazan is a better career role model. He started as an actor, then was an extraordinarily successful director in theater before he tackled film, and by the time he did he was a mature artist."

"I see your point. I'll finish the film, then put it aside until you think the time is right, Dad."

"I don't want you to think I'm going to make all your decisions for you," Stone said, "but I want you to learn to think about them hard before you go off half-cocked."

"I understand."

"There's something else. Your mother and I are delighted that you and Ben have become friends so quickly, but you have to remember that Ben, in spite of your newfound age, has two important years on you, and that's a lot of experience you haven't had yet. Ben is an impulsive young man, and sometimes his impulses have gotten him into trouble. You're going to be put in the odd position of sometimes being the grown-up in the friendship, instead of just going along with what he wants. And, I've no doubt there'll be times when you should just walk away from him, if you disagree with his actions. Being his friend doesn't mean you have to be his abettor. . . , I'm sorry, do you know that word?"

"As in 'aid and abet'?"

"Yes, exactly. New York City is a very fast track for a young man, especially one like Ben, who thinks he's all grown up. You're going to have to have some rules of behavior in this city, and since you'll be living with me, I'm going to make them."

"Yes, sir."

"The first thing is, you must never, ever drink alcohol in any form until after you're legal, at twenty-one, and that means twenty-three for you."

"I've done some reading on the Internet about that, and I know that alcohol can have a bad effect on young brains, and that the brain isn't really mature and fully formed until around the mid-twenties."

"That's true," Stone said, "and I'm

glad you understand the reasons for the rule. It applies to marijuana, too, and that has the additional problem of being illegal. No matter how you feel about whether it should be legal or not, it remains illegal, and the next rule is, you must not allow yourself to commit illegal acts. If you so much as walk into one of the downtown clubs Ben is fond of, you will have committed an illegal act, even if you don't drink. Those places are watched by the police and sometimes raided, and believe me, a night in jail is something you don't want to experience. I was a policeman for fourteen years, and I saw young people make mistakes all the time that had a bad effect on their future. You must make every effort to get through your youth with a clean record, and again, that sometimes means just walking away from situations. If you were living in rural Virginia, this might be a lot easier to handle, but not in New York. You'll have to watch yourself all the time. For the time being, you must not be outside this house after eight in the evening without permission, and that means I must know where you're going and with whom. You are to carry your cell phone at all times, and you are to answer it when I or your mother call."

"I understand, Dad, and I'll try my best."

"I know that your best is very, very good, Peter. There's something else. I think, especially with Ben as a friend, you're going to meet a lot of girls who are older and more experienced than you. Am I correct in assuming that you are acquainted with the rudiments of sex?"

"Oh, yes. I've read a lot about it, and, of course, we had a class at school. I haven't done it yet, though."

"You're going to have to decide for yourself when to start having sex, Peter, because I can't be there with you all the time. But I urge you to act with restraint. You can't get into trouble restraining yourself, but you can get into one hell of a lot of trouble by just plunging into that life. When you think this might happen to you, you must always wear a condom. You are too young to be a father, but nature has made you very fertile. Disease is a problem, too, as you no doubt learned in school.

"Another thing is, now that you are legally eighteen, you must be careful with girls younger than you. Do you know what statutory rape is?"

"Sex with somebody under eighteen, right?"

"Right, and that means even if it's consensual. A girl of fifteen or sixteen can't waive the law on that subject, and girls' fathers can become very angry at young men who violate it. It's a dangerous situation, and you should avoid it at all costs."

"I understand."

"Finally, you'll find it much easier to deal with problems if you're willing to come to me and talk about them. I know you won't always take my advice, but I give advice for a living, and I'm good at it. Take advantage of that."

Peter smiled. "I have no problem talking with you, Dad."

"Good. Now that we've made you into the perfect son, you get on with your day, and I'll work on becoming the perfect father."

Peter ran back to his room, and Stone heaved a huge sigh of relief.

"I heard all that," Joan said from the door.

"Eavesdropper!" Stone said.

"You should take your advice," she said.

16

Stone pressed the button for Joan's extension. "Joan, please find a Timothy Rutledge at the University of Virginia and get him on the phone for me. If he's not there, see if information has a number for him."

"Hang on, boss," Joan said. Thirty seconds later she buzzed him. "Line one."

Stone picked up the phone. "Mr. Rutledge?"

"It's Dr. Rutledge, thank you. Who is this?"

"My name is Stone Barrington. I think you know who I am."

"Not necessarily," Rutledge replied.

"Arrington Calder is visiting me in New York. Does that ring a bell?"

"Maybe."

"All you need to know is that I am an attorney and that I represent Mrs. Calder."

"What do you want?"

"Mrs. Calder has asked me to request of you that you do not attempt to see her or speak to her, except for business purposes—that is, on matters pertaining to the completion of her house in Virginia."

"Why doesn't she say that to me herself?"

"Mrs. Calder informs me that she has already done so, and in no uncertain terms."

"What is this about?"

"I will be happy to put it in writing for you and include a restraining order against you, requiring you not to see or communicate with her, except under the circumstances I have already outlined. I'm told that you are acquainted with restraining orders."

There was a long silence.

"Is there anything you don't understand about Mrs. Calder's request?" Stone asked.

"Yes, I don't understand why."

"She no longer wishes to hear from you, except on business. That is all you need to know. It is also all a judge needs to know. You should be aware that a restraining order is a public document and therefore can be seen by anyone who takes the trouble, and there are media people who take the trouble every day. Do you understand that?"

"Go fuck yourself," Rutledge said.

"Did I mention that this conversation is being recorded?" Stone asked.

Rutledge hung up.

Stone looked up to see Arrington standing in the doorway.

"That was very good," she said. "Very professional. Were you really recording him?"

"Yes," Stone said.

"Was he angry?"

"Yes. He kept saying he didn't understand why you wouldn't see him."

She nodded. "It figures. He was a perfectly nice person, until he heard your name."

"From whom did he hear it?"

"From me. I told him that Peter and I were spending Christmas with you. He demanded to know who you were, and I told him you are an old friend. That didn't help. He started asking questions about you, and I cut him off."

"How long had you been seeing him?" Stone asked.

"Since shortly after construction started on the house. It was foolish of me, I guess, to become involved with someone who worked for me, but you weren't around, and I was lonely."

"Does Peter know him?"

"They've met once. I've kept him away from Tim."

"Well, let's let sleeping dogs lie," Stone said. "He's been warned."

17

Peter put on his overcoat and gloves, tucked his leather envelope under his arm, left the house, first making sure his key was in his pocket, walked up to Third Avenue, and hailed a cab. "Two-oh-five West Fifty-seventh Street," he said to the driver, looking at the address written on the back of his father's card.

The driver said nothing to him but talked rapidly into his cell phone in a language that Peter thought was Arabic or Urdu. The man drove as quickly as possible in the traffic, and arrived at the building in ten minutes. Peter paid and tipped the man, as his father had told him to, and got out of the cab. It was, he reflected, the first time he had been in a New York City taxicab alone. He walked into the building and was greeted by a man in a uniform.

"May I help you?"

"Yes, please. I have an appointment with Miss Letitia Covington."

The man picked up a phone. "Your name?"

"Peter Ca—Barrington," he said, correcting himself quickly.

The man announced him, gave him the apartment number, and told him to go up.

Peter got on the elevator and pressed the correct button. He checked his hair and the knot in his tie in the car's mirror and exited into a vestibule. Before he could ring the bell the door opened and he was greeted by a uniformed maid.

"I'm Peter Barrington," he said, and she took his coat and led him into a sunny living room facing Fifty-seventh Street. A handsome, gray-haired woman of an age he could not determine sat in an armchair.

"Peter? I'm Letitia Covington," she said, indicating that he should sit on the sofa next to her chair.

"How do you do, Miss Covington," he said. He shook the offered hand, which was cool and dry, and sat down.

"Would you like tea?"

"Thank you, ma'am, yes."

"Milk or lemon?" she asked, reaching for the pot on a silver tray before her.

"Lemon, please, and two sugars."

The woman smiled to herself and poured.

"Thank you, ma'am," Peter said, accepting the cup.

She offered him a tray of pastries. "Something to eat?"

"No, thank you, ma'am."

"Well, now," she said, "I'm told you are interested in attending Knicker-bocker Hall."

"Yes, ma'am, I am."

"Tell me why?"

"My goal is to be a film director," he replied, "but my last school had only a limited program."

"I see. I'm told you just graduated. How did you come to graduate in December?"

"I was an advanced student, and at the end of the last term I had an oral examination on the high school curriculum with six faculty members, and they decided to graduate me. They said they had nothing further to offer me, and I agreed with them."

"You must be very bright."

"They tell me so."

"Peter, have you ever had an IQ test?"

Peter felt his cheeks color. "Yes, ma'am."

"And what was your score?"

Peter gulped. "I . . . believe it was one hundred sixty-one," he said.

She laughed. "You mustn't be embarrassed about that," she said. "That's a very high score. You might avoid telling people about it, though, unless they corner you, as I did."

Peter smiled. "Yes, ma'am."

"And why do you wish to be a film director?"

"Well, my stepfather was an actor, and I grew up around a lot of film people when we lived in Los Angeles, and I liked them. Then I started seeing a lot of old films and reading about them, and pretty soon, it was about all I could think about. I guess I was around eight then."

"And what was your stepfather's name?"

"Vance Calder," Peter replied.

Her face brightened. "Ah, I met him a few times," she said. "He was charming, and, of course, he was one of our best film actors."

"Miss Covington, I would appreciate it if we could keep his name between us."

She looked surprised. "Why?"

"Because, ever since we left Los Angeles, people have treated me differently because of his name, and I've never liked it. If I go to Knickerbocker, I want to be just Peter Barrington."

"I understand perfectly," she said, "and I admire you for not using his name shamelessly to advance yourself, the way that many children of famous people have done."

"Thank you, ma'am."

"Have you brought any of your work?" she asked.

Peter opened his leather envelope. "Here is a screenplay I've written," he said.

"Give me a moment," she said, then opened the folder and began to read quickly, turning the pages. She stopped and looked up. "That is an excellent first scene," she said. "I particularly like the dialogue. I'll read it all later."

He handed her his DVD. "I've edited the first seventy minutes," he said. "I expect I'll finish it soon."

"You mean it's already shot?"

"Yes, ma'am."

"Peter, did anyone help you write this?"

"Well, I had a faculty adviser, but he wasn't much help. He was a music teacher."

She smiled. "I see. I was going to ask you if you knew exactly what a film director does, but you obviously do. Why Knickerbocker?"

"I've read about the program, and I think it suits what I want to do very well."

"Tell me what you want to do, beyond directing."

"I want to learn to work with actors and direct theater."

"And how do you propose to learn to work with actors?"

"By becoming an actor myself," Peter replied. "My role model is Elia Kazan."

"Ah, yes, Gadge," she said. "That was his nickname, but he didn't like it. I didn't know that until I read his autobiography. Have you read it?"

"Yes, ma'am," Peter replied. "Twice."

"I see. And what do you want to do after graduation from Knickerbocker?"

"I want to go to the Yale School of Drama," Peter replied, "for the same reasons I want to go to Knickerbocker."

"Peter, I've no doubt that you would fit in perfectly at Knickerbocker," she said. She picked up a folder and handed it to him. "This is an application. Please fill it out and return it to me with a copy of your birth certificate and your transcript from your previous school."

Peter handed her the documents. "I

have those right here," he said. "May I fill out the application now?"

She laughed again. "Yes, you go right ahead. Do you have a pen?"

"Yes, ma'am," Peter said.

"I'm going to give you a few minutes to complete the application, and then I'll come back," she said, rising.

Peter stood with her, and she left. He opened the folder and began to fill in the blanks.

Letitia Covington went into her study, sat down at her desk, picked up the phone and dialed the number of the headmaster of Knickerbocker Hall, who lived on the floor below her. "Arthur," she said, "it's Letitia."

"Good afternoon, Letitia. How did you know to find me at home?"

"Because I know what a lazy old fart you are, and that you often leave school early."

"I come home to do paperwork," he protested. "They won't leave me alone if I'm at school."

"I want you to come up here right now," she said.

He laughed. "What's up, Letitia?"

"I have a candidate for you, sitting on my living room sofa, filling out his application, right now."

"Letitia, you know we have a waiting list."

"You're going to forget all about that when you meet him," she said. "Now get your ass up here!" She hung up and went back to the living room.

Peter rose as she entered and handed her the folder.

"Already finished?"

"Yes, ma'am. I put my birth certificate and my transcript in the folder, along with a recommendation from the headmaster."

The doorbell rang, and the maid led in a man wearing a seedy cardigan and a necktie loose at the collar.

"Peter, this is Arthur Golden, our headmaster at Knickerbocker."

Peter stood and offered his hand, noticing that he was taller than Golden. "How do you do, sir?"

"Sit down, sit down," Golden said.

"I'm not accustomed to good manners from students."

"I'm afraid, Arthur," Miss Covington said, "that Peter doesn't know how to behave any other way." She handed him the screenplay. "Read the first scene," she said. "We'll wait."

Golden sat down, put on the glasses that hung from a string around his neck, and began to read. Finally he stopped and began asking Peter all the questions Miss Covington had asked him.

When Peter had dutifully answered them all, Golden looked at Miss Covington and nodded. "Peter, I'd like you to come to the school tomorrow morning, meet some people and have a look around. Please bring your parents, if you like."

"I'd like that very much, Mr. Golden," Peter replied.

"Don't wear a jacket and tie," Golden said. "You'll frighten the other students."

18

Peter ran into Stone's office, breathless. "I think I got in!" he shouted. "Miss Covington was just great, and she made the headmaster, Mr. Golden, come up to her apartment to meet me!"

Stone helped him off with his coat and steered him to the sofa. "Sit down and take a few deep breaths," he said, and got the boy a bottle of water from the fridge.

Peter gave him a blow-by-blow account of his meeting. "I'm going to the school tomorrow morning. They said you and Mom could come, too!"

"I'm available," Stone said, "and I'm sure your mother is, too."

That evening they attended *The Lion King*, which Stone liked much better than he thought he would, and they dined at Sardi's. Stone explained the history of the restaurant, and they played at recognizing the faces in the caricatures hung in rows on the walls. Peter did better than Stone.

Later, as they climbed into bed, Stone pulled Arrington close to him. "I love you," he said.

"I love you, too."

"Good. Will you marry me?"

She pushed him back and looked at him. "Stone, are you just trying to make an honest woman of me?"

"Among other things. In addition to all the other good reasons for getting married, I don't think Peter ought to have to explain our relationship to people."

"What about this separate living in New York and Virginia?"

"That's still to be negotiated, after we've settled the basic question."

"Yes, I'll marry you," she said, "gladly and with enthusiasm." They kissed for a long time.

Finally, Stone broke free. "Wait right here," he said, getting up.

"Did you think I was going somewhere?"

Stone padded across the bedroom to his dressing room, where he pushed back some suits and opened his safe. He felt around at the rear of the steel box until he found it, then he locked the safe, went back to Arrington, and handed her the box.

She looked at him, mystified, then opened it, revealing the ring inside, along with a matching diamond wedding ring.

"It's not as big as your old one," Stone said, "but it's more, ah, tasteful."

"It's gorgeous," she said. "When did you buy this?"

"Before our planned trip to the islands," he replied. "I had planned to give it to you when we were in St. Marks, but we didn't quite make it there, at least, not together. It's been in my safe ever since."

Arrington slipped it on. "It's perfect. What is it, six carats?"

"Five and a bit, nearly flawless."

"You couldn't afford this in those days."

"I managed. Now it seems like a good investment; it would cost five times as much now."

She sat up in bed next to him, naked, looking nymph-like, looking at her ring on her finger. "We have some things to work out."

"Yes, we do. Before we start, remember that I have a career in New York, more than ever."

"I am cognizant of that," she said. "But you have to remember that I'm building a new house, and that it's almost finished. I have work to do there, and I'll want to spend a lot of time there. I admit, I'm enjoying New York more than I did when I last lived here, and I love your house, too."

"You have a fast airplane," he said. "You can come and go as you wish. I hope you'll miss me, though."

She sighed. "I'm sure I will. And I think we should go ahead with the hotel project in Los Angeles."

"All right." Arrington's house in Bel-Air rested on eighteen acres, and Stone had put together a plan to develop it as a hotel. "Do you think you'll have to spend a lot of time there?"

"No, I don't. I'll make the architects and landscapers come to New York or Virginia with their plans, and I'll try not to go until my house there is finished." Part of the deal was that the developers would build her a house on the hotel grounds.

"Sounds good."

"You and Woodman & Weld have done a superb job of putting my affairs in order. That's why I think I can go ahead with the project."

"On behalf of Woodman & Weld, I thank you. You have a lot to thank Mike Freeman for, too. He's put together a great group of investors and brought in the hotel management group, too."

"I'll write him a note on my best stationery," she said.

"Order some new stationery tomorrow," Stone said.

"That brings up another problem, a very big one," she said.

"Stationery?"

"Yes. I cannot be Arrington Barrington."

Stone burst out laughing. "This could wreck the whole thing, couldn't it?"

"It certainly could."

"I have a solution."

"I hope so. Tell me."

"Your maiden name is Carter; call yourself Arrington Carter Barrington. You could even hyphenate it, if you're feeling posh."

"Arrington Carter Barrington. That makes all the difference, doesn't it?"

"All you needed was a little air between the two names."

"Lots of people use names like that these days," she said, repeating it.

"They do, don't they?"

"When do you want to get married?"

"Well, for purposes of our visit to our son's new school tomorrow, I think we should style ourselves Mr. and Mrs."

"Good idea."

"After we see the school, we can run down to City Hall and pick up a license, then we can speak the vows at our leisure."

"Listen, Stone, we have to be very careful, very private about this. I don't want to see stories in the newspapers about us. That might make things difficult for Peter, if he has to start explaining his new name to people."

"We'll do it as secretly as possible, and let people find out as it comes up."

"You'll want Dino for best man, won't you?"

"Yes. Whom do you want for maid of honor?"

"I don't know; I'll have to think about it. I don't have a lot of girlfriends."

"No rush."

She stretched out in his arms again. "Arrington Carter-Barrington," she said. "With a hyphen. Will you be Stone Carter-Barrington?"

"Ah, no."

"Oh, all right." She kissed him for a long time, then nature took its course.

19

Stone went down to the office for a few minutes before leaving for Knicker-bocker Hall, and Joan buzzed him. "Seth Keener on one," she said.

Stone picked it up. "Good morning, Seth."

"Morning, Stone. A couple of things: it seems the New York State legislature is going to pass a no-fault divorce law sometime soon. We have to decide whether to wait for that or go ahead with the present petition."

"The present petition has been filed; let's stick with it. It might even get resolved more quickly, because of the impending no-fault law; some cases might be withdrawn to wait for no-fault."

"All right. The other thing: I'm hearing rumors that *60 Minutes* is about to do an investigative piece on the island of Monoto."

This was the Pacific enclave of the wealthy where Stephanie Fisher and her brother had run after looting the family firm. "What does that have to do with the divorce?"

"I'm not sure. It depends on how big an effect the program has."

"I don't think it matters what effect the show has. The petition is filed. If you know anybody who can rush it, that's fine with me and, I'm sure, with my client."

"Okay, I'll get on it."

"Does Stephanie know about *60 Minutes*?"

"I don't know."

"If I were you, I'd wait for her to bring it up. No point in getting her upset now."

"You have a point." Keener hung up.

Peter and Arrington appeared in his

office, Peter dressed in a sweater and an open shirt.

"Where's your necktie?" Stone asked.

"The headmaster told me not to wear one."

Stone shrugged. "Okay. Peter, for purposes of this interview, your mother and I have decided to style ourselves as Mr. and Mrs."

"Whew," Peter said. "That's a relief."

"In fact," Arrington said, "Stone and I have decided to make that styling permanent, and quite soon."

Peter smiled broadly. "Then I won't be a bastard?"

"Peter!" his mother said.

Stone laughed. "I don't think you'd better bring that up again, and especially not at the school."

They got out of a cab at Knickerbocker Hall, which occupied a large building in the East Nineties.

"It looks very well kept up," Arrington said.

"They must have a big endowment,"

Stone replied. "I imagine we'll be hearing a lot about that."

"You mean, we'll have to make a contribution to get Peter in?"

"Oh, I think they'll be more subtle than that," Stone said.

They climbed the front steps and made their way to the administrative offices. Someone took their coats, then Arthur Golden, the headmaster, met them in the reception area and introduced himself. "Peter and I have already met, of course. This is a good time for our tour, since everyone is in class. In forty-five minutes, the bell will ring, and all hell will break loose."

He led them down the main hallway, and they peeked into two or three classrooms. "The classes are quite small," Arrington said.

"We're proud of that," Golden said. "Never more than twenty, and more often, fifteen or so." He showed them the science labs, which were impressive, then he opened a large door that led to the next building.

They saw a life art class, featuring a not-quite-nude model, and a sculpture gallery. Then they went through a door and emerged into the balcony of an auditorium from which all the seats had been removed. A set had been constructed, and a student director was speaking with a small group of actors.

Golden pressed a finger to his lips.

Peter hung over the rail of the balcony to get a better view, and they all watched the scene performed. Golden led them out into the hall. "That will be filmed later; they have to move the camera from another set."

"You have only one camera?" Peter asked.

"Two are being repaired," Golden replied. "It seems they're always in the shop. And they're not digital." He led them through another door that led to a corridor containing a number of rooms that were used as editing studios.

"You're still using Moviolas?" Peter asked, referring to the editing machines.

"We have a Steenbeck," Golden replied, "but we need new equipment."

After their tour they returned to Golden's office, where they were offered tea.

"We'd like very much to have Peter

as a student here," the man said. "I've talked about his situation with some of the faculty, and we think that his time should be divided equally between film classes and courses from the university curriculum for the freshman year."

"I've already taken most of those courses," Peter said.

"I saw that from your transcripts, but we think you need more history, a phi-losophy course, and a language."

"I've been tutored in French," Peter said, "but I never had a course at school."

"We'll evaluate you to get a sense of your level, and go from there," Golden said. He handed Stone an envelope. "Here is a schedule of our fees."

"Peter," Stone said, putting the enve-lope into a pocket, "is Knickerbocker your choice?"

"Oh, yes, sir!" Peter said. "It certainly is."

"Then you may join us at the begin-ning of the next semester, in January," Golden said, "and we look forward to having you as a student, Peter."

Everyone shook hands, and on the

way out Golden said to Stone and Arrington, "Frankly, considering what I've seen of Peter and his record, I'm not sure how long we can hold on to him before he'll be going to Yale."

Stone and Arrington left Peter at the house, then took a cab down to City Hall, where they stood in line for a marriage license. Stone saw a man with a camera in a corner of the room and stepped between him and Arrington. "Just act natural," he said to her. "This will be over soon."

They left the building with their license in hand, and the man with the camera followed them, but Stone made sure he shielded Arrington and that his back was to the camera.

"Who was that man?" Arrington asked when they were in a cab.

"I don't know. He's probably a stringer for one of the columns, looking for celebrities."

"Do you think he recognized us?"

"You haven't been in the papers much since Vance's death," Stone said. "It's more likely that he might have seen me at Elaine's. I wouldn't worry about it."

They joined Dino at Elaine's, and Stone told him they had a marriage license. "That's good news," Dino said. "Eduardo will want to know that. Do you mind if I tell him?"

"No, go ahead," Stone said, and Arrington nodded. "I'm looking forward to meeting Eduardo," she said.

20

The following day Stone was working at his desk when Joan buzzed him. "Eduardo Bianchi, on line one," she said.

Stone picked up the phone. "Hello, Eduardo," he said.

"Good day, Stone," Eduardo replied in a voice still youthful, given his great age. "I'm so happy you are joining my family and me for Christmas dinner."

"Arrington and I are looking forward to it," Stone replied, "and she's looking forward to meeting you."

"I wonder if I may tender an invitation of another kind?"

"Of course."

"Dino has told me of your plans to marry soon."

"That's right, we got a license yesterday."

"There will be an official present at our Christmas dinner who would be pleased to marry you, I'm sure, if you can come half an hour early."

"What a lovely thought," Stone said. "I'd be delighted, and I'm sure I can accept on Arrington's behalf. You're acquainted with Bill Eggers, managing partner at Woodman & Weld, I know."

"Of course."

"I'd like very much to invite Bill to the ceremony," Stone said.

"Of course you may. I'd be very pleased to have Bill and his wife to dinner, as well, if he doesn't already have plans."

"I'll ask him and let you know."

"Very well, then, please be here promptly at twelve-thirty on Christmas Day."

The two men said good-bye, and Stone hung up. Stone called Eggers, told him of their plan, and invited him.

"Marian and I would love to be with you," Eggers said, speaking of his second wife. "It's Betty's year to have the kids for Christmas, so we don't really have any plans. I'll call Eduardo myself and accept, and we'll see you Christmas Day."

Stone, Arrington, and Peter lunched in the kitchen, and he told Arrington of Eduardo's invitation.

"How very nice of him," Arrington said. "I hope you accepted."

"I did, and I'm glad you're happy about it."

"Please tell me more about Eduardo," she said.

Stone took a deep breath. "He's a remarkable man. There are rumors that, in his youth, he became an important figure in the old Mafia, and that he may even still be involved in some way, but no one has ever been able to substantiate that, and I've never had the courage to ask him for fear of offending. If the rumors are true, then he's always been able to keep that association buried deep in his background.

"In any case, Eduardo has succeeded brilliantly in a number of fields. He founded an investment bank and became a major shareholder in a couple of big brokerage houses and serves on a number of big corporate boards. He's also on the boards of the Metropolitan Museum of Art and the Metropolitan Opera, among other nonprofits, and he wields more personal influence in more areas than any man I know or have ever heard of."

"That's impressive," Arrington said.

"Peter, Eduardo is also Ben's grandfather. His daughter Mary Ann was married to Dino."

"Didn't Mary Ann have a sister?" Arrington asked.

"Yes, Dolce, but she's mentally ill and is in some sort of facility in Sicily." Stone didn't mention that he and Dolce had once been married in a civil ceremony in Venice, and that, when Dolce went mad, Eduardo had seen that the marriage document was removed from the city's records and sent to Stone. He had burned it.

"Where does Eduardo live?" Peter asked.

"Way out in Brooklyn, on the water, in a very impressive house, and you should remember to call him Mr. Bianchi, unless he asks you to do otherwise."

"Of course," Peter said. He produced his leather envelope and took out a document. "I want to send in this application to Yale," he said, "and I'll need your signature."

"Good idea to apply now," Stone said, and Arrington agreed. "Do you think two semesters at Knickerbocker will be enough for you?"

"I think so. There's always summer school, too."

"Oh, I'd like you to spend at least some of the summer in Virginia," Arrington said.

"If that's what you want, Mother."

"So nice to have a dutiful son," she said. "What are your plans for the afternoon, Peter? Will you be working on your film?"

"No, there's an Orson Welles series

at the Film Forum, and Ben and I are going to go. He's never seen a Welles film."

"He has a treat in store," Stone said.

"Yes, he does," Peter agreed. "He's gotten very excited about film. I don't think he'd given it much thought until we met, but now he wants to see *everything.*"

"You're a good influence," Stone said. "If Ben weren't seeing so many movies with you, he'd be getting into some sort of mischief. That's what his father says, anyway. Dino is very happy about your friendship."

"So am I," Peter said.

21

The lights came up at Film Forum after *Citizen Kane*, and Peter and Ben rose and shuffled out of the theater with the crowd.

"You're awfully quiet," Peter said.

"That's because I'm stunned," Ben replied. "I want to see it again."

"I have it on DVD," Peter said. "Come on back to the house, and I'll rack it up for you."

They took a bus back to Turtle Bay, and Peter let them into the house with his key. Stone was standing just inside the door taking off his overcoat and hanging it in the hall closet.

"Hey, fellas," Stone said. "How was the movie?"

"Movies," Peter replied. "Ben liked them."

"Especially *Citizen Kane*," Ben said.

"We're going to go upstairs and watch it again on DVD," Peter said, "so please excuse us."

"Of course, go on up."

The boys ran up the stairs to Peter's room, and he found the disc for *Citizen Kane*.

"Did you say Welles was twenty-four years old when he directed this movie?" Ben asked.

"That's right, and he was already a big actor and director on Broadway and on the radio."

"That's unbelievable," Ben said.

"We can beat that. Sit down." He pointed Ben at a chair, then sat down himself. "Ben, I think you're a smart guy."

"That's true, but I'm not as smart as you."

"If that's true, it's an accident of nature, so don't worry about it. What's more important is, you're a good guy, too."

"Thanks, Peter. I feel the same way about you."

"For the next four years or so, I've got to keep you out of trouble."

Ben laughed. "You've been talking to my dad."

"No, I've been talking to *my* dad, but he feels the same way about it as your dad. The thing is, they're both right."

Ben looked sheepish. "Yeah, I have been in a few scrapes, but I had some fun, too."

"We've got to find some new ways for you to have fun," Peter said, "because I'm not going to get involved in any scrapes. There's too much at stake."

"What's at stake?"

"Have you ever noticed when some young celebrity gets into drugs or gets arrested for drunk driving, how long it takes him to get over those things? I mean, they end up in jail, then in court, then in rehab, then in community service, and most of them have to go through that two or three times before they finally get it. The ones who don't get it end up in prison or dead."

"Well, yeah, I've noticed that."

"All that stuff they have to do to get straight takes up years of their lives. You and I don't need to waste that kind of time getting out of trouble we should never have gotten into in the first place."

"You have a point," Ben conceded.

"Ben, I think you would make a terrific movie producer."

"Really?"

"You're smart, you're good with money, you're well organized. But you're not motivated—not yet, anyway."

"What should motivate me?"

"Would you like to be a movie producer?"

"Yeah, sure I would. Who wouldn't?"

"Okay, everybody, but only a few are suited to the work. First of all, you love the movies."

"Well, I love everything you've shown me."

"A good motivation to have would be to want to make movies as good as or better than those."

"Yeah, I can see that."

"If you're motivated, then making that happen becomes the most—well, one of the most important things in your life, and you do the things you have to do to achieve that ambition."

"What are the things I have to do, if I want to be a movie producer?"

"First of all, you have to do the things that everybody ought to do anyway, like getting an education and behaving yourself. Then you have to pick out a few things to do that lead you toward your goal."

"Such as?"

"Such as coming to Yale Drama School with me, instead of going to Columbia."

"Drama school? *Me*?"

"Why not? In drama school you'll learn how to produce a play and a movie, and you'll meet the kind of people you'll later be working with when you're a producer: directors, actors, writers, technicians. And while you're at it, you should take some business courses, too, particularly accounting and marketing. Then, maybe, you should get an MBA."

"Drama school, business school," Ben mused, half to himself. "You know, that makes a lot of sense—*if* I decided I wanted to be a movie producer."

"Do you have some other career in mind?"

"My dad wants me to go to law school. I think he wants me to be like Stone."

"He'll get over it. What does your grandfather want you to do?"

"He says I should do something I love, and he'll help me get to the top of it."

"Can he help you switch from Columbia to Yale?"

"Just between you and me, Peter, I think my grandfather can make *anything* happen."

"Then he's a valuable ally. From what I've heard about him, he's very rich, too."

"Yeah, I guess he is."

"And you're his only grandchild, aren't you?"

"Yeah."

"That means you're going to have a lot of options other kids don't have."

"I never thought of it that way," Ben said, "but you're right."

"How does this sound, Ben." Peter raised a hand as if framing a big sign. "A BEN BACCHETTI PRODUCTION OF A FILM BY PETER BARRINGTON."

Ben laughed. "Hey, that sounds pretty great!"

"It can be great, if it's what we both want. What do you want, Ben?"

Ben took a deep breath. "I want that."

"Are you willing to do the things you have to to get it? Now, I don't mean stabbing people in the back, the way they seem to do in Hollywood. I mean, are you willing to do the things you have to do to learn how to do it and be great at it?"

"Yes," Ben said firmly. "I'm willing to do those things."

"And are you willing not to do the things you shouldn't do?"

"Yeah, I'm willing not to do those things."

"Great! We'll have a lot more fun if I'm not bailing you out all the time."

Ben laughed. "You know, my dad is always saying stuff like this to me, but coming from you, it makes a lot more sense."

"I'm glad, Ben. Now, because you're my friend and I trust you, I want to tell you a couple of things that nobody else knows and that I don't want anyone else to know until the right time."

"You're right, Peter, you can trust me."

"First of all, you've probably already figured out that Stone is my biological father."

"Well, yeah."

"And he and my mother are getting married."

"Great!"

"It's better if all that doesn't get around."

"I understand."

"Second, it should help motivate you to know that my mother owns about forty percent of Centurion Studios."

Ben stared at him blankly. "The actual Hollywood studio?"

"That's right. My stepfather, Vance Calder, was Centurion's most important star for fifty years, and during that time he bought the studio's stock every chance he got. A couple of times, he even took payment for acting roles in studio stock."

"That's amazing."

"Yes, it is, but it's going to be even more amazing for you and me. Get your mind around this: one day I'm going to own all that stock, and it's going to allow me to make any film I want to make at Centurion, and it's going to allow you to produce it. And it's going to allow the two of us to run Centurion Studios."

Ben sank back in his chair, looking stunned.

"Now, before you get over that idea, I've something else to tell you."

"I'm not sure I can stand it," Ben said.

"I'm not sure you can, either, but here goes: Ben, I'm only sixteen years old."

Ben sat bolt upright, looking at Peter's face for some sign that he was kidding. "I'm going to be eighteen next month; you mean you're two years younger than I am?"

"You're good at math, Ben."

"I can do eighteen minus sixteen."

"Now, Ben, my age makes me a freak, at least until I'm in my thirties, when it won't matter. But, if people think I'm eighteen, then I'm not a freak, and life will be so very much easier for me. Can you understand that?"

"Sure, I can. Your secret is safe with me, Peter."

"Good. And I have a legal birth certificate to prove I'm eighteen. Please remember: life will be easier for both of us if you continue to treat me as if I'm eighteen."

Ben smiled broadly. "No sweat, pal."

"That means I'm not going to drink until I'm twenty-one, which means until I'm twenty-three. I'm not suggesting that you should wait that long, but you'll have a better brain in your head if you do."

"I'll think about that."

"I'm probably not going to have sex for a while, either, and I don't need you to give me a hard time about it."

"Up to you, Peter."

"And it will help our career plan if you don't get anybody pregnant."

"Good point."

"Great. Now, are you ready to watch *Citizen Kane* again?"

"Are you kidding? I'm ready to produce it!"

22

On Christmas Day Stone and Arrington were dressing.

"Do you think this dress will be all right?" Arrington asked.

"It's beautiful," Stone said, "even if it's not white."

"I think I'm a little beyond the white dress," Arrington said.

Stone kissed her. "You look like a virgin bride to me."

She laughed. "It's going to be fun being married to you."

"Let's be sure to keep it that way," he said, zipping up her dress.

"Who did you say is going to marry us?"

"Eduardo said, 'an official.' That probably means a judge. He knows a lot of people like that." Stone went to his dressing room and came back with a clear plastic box. "Here's your bouquet," he said, handing it to her.

"Oh, it's beautiful, Stone. I wouldn't even have thought about that. Where's the wedding ring?"

"In my pocket," Stone said, "for Dino to convey."

"Who's going to give me away?"

"How about Peter?"

"Perfect. I don't guess we'll have a rehearsal."

"No, but if I know Eduardo, we'll have one hell of a wedding feast."

She looked at herself in the mirror. "Am I ready?"

Stone looked over her shoulder at her reflection. "I don't think it's possible to improve on that image."

Peter knocked on the door and came into the room. "Are we ready to go?"

"We are," Stone said. "What's in your leather envelope?"

"Just some stuff for Ben."

"Let's get out of here, then." They took the elevator down to the garage. Stone got them into the car and backed out into the street.

Peter rolled down the window a little. "Wow," he said, "how come the glass is so thick? It wasn't this thick on our Arnage, in L.A."

"Because it's an armored car."

"Why do you need an armored car?" Peter asked. "Is this something I should worry about?"

"No. When I bought my last car it was already armored, and it turned out to be very helpful a couple of times, especially when I rolled it end-to-end. Mike Freeman's company has a division that armors vehicles, and when I was out of a car, he lent this to me. I liked it, so I got the law firm to buy it for me. Mike gave them a good deal."

"What was the other occasion when having an armored car helped?" Peter asked.

"Somebody threw something at me from a motorcycle that might have hurt me, except for the armored glass." Stone didn't mention that what had been thrown at him was a bullet.

They drove out to Brooklyn and beyond and pulled into Eduardo's driveway at exactly twelve-thirty. Pietro, Eduardo's butler, valet, and probably bodyguard, stepped out the front door and got the car doors for them. "Everybody is ready," he said. He took their coats in the foyer, then led them down the hall in a direction Stone had never been in the house. He opened a set of double doors, and they stepped into a small, quite beautiful chapel.

Eduardo greeted them, and Stone introduced Arrington and Peter. Dino and his former wife, Mary Ann, and Ben were there, as were Bill and Marian Eggers, and then they were surprised to be introduced to the mayor of New York.

"His Honor will perform the ceremony," Eduardo said.

"Do you have the license?" the mayor asked.

Stone handed it to him.

Eduardo arranged everybody in front of the altar, and the mayor read the ceremony from a small book. Dino dealt with the ring, Peter gave away his mother, and Marian Eggers served as matron of honor. Stone and Arrington kissed and the mayor dealt with the paperwork. "I'll see that everything is filed," he said.

Eduardo led them to his large living room, where his elderly sister supervised the pouring of champagne, and toasts were offered. Then Pietro opened the doors to the dining room, they found their place cards, and were seated. There followed a parade of food that could have fed everyone in a Salvation Army chapel, where, Dino whispered, most of it would end up, with the mayor delivering it personally.

After Christmas dinner they adjourned to Eduardo's handsome library for coffee. Ben came over to Peter, whispered something to him, and Peter handed him an envelope from his little leather case. Ben went to his grandfather and asked if he could speak to him alone for a moment. They were out of the room for, perhaps, ten minutes, then returned. Ben flashed Peter a thumbs-up.

Stone leaned over to Peter, who sat between him and Arrington. "What was that all about?" he asked.

"Ben's grandfather is going to help him change from Columbia to Yale, so that we can go to college together. He's going to pass along my application, too."

"You shouldn't have asked Eduardo to do that without talking with us first," Arrington said.

"I didn't ask him, Ben did."

"Still."

"Mom, he's just passing along my application. I think it's better than mailing it in, don't you?"

"I hope you both get in," Stone said.

"We've both got the qualifications," Peter replied. "It's the interview that's important, and at least they'll know who we are when we get there."

Stone looked at Arrington. "I don't

think Dino and I could have dealt with this as well as the boys have."

Dino pulled up a chair. "I'll second that," Dino said.

Peter went over to talk with Ben and his grandfather.

"Ben's not going to law school," Dino said. "He wants to be a movie producer."

"I can imagine where he got that idea," Arrington said.

Stone spoke up. "I think it's a good idea that they go to college together."

"I'm for that, too," Dino said. "I suppose you dealt with Peter's birth certificate."

Stone nodded. "Bill Eggers did it through an L.A. judge with whom we both went to law school."

Later, Stone had an opportunity to talk with Eduardo.

"I'm very impressed with your son," the older man said.

"To tell you the truth, so am I," Stone replied. "He surprises me every day."

"Benito has told me of their plans to

work together after Yale," Eduardo said. "I think it's good that he has a friend with a good head on his shoulders."

"I'm glad Peter has such a good friend, too, Eduardo," Stone replied.

He was going to have to ask Peter about this plan he had, since he had heard nothing of it.

23

Kelli Keane was at her tiny desk in a corner of the Page Six offices at the *New York Post* when she got a call from the young man with whom she had slept the night before, who happened to work on the outer periphery of the mayor's staff.

She listened through her earpiece while simultaneously typing on her computer keyboard. "Go," she said.

"Word around the office is that the mayor married somebody yesterday."

"I thought he wouldn't do that."

"Only in exceptional cases, and in

this case, secret ones. It happened at the home of Eduardo Bianchi."

"Who?"

"Big shot, lives way the hell out in Brooklyn; on a lot of boards, corporate and charitable."

"So, who got married?"

"That's the mystery. The mayor has had Christmas dinner booked there for weeks, and after the dinner he took all the considerable leftovers to some mission down on the Bowery."

"Come on, Bruce," she said, "who are the happy couple? They must be somebody special."

"You're right, but it beats me."

"Who were the other guests for Christmas dinner?"

"I don't have anything hard on that; I'd have to guess."

"So, guess."

"Well, Bianchi has two daughters, but one of them is supposed to be in a loony bin somewhere, so the one daughter must have been there. She used to be married to Lieutenant Dino Bacchetti, who runs the detective squad at the

Nineteenth Precinct, and they have a son, so he must have been there."

"How about Dino, was he there?" She had seen him often at Elaine's.

"Maybe, who knows? Bianchi has an old battle-ax of a sister, who acts as his hostess when he entertains. That's all I can think of."

"Thanks, Bruce."

"See you this week?"

"Maybe. Give me a call." She hung up and thought for a minute, then she got up and maneuvered her long legs toward a bulletin board across the room. There was a photograph, taken at the marriage license office downtown, of a couple standing in line for a license. They were noticeable, because they were so much better dressed than anyone else in the room, but the woman stood behind the man, and her face was visible only from the eyebrows up, while the man's back was halfway to the camera. A Post-it was stuck to the picture and the words "Who are these people?" were scrawled on it. Kelli unpinned the picture and walked back to her desk with it.

Who, she wondered, was that guy who was always with Dino Bacchetti at Elaine's? Kelli was new at Page Six, having come up from Philly, so she was new in the city as well. She had been told this guy's name, but she hadn't written it down. He was tall and good-looking and always well-dressed, like the man in the photograph. She phoned her friend Gita, who worked in sports.

"Gita," the woman said. "Speak."

"It's Kelli. Remember when we were at Elaine's last week?"

"Yeah, sure." The two women had had a few drinks at the bar.

"Remember the cop Dino Bacchetti was there?"

"Yeah; he almost always is."

"And who's the good-looking guy he hangs with?"

"That's Stone Barrington. All the girls at the bar want to screw him."

"Who is he?"

"Lawyer, sort of a fix-it guy for Woodman & Weld."

"What does he fix?"

"Whatever needs fixing, I guess."

"Is he married?"

"No, famous bachelor. What, you want to screw him, too?"

"Not that I would mind, but no. We have a picture of somebody who looks like him standing in line for a marriage license the other day."

"That would definitely *not* be Stone Barrington; he'd rather be struck by lightning."

"There were some other people with him and Dino that night—a woman and a couple of kids."

"One of the kids was Dino's son—I don't know his name. No idea who the others were."

"Thanks, sweetie." Kelli hung up. Her stomach growled; it was nearly eight p.m. She turned to her computer and wrote: "Item: At whose marriage did the mayor officiate at Eduardo Bianchi's house on Christmas Day? We thought Hizzoner didn't hitch folks."

She printed it out and dropped it in the day editor's in-box on the way to the elevator. She pressed the down button and waited, then the day editor appeared with a sheet of paper in his hand and thrust it at her.

"This won't fly," he said.

"Why not? My source is good."

"You don't fuck with him."

"The mayor? We fuck with him all the time."

"That's right, you're new in town, aren't you? We don't fuck with Eduardo Bianchi. Nobody in this city does." He turned and went back to his desk, and Kelli followed him.

"So who the fuck is Eduardo Bianchi," she demanded, "that we can't fuck with him? I thought we could fuck with anybody, if the source was good."

"Almost anybody," the editor said, sinking into his chair. "We don't fuck with Rupert Murdoch, and we don't fuck with Eduardo Bianchi."

She started to ask why, but he held up a hand.

"Don't ask," he said. "Ever."

Kelli walked back to the elevator, fuming, and rode down to the lobby. She went outside and threw herself in front of a cab. "Eighty-eighth and Second Avenue," she said to the driver. All the way uptown she turned the thing over in her mind. By the time she got to Elaine's she was determined to get to the bottom of this.

She walked in and was greeted by Gianni, one of the two headwaiters. She ordered a drink at the bar, then grabbed Gianni's sleeve when he came back from seating a party. "Gianni, you know everything; who were those people with Dino and Stone the other night?"

"What people are those?" Gianni asked.

"A beautiful blond woman and a couple of kids, one of them Dino's."

Gianni looked at her evenly for a moment. "I don't know who you're talking about," he said.

She started to pursue it with him, but he stopped her.

"And let me give you some advice: don't ask Elaine, either." He walked away.

She turned away, her cheeks burning. Gianni knew who she worked for, so she was going to have to be careful, if she didn't want to get eighty-sixed from Elaine's.

A man came into the restaurant and sat down beside her at the bar. She cased him in the mirror: slicked-back black hair, Italian suit, cashmere overcoat.

"Hi," he said to her, holding out a hand. "Anthony Cecchini."

"Kelli," she said, shaking the smooth hand. The guy was definitely not a stevedore.

"Kelli what?"

"Keane, with an 'a' and an 'e' on the end."

"Buy you a drink, Kelli?"

"I've got one, thanks."

"The next one, then."

"Sure, why not." He was kind of good-looking. "I perceive that you are Italian," she said.

He laughed. "You're very perceptive."

"Tell me, Anthony, does the name Eduardo Bianchi mean anything to you?"

He froze. "Where did you hear that name?" he asked.

"Oh, around."

He turned to the bartender. "Kevin, her next drink is on me," he said, then he got up and moved to the other end of the bar.

Kelli was flabbergasted, and she didn't flabbergast easily. What the fuck was going on here?

24

A couple of days after Christmas Stone was catching up on his corporate reading, when Joan buzzed him.

"A Mr. John Ellis, from Knickerbocker Hall, on one."

Stone picked up the phone. "Stone Barrington."

"Good morning. Mr. Barrington," the man said. "I'm John Ellis from Knickerbocker."

"Good morning."

"I run a little office at the school that deals with keeping our budget on an even keel," he said.

"Oh?"

"I'm afraid that running the school on tuition fees just isn't possible, and we rely on the kindness of our alumni and the parents of our students to help us keep the ship upright."

"How can I help you, Mr. Ellis?"

"I understand that when you took the tour last week you had a look at our film school facilities."

"That's correct, we did."

"Perhaps you'll recall that two of our three cameras were out of service."

"My son certainly remembers that," Stone said.

"Also, that our editing equipment needs updating."

"He recalls that, too."

"The school would be very grateful if you could manage a donation that could help us with the modernization of our film school."

"I see. I expect you have a figure in mind."

"We were hoping that you might think a donation of one hundred thousand dollars would be reasonable, given your very bright son's deep interest in film-making."

"Let me speak with his mother about it, and I'll get back to you."

"Of course, Mr. Barrington. Let me give you my direct line."

Stone wrote down the number, hung up, and buzzed Arrington.

"Hello, there."

"Are you awake yet?"

"More or less."

"You recall that I mentioned that Knickerbocker might put the bite on us for a donation?"

"Yes, I recall."

"Well, they've taken less than a week to get around to it. A Mr. Ellis just called and mentioned that their film school equipment badly needs upgrading. They're looking for a hundred thousand."

"I talked with Peter about their equipment," she said. "From what he's told me about the cost of such stuff, I'd think it would take half a million to make a difference for the film department."

"I can't argue with that," Stone said, "but—"

"Oh, Stone, just tell Joan to write the check on my account and to bring it up to me for a signature. We should get signature cards for my accounts, too, so we can add yours."

"As you wish, love."

"See you at lunch."

Stone hung up and buzzed Joan. "Have you got Arrington's checkbook?"

"Yes, she gave it to me when she got here."

"She wants to make a donation to Knickerbocker Hall of five hundred thousand, and she's asked that you write the check and bring it upstairs for her signature."

"Will do."

"Also, she wants me to be a signatory on some of her accounts. Ask her which ones and call them for the proper paperwork. And make her a signatory on my accounts, too."

"Again, will do."

Stone called back John Ellis.

"Yes, Mr. Barrington."

"We'd like to make a donation of five hundred thousand, Mr. Ellis."

Ellis's voice lit up. "Well, that's *very* generous, Mr. Barrington."

"And we'd like your personal assurance that the entire sum will be spent on the upgrading of your filming and editing equipment," he said, "and we'd like to do it anonymously."

"Of course, of course."

"The check will go out today." Stone said good-bye and hung up before Ellis could enthuse further.

Stone and Arrington were having coffee after lunch. Peter and Ben had gone to the movies.

"I told Joan to get you put on all my accounts at Chase," Arrington said. "Banking and investment."

"If that's what you want," Stone said.

"We have to get something straight," Arrington said.

"All right."

"I don't know exactly how much money you make, and I don't care, but I don't expect you to make gifts of half a million dollars from your own resources. We're married now, and as far as I'm concerned, what's mine is yours. We'll have joint accounts on everything. I've asked Joan to get us new checks reflecting that."

"I'd prefer to go on paying for everything I'm accustomed to paying for," Stone said.

"Whatever you wish," she replied. "Just know that we're never going to have an argument about money. If you think we should give Knickerbocker another million, just write the check."

"I would be very uncomfortable doing such a thing without consulting you first," Stone said.

She kissed him. "I trust you completely," she said. "I'm aware that in the year since you and Woodman & Weld have been handling my finances, my net worth has increased more than thirty percent. That would never have happened under my old arrangement."

"Thank you."

"I also spoke to Bill Eggers about making a new will," she said. "He suggested that you might feel better if I worked directly with him on that, instead of involving you."

"Bill was right," Stone replied.

"I have an appointment with him this afternoon. I know there are major tax issues, and I want everything taken care of immediately."

"I recall that you were never a procrastinator," Stone said.

"Not now or ever," she said, laughing.

Late in the afternoon, Arrington came into Stone's office and handed him two blue legal envelopes. "Here is the original of my will and one copy. Isn't word processing wonderful? We got the whole business taken care of in two hours."

"I'll put them in the safe," Stone said, buzzing Joan.

Joan came in, and he handed her both envelopes. "This is the original and a copy of Arrington's new will," he said. He took off his signet ring and handed it to her. "Seal both with wax, write the date on the envelope, and put them in the safe. I don't ever want to see them."

"Will do, boss," she said, then she handed him a sheaf of papers. "Chase messengered over these documents and the new checks. You both need to sign them."

Stone and Arrington signed at the places indicated.

"There," Arrington said, kissing him. "Now we are truly one, blessed by the Chase Private Bank."

25

Kelli Keane got off the elevator and stopped at the day editor's desk on the way to her own. "Do we have someone who can search public records for us?"

"Yes," the editor replied, without looking up from his screen. "You."

Kelli went to her desk and dropped her large handbag, then phoned her acquaintance at City Hall.

"Yes?"

"It's Kelli."

"Well, hi, there. We getting together this week?"

"You can buy me dinner tomorrow

night at Elaine's, eight-thirty. You book the table."

"Done."

"Do you have anything more on who got married at what's-his-name's house?"

"Not a word. I don't think anybody here knows."

"Were they friends of what's-his-name or the mayor's or both?"

"No idea."

"I want more information tomorrow night," she said, "and I want you to get me a copy of a recently issued marriage license, since you're so conveniently located."

He sighed. "All right, who?"

"Stone Barrington."

"Is Stone the first or last name?"

"First. Barrington, Stone. E-mail it to me before lunch, will you?"

"You're very bossy."

"I'll make it worth your while," she breathed into the phone.

"Before lunch," he said.

Kelli Googled Stone Barrington and found only a few dozen references, mostly dealing with legal cases he had

worked on, and there was an announcement from a year ago that he had been
made a partner of Woodman & Weld.
She was surprised to learn that he had
been involved in the investigation of the
murder of the movie star Vance Calder,
fifteen years before. Kelli, being in her
twenties, knew of Calder only from his
old films on various cable channels. She
had never watched one. She looked up
the actor on Wikipedia and was surprised at the length of his entry, his film-
ography of seventy-five and his five Os-
cars. There was little about his personal
life, only that he had married in his late
sixties and fathered a child.

She looked up from her screen and
found the day editor staring down at
her. "What?" she asked.

"What are you working on?"

"Something really interesting," she
said.

"How interesting?"

"Interesting enough for me to devote
a few days to the story and not be
pecked to death by lesser assignments."

"Tell me about it."

"You have a way of cutting me off at

the knees whenever I come to you with interesting information, so I'm not going to tell you about this one until I have it fully sourced and sewn up." He stared at her for a long moment, and she realized he was looking at her cleavage. "What else can I do for you?" she asked, leaning forward to give him a better view of her unfettered breasts. He turned around and walked back to his desk, and Kelli breathed a sigh of relief.

She checked her e-mail and found one from her contact in the mayor's office. She opened it, then the attachment, printed it and saved it under a new file name, then she took the sheet of paper out of the printer and examined it.

Stone Malon Barrington had been granted a license, dated December 22, to marry Christine A. Carter. His address sounded like Turtle Bay, and hers was the same. She Googled Carter and learned that she was a freelance writer and had had many magazine articles published, including, some years before, a profile for the *New Yorker* of Vance Calder. There was no article newer than that and nothing newer in her Google search, either. So the only nexus of Carter and Barrington was Vance Calder, fifteen years before. Odd, she thought, since they were both New Yorkers and Calder had lived in Los Angeles.

She went back to her Google search of Calder and looked for a biography. Two had been written, both more than twenty years ago, so they were of no use. She called a young man in the Arts section, with whom she had had a dalliance.

"Jess."

"Kelli, how you doing?"

"Okay. You're a film buff, right?"

"Gee, how'd you guess? Could it be because I review them for the paper?"

"Tell me about Vance Calder."

"Hollywood great, up there with Jimmy Stewart, Spencer Tracy, and Cary Grant; five Academy Awards, eighteen nominations, both records for an actor. What else do you need to know?"

"Personal stuff."

"Bachelor for most of his life, lived quietly, didn't give interviews—print or

TV, except once for a *New Yorker* pro-file. The old-timers like Calder didn't do the publicity thing much."

"How come?"

"They didn't need to. The studios handled publicity but kept the press off their backs. I mean, you never saw Clark Gable on *The Tonight Show*, did you?"

"Then why would Calder sit still for a *New Yorker* profile?"

"The most prestigious of all magazine pieces, and he was nearer the end of his career than the beginning. It made quite a splash at the time, as I recall."

"Do you know anything about Christine Carter, who wrote the piece?"

"Was that her name? I forget."

"She apparently hasn't written anything since."

"Maybe she got married and quit."

"Not until Christmas Day of this year, I think."

"Married or quit?"

"Married."

"I don't know if you've heard about this, Kelli, but people sometimes marry more than once."

"Yeah, yeah. Thanks, Jess." She hung

up. Now, how the hell could she research somebody who fell off the map
fifteen years ago? There was no résumé
attached to a marriage license.

Then she had a thought. She checked
her makeup, then walked across the
room and down a corridor where senior
people had actual, enclosed offices,
some of them with windows. She
stopped before one; the name on the
door was Prunella Wheaton. Prunella
was an old-line gossip queen whose
column had been running in the paper
for something like fifty years. The door
was open, nobody home.

"Can I help you?" a deep female voice
said from behind her.

Kelli turned to find her—tall, slim,
beautifully dressed, and with just enough
surgical work done to keep her breasts
high and her wrinkles in check. She had
to be eighty, but she didn't look a day
older than sixty. "Oh, Miss Wheaton,"
Kelli gushed. "I'm Kelli Keane. I'm on
Page Six. I wonder if I could talk with
you for a moment?"

Wheaton shrugged. "Come on in,
sweetie, and take a pew."

Kelli perched on a chair across the desk from the woman. "I'm looking for information on Vance Calder, the actor."

"Of course," Wheaton replied. "What do you need?"

"Did you know him, by any chance?"

Wheaton leaned back in her chair. "Know him? I fucked him."

26

Kelli laughed in spite of herself.

"And not just once or twice," Prunella Wheaton said, smiling a little. "Often, and with enthusiasm, for the better part of a year."

Kelli started to ask a question but decided it was better to shut up and listen.

"Vance had won an Oscar for his first film outing, a western called *Bitter Creek*. During filming his girlfriend, whose name I've forgotten, was murdered by some maniac, and he was very depressed about it for a while. I was an aspiring actress then, and I went to Centurion for an audition, which he attended, and I guess I caught him on the upswing. Vance was about twenty-one but looked five or six years older. I was about your age, and I got the part, a good one. I had a couple of other decent film parts, then I made a stinker that marred my career. I cried on the shoulder of Louella Parsons, and she took pity on me and offered me a job as her assistant. I learned the trade from her, and when Louella kicked off, I got my own column."

"Did you continue to see Vance after that?"

"Occasionally. We remained on good terms, and he would let me call him now and then for a confirmation on a story. He never leaked, though, and I respected him for that." She smiled again. "In addition to being the hand-somest man I ever met, Vance was also the best lay I ever had—really adventurous and a sweet lover. I never did as well again."

"Did you know his wife? The one he married in his sixties?"

"No, by that time I was in New York and out of touch with Vance. The only time I heard anything about them was when a rumor circulated that she had been kidnapped—someone wanted something from Vance, I forget what. I called him, and he denied the whole thing, and so did the police, so that was the end of it.

"The last time I heard anything about her was a year or so ago when some L.A. developer took a run at Centurion. He wanted the back lot to build an office complex and hotel on, and Mrs. Calder opposed him and won. Vance had been buying stock in the studio since the early days and I hear owned at least a third of it."

"So Mrs. Calder inherited that?"

"That and a great deal more. Vance was very smart and a very good businessman. He worked all the time, for big money, and he invested brilliantly, the way Bing Crosby and Bob Hope had done. I don't think there was ever a richer actor in Hollywood. Some reports said he was worth more than a billion dollars."

"Wow. And then he was murdered."

"That's right."

"Who killed him?"

"Some woman he'd been having an affair with, I think. His wife was a suspect for a while, and she was dodging the police, but the thing was settled when the other woman committed suicide and left a note, as best I can recall."

"Are you acquainted with someone called Stone Barrington?" Kelli asked.

"Lawyer, habitué of Elaine's. I don't go so much anymore."

"He was apparently involved in the investigation into Calder's death."

"Oh? I don't remember that."

"Was Mrs. Calder's name Christine?"

Wheaton shook her head. "No, not Christine. Funny, I can't remember it now."

"Thank you, Miss Wheaton," Kelli said, rising.

"You're a beautiful young thing,"

Wheaton said. "Call me Prunie; everybody does."

"Thank you, Prunie."

"Come see me anytime."

Kelli thanked her again and went back to her desk. She got on her computer and went into the paper's archives, business section, and started a search beginning a year before. "Centurion, Calder" brought up the headlines about the stock battle at the studio and Mrs. Calder's part in it. She read the accounts without ever seeing Mrs. Calder's first name, but then, at the very end was a short piece saying that Michael Freeman, chairman and CEO of Strategic Services, who had voted his stock with Mrs. Calder, and Stone Barrington, of the law firm of Woodman & Weld, had joined the board of directors of Centurion Studios.

Kelli knew of Strategic Services as some giant security company that supplied bodyguards and armored cars to companies all over the world, and if the company was a major stockholder in Centurion, it made sense that Freeman might become a director. But Stone

Barrington? He was a fixer for Woodman & Weld, who had been a partner
for only a year. What was he doing on
Centurion's board?

27

Stone and Arrington were having breakfast in bed when Peter appeared, wearing a parka over a sweater and jeans, and carrying a leather tote bag. "Good morning," he said, "I'm off to school."

"Sweetheart," Arrington said, "are you sure you don't want us to drive you?"

"Oh, come on, Mom, I'm way beyond that. I'll get the bus and walk a couple of blocks. I can't be seen arriving at the front door in a Bentley."

"He's right, you know," Stone said.

"Did Joan give you your Metrocard, Peter?"

"Yep, I'm all set."

"You need lunch money?"

"You gave me a hundred bucks a few days ago. I haven't eaten my way through that, yet."

"Okay, sport, go get 'em."

Peter gave them a little wave and left.

"God," Stone said, "I never thought I'd be sending a kid off to school."

Arrington laughed. "Thank your lucky stars that you never had to change his diapers."

"I thank my lucky stars."

"What are we doing for dinner?"

"Meeting Dino and Ben at Elaine's, what else?"

"You're right, what else?" she said.

Kelli Keane and her friend from the mayor's office, Bruce Sirowitz, arrived at Elaine's at eight-thirty, and were given a decent table along the main wall, but near the back of the restaurant.

"Good work," she said.

"It's not my first time here," Bruce replied.

They ordered drinks, and Kelli leaned out into the aisle and looked again at the tables up front. "They're not here yet," she said.

"Who's not here?"

"Dino Bacchetti and Stone Barrington."

"Bacchetti from the Nineteenth Precinct? He's one of the mayor's favorite cops."

"He was at that wedding at what's-his-name's house on Christmas Day, wasn't he?"

"Kelli, don't start that again."

"It was Barrington who got married that day."

"You don't know that. You know only that he got a license earlier."

"It makes sense. What doesn't make sense is who his wife is."

"It was on the marriage license, wasn't it?"

"Yes: Christine A. Carter. She's a blank on Google for fifteen years. Wrote magazine pieces, did a profile of Vance Calder for the *New Yorker*. I think she may have married him." She grabbed his wrist and squeezed. "I was right; here they come."

Barrington, Bacchetti, a beautiful blonde, and two late-teen boys came into the restaurant together. The adults were seated up front, but the boys were given their own table farther back, a couple of tables from where Kelli and Bruce were seated.

"I think Mrs. Barrington was married to Vance Calder," Kelli said.

"That's quite a leap, given what you've got," Bruce replied. "Anyway, she's too young to have been married to Calder. He was in his seventies when he died, and that was years ago. I mean, look at her."

"Wouldn't be the first May-September romance in Hollywood," Kelli said.

"Why are you obsessed with this?" Bruce asked.

"I'm thinking of doing a biography of Vance Calder," she said.

"Good God, why?"

"Because there hasn't been one for more than twenty years, and a lot happened to him late in life, like getting married, having a kid, and getting murdered. Did you know his wife was a suspect?"

"Where did you hear that?"

"From Prunella Wheaton."

"How do you know her?"

"We work at the same paper, on the same floor," she pointed out. "I just introduced myself, and we had a conversation about Vance Calder. She told me she fucked him, and that he was the best lay she ever had. She used exactly those words."

"And she looks like such a lady."

"She's a tough old bird," Kelli said.

"I don't doubt it."

"Excuse me for a moment," Kelli said. She got up and walked over to where the two boys sat, drinking Cokes. "Hi, fellas," she said. "My name's Kelli. What's yours?" To her surprise, both boys stood up.

"Hi, I'm Ben," one of them said. "This is—"

"Joe," the other said quickly.

"Glad to meet you both. Tell me, guys—"

Then Frank, one of the headwaiters,

was positioning his large frame between Kelli and the table. "No, Kelli," he said. "You don't bother the customers."

"Take it easy, Frank," she replied, returning reluctantly to her own table.

"You're lucky Elaine isn't here yet," Frank said, then walked away and positioned himself near the boys' table.

"What was that all about?" Bruce asked.

"That was about me doing my job," she replied.

"Well, stop doing your job," Bruce said. "I don't want to get thrown out of here and eighty-sixed."

Two tables down, Ben said, "How come you told her your name is Joe?"

"She's press," Peter said. "I could have spotted her when I was six. Don't ever talk to her."

"Gee, I'd like to jump her," Ben said.

"And she'd probably let you, for a story," Peter replied. "But you'd regret it."

"I don't think so," Ben said, sneaking another peek at her legs.

"Ben, you're going to have to learn how that game is played," Peter said. "You're going to see a lot of it when we're in the film business."

"If you say so," Ben replied.

"Didn't you see what Frank just did? He rescued you from making an ass of yourself. You watch Gianni and Frank; they know who's who around here."

Frank came over. "I'm sorry about that," he said.

"Who is she?" Ben asked.

"Kelli Keane. She works on Page Six at the *Post*."

"Didn't I tell you?" Peter said.

"What did she ask you?" Frank asked.

"She wanted our names," Peter said. "I lied to her."

"You're a smart boy," Frank said, then went to meet some customers.

Ben sighed. "You were right," he said, "but I'd still like to jump her."

28

Kelli left Elaine's pissed off, and her anger kept her awake that night. The following morning she went back to see Prunella Wheaton.

"Good morning, Kelli," Wheaton said. "Have a seat. Would you like some coffee?"

"Thank you, Prunie, yes," Kelli replied, taking a chair.

"So, how are things?"

"I'm having trouble on my story," she said, "and I want to ask your advice."

Wheaton handed her coffee on a small tray, with milk and sweeteners and a cookie. "Frankly, I get bored around here. I do my work on the phone, more often than not, so I'm glad to have some company."

"I asked you before about Vance Calder," Kelli said.

"I remember."

"Let me go back to the beginning." She told Wheaton about the wedding at the Bianchi house, the mayor and Stone Barrington and Christine Carter. "I think she may be the woman Calder married, but I just can't get any confirmation. In the business reports about Centurion last year, she was always referred to as Mrs. Vance Calder. Now, if Carter turns out to be Mrs. Calder, there's a juicy little story in all this, particularly if she's as rich as you say she is. There might even be a book in it—a new bio of Calder."

"Do you know who Eduardo Bianchi is?" Wheaton asked.

"No, except that he's on a lot of boards. Nobody will talk about him, not even a guy I met in a bar."

"Who did you meet?"

"Somebody named Anthony Cec-chini."

"I see," Wheaton said. "The buzz for decades on Bianchi is that he was once a very powerful mover in the Mafia, although entirely behind the scenes. Early on, he saw a better way ahead by becoming a respectable financier and a big philanthropist, though he was said to keep a hand in with his Italian friends."

"If he's so respectable now, then why is everybody afraid of him?"

"Sweetie, there are people out there in this life that you never want to mess with."

"Like Rupert Murdoch."

"If you work at this paper, sure. Bianchi has so many good friends and contacts in this town that if you spoke ill of him or invaded his privacy, he wouldn't have to lift a finger to make life difficult for you; his friends would do it for him. A phone call would be made by someone, or a few words exchanged at some club, and next thing you knew, you'd be out of work and never even know why."

"That's scary," Kelli said.

"And you should know that your new

acquaintance, Mr. Anthony Cecchini, is the grandson of one Onofrio Cecchini—also known, improbably, as Irish Mike—who has probably been responsible for more sudden deaths than you have pubic hairs, if indeed you do, in this age of the Brazilian. I don't understand why a woman would endure that kind of pain just so her boyfriend won't get hairs in his teeth."

Kelli laughed.

"But I digress," Wheaton said. "If Cecchini *petit-fils* heard you mention Eduardo Bianchi, and if he knows what you do for a living, then Mr. Bianchi or someone who feels beholden to him knows, too."

"I just asked him if he knew who somebody was named Eduardo Bianchi. He immediately moved away from me at the bar, and he left as soon as he finished his drink."

"Could he have asked the bartender about you?"

"I didn't see them have any conversation."

"Good. If I were you, from this moment on, I would not let Mr. Bianchi's name pass my lips, nor would I utter the mayor's name in conjunction with his."

"Well, there goes my item," Kelli said sadly.

"If you were contemplating something along the lines of 'The mayor wedded Stone Barrington to the widow of Vance Calder at the home of Eduardo Bianchi,' then certainly your item is gone— or you are. Take your pick."

Kelli nodded. "I get it."

"Now, it would not be off-limits for you to connect the studly Mr. Barrington to the Calder widow and her fortune if, indeed, you can substantiate that such nuptials actually took place. Page Six thrives on that sort of thing." Wheaton picked up her phone and leafed through a fat Rolodex. "Go to the powder room, take your time, then come back."

Kelli set down her coffee cup and left Wheaton's office. She visited the ladies', did her business, touched up her makeup, then returned. Wheaton was just hanging up.

"Good timing," she said, pointing at the visitors' chair. "I just spoke to an old friend of mine, Rick Barron. Does that name mean anything to you?"

Kelli shook her head.

"Of course not; you are hardly contemporaries. Rick was, for many decades, a *macher* at Centurion. He put Vance Calder under contract when he was nineteen, at the suggestion of his wife, Glenna Gleason." She raised her eyebrows questioningly.

Kelli shook her head again.

"Major singer and movie star from the late thirties up to the sixties. They've been married for at least sixty years. So, here's the dope. Vance Calder was visiting New York around fifteen years ago when he met a young woman named Arrington Carter."

"Then Arrington is the "A" in Christine A. Carter."

"Correct. Arrington had been seriously seeing Stone Barrington for a while, living with him for much of the time, but when she did the profile on Vance, he swept her off her feet, took her back to L.A., and married her. Almost exactly nine months later, she produced a son, Peter. They lived happily ever after, until someone deposited a bullet in Vance's carcass.

"When that happened, she was a suspect, being the spouse, and she apparently called on Stone B. For help. He went out there and helped straighten out things for her. Again, last year, when the corporate raider made a run on Centurion, she called on Stone, and he was very helpful. About that time she fired her attorney and hired Stone to represent her in all things, among them, dealing with her very large interest in Centurion by serving on its board. Bringing her in as a client probably resulted in Stone's being made a partner at Woodman & Weld. Rick knows Stone and was not terribly surprised to hear that he and Arrington have married. By the way, Arrington has lived for a number of years in the environs of Charlottesville, Virginia, where she is currently building a house."

"And you got all that from one phone call?"

"You can do that, if you call the right person," Wheaton said, stroking her Rolodex like a puppy.

"Tell me, Prunie, did your contact address the issue of the father of the nine-month baby?"

Wheaton's eyebrows went up. And she smiled broadly, revealing perfect dental implants. "No, my dear," she said, "but I think you have a future in the gossip business."

29

When Stone arrived at his desk Joan handed him a slip of paper. "Mike Freeman would like you to have lunch with him and a friend at the Four Seasons, at one o'clock," she said.

Stone looked at the paper. "Who's his friend?"

"He didn't say, even when I asked him, but there's nothing else on your calendar, so I accepted for you."

"All right," Stone said.

"Also, Herbie Fisher's divorce petition has been granted."

She handed him a document. "Here's his copy of the decree."

"That was unusually fast," Stone said.

"My information is that a lot of petitions have been withdrawn, pending the new no-fault law coming into effect."

"Get Herbie for me, please."

A moment later the phone buzzed, and Stone picked up. "Good morning, Herbie."

"Good morning, Stone. You got me on the way out to class."

"I won't keep you. Your divorce petition has been granted; you're a free man again."

"That's great news, Stone."

"Try and hang on to your freedom for a while, will you?"

"I'll see what I can do. Bye." Herbie hung up.

Stone shook his head. He fully expected to hear soon from Herbie that he had found The One.

Stone walked up the stairs at the Four Seasons and immediately spotted Mike

Freeman at his regular table in the Grill, along with another man. As he approached the table, Stone saw a thickly built gentleman in a good suit with short, salt-and-pepper hair, whom he did not recognize.

Mike stood when he saw Stone coming and offered his hand. "Stone, I'd like you to meet Hank Hightower. Hank, this is Stone Barrington."

Stone shook the man's hand and sat down.

"Drink?"

"I'll stick with San Pellegrino," Stone said.

Mike ordered the water for them all, and menus arrived. He waited until lunch was on the way before continuing. "Stone, Hank is CEO of Steele Security, the insurance company."

"Ah, of course," Stone said.

"Steele, as you probably know, is a broad-based insurance company, offering just about every sort of coverage."

"Yes, I've seen the ads," Stone said. "You're an old-line company, aren't you, Hank?"

"Since 1850," Hightower replied.

Mike continued. "Hank and I have worked out a way for Steele to offer its best customers additional coverage from Strategic Services: personal security, various travel coverages, et cetera. For instance, many of Steele's clients when traveling domestically or abroad take along expensive items, like jewelry."

"Yes," Hightower said, "and these days, with all the terrorism in the world, many of our customers are feeling a bit nervous about the personal safety of themselves and their families—kidnapping, robbery, that sort of thing."

"I can understand that," Stone said.

"We're going to need a legal framework to cover our collaboration," Mike said, "and we'd like your firm to draw that up."

"We'd be very happy to do so," Stone replied. "Hank, can you supply me with an outline of your collaboration, the specific services involved, and your various responsibilities to each other?"

"I can," Hightower said, "and I will have it in your hands by tomorrow."

"Then I should think that, in a week or so, Woodman & Weld will have a draft agreement for you both to review."

"Thank you, Stone," Hightower said. "There's something else: we've been with a large law firm downtown for a dozen years or more, but for the past year or two we've been feeling neglected. I know you've heard this before: we're not getting the kind of prompt attention to our needs as in the past, and we're not getting the attention of the senior partners. In short, we're being taken for granted."

"I'm sorry to hear that, Hank," Stone said with a straight face, although he was delighted to hear it. "May we be of service?"

"I think that's a very good possibility," Hightower said. "I'd like to meet some of your people."

"I'll be very happy to arrange that," Stone said. "I think we should start by having you meet our managing partner,

Bill Eggers, and perhaps you might bring your in-house counsel, as well. Bill can give you both a precise description of the breadth and depth of our services and how we might be of help to you."

"I'd like that," Hightower said.

They talked further over lunch, and Stone left them with a promise to get back to Hightower with a firm appointment to meet with Eggers.

Stone didn't go home immediately. Woodman & Weld was located in the Seagram Building, upstairs from the Four Seasons, so he took the elevator and went straight to Eggers's office. The secretary showed him in.

"Afternoon, Stone," Eggers said. The debris of his lunch was still on his desk, and the secretary cleaned up. "What's on your mind?"

"New business," Stone said.

"Glad to hear it. Anybody I ever heard of?"

"Steele Security."

Eggers's eyebrows went up. "Are you serious?"

"I am. I just had lunch with Hank Hightower, their CEO, and Mike Freeman. They've asked us to put together an agreement between Steele and Strategic Services to cover some joint services they're going to be offering."

"Sounds interesting. Could be a wedge to get some more business from Steele."

"We don't need a wedge," Stone said. "Hightower says they're feeling neglected by their current firm and are looking for new representation. He'd like to bring his in-house counsel to meet with us."

Eggers placed a hand on his chest. "Be still my heart," he said. "Set it up. I'll make time whenever they want to come in."

Stone dug Hightower's card out of his pocket, walked over to Eggers's sofa, sat down, and picked up the phone. Five minutes later he hung up. "Three o'clock tomorrow afternoon," he said.

"Done," Eggers said, making marks on his calendar to block out the time.

"And you'll be there, too." It wasn't a question.

"Of course, though please remember that I don't know a hell of a lot about insurance."

"Maybe not, but you know how to tap-dance. I'll get a couple of department heads in on this, too."

Stone got up to go. "Bill, thanks for handling Arrington's will with such dispatch. I'm happy not to have been involved in that process."

"Have you read the will?"

"No, and I don't intend to."

"As you wish," Eggers said. "If you ever get around to it, I think you'll be pleased with the way we've organized her estate."

"I'm sure I will."

"How's the new school for Peter?"

"He's eating it up. He's going to screen the rough cut of his film for them next week."

"I made a call to Yale on the subject of his and Ben's applications," Eggers said, "and learned that Eduardo was in ahead of me."

"Thanks, Bill. Peter wants Yale badly."

Stone excused himself and walked slowly back to the house, thinking he had had a pretty good day. He walked into his office and found Arrington waiting for him, and she was in tears.

30

Stone sat down on the sofa next to her. "What's wrong, sweetheart?"

Arrington grabbed a tissue from the box on the coffee table and blew her nose. "I just had a call from an old friend of Vance's, Prunella Wheaton?"

"The gossip queen? What did she want?"

"She said she got wind of somebody looking into you and me."

"Come on, tell me the whole thing."

"Someone got ahold of a copy of our marriage license."

"That's a public record. What else?"

"Well, they've figured out that we were married at Eduardo's house and about the mayor, too, but they're afraid of printing anything about that for fear of angering some of Eduardo's friends."

"So far, so good. Is there more?"

"They've figured out that I'm Vance's widow and that I have a son."

"None of this is really a secret," Stone said. "Nobody could make very much of that."

"They might, if they can count," she said.

Stone thought about that. "I think we might have that covered with the change of birth certificate." He thought some more. "Is Prunella Wheaton a friend of yours, too?"

Arrington shook her head. "No. I met her once, when I was lunching with a group of women in L.A. She and Vance had an affair when they were very young, long before I knew him."

"And Wheaton didn't say where she heard all this?"

"No, she said it was just a rumor."

"Did you get the impression that it was somebody at the *Post*? Because that's where Wheaton's column runs in New York."

"She didn't say."

"Apart from sharing this rumor, did Wheaton ask you any questions?"

"Just girl stuff. She congratulated me on the marriage and asked how Peter is."

"What did you tell her about Peter?"

"She asked where he was in school, but I dodged that one."

"What else?"

"She asked where I'm living, and I said in New York, then I made an excuse and got off the phone."

"I think that was a good idea," Stone said. "I think this rumor may be a fiction and that Wheaton is the one who's interested. Why would a gossip columnist warn you that another gossip columnist is interested in you? This doesn't pass the smell test."

"What should we do?" Arrington asked.

"Let me make a couple of calls," Stone said, "then we'll make a plan."

"What sort of plan?"

"I don't know yet, but we don't want

to be caught off guard if she calls again, or if someone else does."

"I see."

"Did you confirm where and when the wedding took place and that the mayor performed the ceremony?"

"No, but I didn't deny it, either."

"For somebody like Wheaton, the lack of a denial is as good as a confirmation. You go upstairs and lie down, and don't answer the phone for a while. Let Joan deal with it."

Arrington stood up, and they hugged. "Thank you for being so calm," she said. She got into the elevator and went upstairs.

Stone called Bill Eggers. "Do you know Prunella Wheaton?"

"In a manner of speaking," Eggers said. "I've been at a couple of dinner parties where she happened to be, but I've always tried to bore her rigid when she tried to talk to me. Sometimes being boring is the best defense with somebody like that."

"Wheaton has caught wind of our wedding and its circumstances. Apparently, she's afraid to mention Eduardo, but we might see the mayor's presiding in print."

"He won't like that," Eggers said. "Rupert Murdoch will get an earful."

"Wheaton knew Vance Calder, and she met Arrington once. She was digging for information about us and Peter. I figure we're covered on the birth certificate, but I'd like for you or someone to call Peter's old school and warn them about giving out any information about him, especially his age."

"I see where you're going," Eggers said. "I'll take care of it, and I'll talk to the attorney in Virginia who's handling the name change."

"Good, Bill, I appreciate that."

"Do you want me to have someone call Wheaton?"

"No, don't do that; it will just pique her interest."

"Right."

Stone hung up and called Joan in. "Arrington got a call from Prunella Wheaton today," he said.

"That old bat? What did she want?"

"She said she'd heard a rumor that someone is prying into our lives, but I

think that she's the one doing the prying."

"If she calls back, I'll squash her like
a bug," Joan said.

"No, don't do that. Put on your sweet
act."

"What sweet act?"

"The one you use when you want
something from somebody you hate."

"But I don't want anything from her;
it's the other way around."

"Exactly."

"Oh."

"Arrington is always out shopping or
at a meeting or taking a nap, or something. Always take her number, but we
won't call back. Be careful about giving
her any information at all."

"I won't give her the time of day."

"But be sweet about it."

"Butter won't melt in my mouth." Joan
went back to her office.

Stone went upstairs to check on Arrington, who was stretched out on the
bed but awake. "When Peter was born
was there a birth announcement?"

She shook her head. "No, Vance told
the publicity department at Centurion

that he wanted no mention of it in the press."

"How about the columns? Did any of them print anything?"

"No, nothing at all. I spent much of my pregnancy in bed—doctors' orders—so I wasn't seen around town with a belly."

"Good," Stone said. He had a feeling that they were now going to learn how good a job they had done with Peter's name and age change.

31

The following afternoon Stone attended the meeting between Hank Hightower and his people and Eggers's department heads at Woodman & Weld. He drank a double espresso after lunch, which kept him from dozing off and having his head strike the conference table at an inopportune moment. Too many facts about the insurance business traveled into one ear and out the other, without stopping in his brain. Once or twice he was called on to nod sagely or speak an encouraging word, and at the end of the meeting, when everyone stood and shook hands and walked to the elevators together, he was of the impression that the meeting had gone very well and that a new and important client was in the offing.

"I thought that went very well," Eggers said, as Stone walked with him back to his office, "and that we may have a new and important client in the offing."

"I couldn't have put it better myself," Stone replied. "I was very impressed with how you made it possible for me to attend the entire meeting without having to voice an opinion or make any other substantive contribution."

"And that double espresso kept you bright-eyed," Eggers remarked. "I must pour that stuff into all our people before after-lunch meetings."

"Cocaine might work, too," Stone suggested.

"Well, we wouldn't want anyone to giggle or break into song, would we?"

"You have a point."

"I want to congratulate you, Stone," Eggers said. "In the space of a year you have brought three large and profitable clients into the fold. That's an impressive achievement, even if you did have to marry one of them."

"I regret that I have but one bachelorhood to give for my firm," Stone replied.

"I've spoken to the attorney in Virginia, who has already accomplished the name change in that state. The petition was advertised in a weekly publication aimed at tobacco farmers, so it is unlikely to be noticed by gossip rakers. Our partner here, who is a board member of Peter's old school, has had a discreet word with the headmaster. No information of any kind about Peter will be conveyed to anyone outside the school, which, in any case, is their longtime policy on privacy for students."

"Thank you, Bill. By the way, Peter got a letter from Yale after he left for school this morning."

"Good news?"

"Joan tried to get me to let her steam it open, but I resisted. I think, whatever information it contains, it would be best if Peter were the first to read it."

"Well, let me know," Eggers said. "I

think I'm more nervous about this than you are."

"Peter feels that both he and Ben Bacchetti are very well qualified to be accepted at Yale, and that the interview, should they be invited for one, will be the crucial test."

"How did they do on the SATs?" Eggers asked.

"Ben did extremely well in all three categories, coming out with a combined score of 2140 out of 2400."

"And Peter?"

"He aced the thing."

"A 2400?"

"That's right. They both did lots of activities in prep school as well, including working for charities, which is looked upon with favor these days. Ben was the editor for his school paper and wrote a column, and Peter has a nearly complete film to show."

"You'd think that would get them into any school in the world," Eggers said.

"Who knows?" Stone replied. "It was a lot easier when you and I were applying to NYU Law School. These days you can't know how these admissions committees work."

"Do they have backup schools?"

"Ben has already been accepted to Columbia, but Peter has no backup."

"It might not hurt if he did."

"The better I get to know Peter, the more I realize that he habitually assesses the possibilities and alternatives of any situation and chooses what he thinks is the best path. If he felt he needed a backup, he'd have one."

"He has a lot of confidence."

"He calls it structured optimism."

Eggers laughed. "I like that."

"Let's hope Yale likes it, too."

"What are you doing this evening?"

"Ben's off to Choate next week, and we're having an eighteenth birthday party for him at the house. I've rearranged my gym to provide a dance floor, and we've hired a DJ, and they'll all eat in the kitchen."

"Are you chaperoning?"

"Joan and Helene, my housekeeper, are handling that; they're a lot tougher than either Arrington or I would be. I'm setting the motion detectors on the first floor so that if anybody tries to make it to a bed, the alarm will go off and lights will flash."

"Smart move. Good luck."

Stone got back to the house in time to be there when Peter returned from school. Joan handed him the letter, and he carried it to Stone's office.

"I got a letter from Yale," he said, holding it up.

"Good," Stone replied.

"I'm going to read it now."

"Good idea."

Peter stared at the envelope a little longer, then he picked up a letter opener and carefully slit the envelope flap and removed the letter. He unfolded it and read aloud: "'Dear Mr. Barrington, we are in receipt of yours and Mr. Benito Bacchetti's applications and their relevant enclosures. We have scheduled an admissions committee meeting for 11:00 AM this Friday, the 7th, and we invite you and Mr. Bacchetti to be interviewed at that time. If this is seriously inconvenient, please phone my office to make other arrangements.'"

Peter flopped down on the couch and heaved a huge sigh. "Wow!" he said. "It's signed by the dean of the School of Drama."

"I'll drive the two of you up to New Haven on Friday morning, if you like," Stone said.

"I like," Peter replied. "Ben likes, too. Holy cow, I have to call him!"

"Call him from your room, if you will. I have work to do here, and I don't want to listen to your squeals."

Peter ran up the stairs, waving the letter.

Joan came in. "I was listening," she said. "This is so great!"

"Isn't it?" Stone said. "Where's his mother?"

"Out shopping."

"I didn't think I could make him wait until she returned to open the letter. He would have exploded."

32

At the appointed time for Ben's birthday party, Stone and Arrington had a pizza delivered and repaired to the master suite, where they watched Peter's film, rapt.

Halfway through, Stone put down his glass of beer. "He did this by himself?"

"He and the other boys," Arrington replied, "but knowing Peter, I'm sure he took the weight of it on his own shoulders."

"I didn't know he had acted in it, too."

"Neither did I. He's good, isn't he?"

"He is, and so is everything else. Now

I see why Leo Goldman at Centurion was so impressed."

They continued to watch until the final fade-out, then Stone put on some music. "You know that Peter sent his screenplay and the DVD along with his application to Yale, don't you?"

"Yes," Arrington said.

"When Leo called me and wanted to buy the film, I insisted that he return his copies to me and keep absolutely quiet about the film, but now I don't think it can be kept quiet. They'll see it at Yale, and word is bound to get around that the thing is, well, brilliant."

"Uh-oh."

"Yes."

A faint throbbing could now be felt from three floors below.

"The party seems to be at its peak," Stone said.

"I've told them to have everybody out of the house by eleven," Arrington said.

"I hope there's still a house left by then," Stone said.

———

Early on Friday morning Stone got the two boys into the car and started for New Haven. Ben had stayed the night before. They reached New Haven in plenty of time, and Stone followed the map that Peter had printed out from the Internet. They found the administrative offices, and took seats in the waiting room. Ben was called in first for his interview.

"Peter," Stone said, "your mother and I watched your film last night, and we thought it was absolutely terrific."

"Thank you, Dad."

"You remember our conversation about Leo Goldman liking it, and how I asked him to keep it a secret?"

"Sure."

"Somebody at Yale, maybe more than one person, has seen it by now, and it may be difficult to keep it quiet."

"It had occurred to me that that might happen," Peter said, "but I thought my chance of being accepted here would be better if they saw it."

"I expect that's right, but you might see if you can find out how many people have seen it and ask them to keep quiet about it."

"I can ask, I guess," Peter said.

Forty minutes passed, and Ben came out of his interview. "They'll be ready for you in a minute, they said." He plopped down beside Peter. "Whew!"

"Was it tough?"

"Not exactly, but they sure had a lot of questions. They didn't like it that I hadn't done any sort of audition, but they seemed to like it that I want to study production and get an MBA. They have a program for that."

"Good," Peter said.

A woman came and took Peter down a hall to a large office, where two men, one of them the dean of the school, and a woman waited. Introductions were made, and they all sat down at a small conference table.

The woman began. "Peter, please tell us why you want to study at the Yale School of Drama."

"For the past seven months," Peter said, "I've read up on about fifteen schools, and I concluded that Yale has the best program. It's as simple as that."

"Do you know anyone who has attended here?" she asked.

"No, but I know that Elia Kazan trained here, and as far as I'm concerned, that's the best possible recommendation."

"Have you read his autobiography?"

"Yes, twice," Peter replied.

"You've indicated in your application that you want to study both acting and directing. Why?"

"My intention is to direct, but I've enjoyed the acting I've done in school productions, and if I'm going to direct, I'll need to understand how actors think and how to work with them. I'm interested in everything you teach here, but I suppose I have to concentrate on something, so I chose acting and directing."

"You understand, don't you, that this is a professional school, and that it's very time-consuming, so you won't have an opportunity to take a lot of college courses simultaneously."

"Yes, I understand that, but by the autumn I will already have taken all of the standard liberal arts curriculum, and I've done most of the reading required to get a BA."

The three exchanged a glance. "I see," the woman said. "Who are your favorite writers?"

"Mark Twain and Jane Austen," Peter replied without hesitating. "In the theater, Tennessee Williams, Arthur Miller, and Noel Coward."

She smiled. "I believe that's the first time I've heard an applicant mention Coward," she said, half to herself. "What have you read that you would most like to direct?"

"I'd like very much to make a film of *Pride and Prejudice*," he said. "I know it's been done, but it seems to get redone every generation or so."

"What would you like to direct onstage?"

"My own plays," he replied.

"Have you written any plays?"

"My screenplay was originally intended for the stage, but my faculty adviser cautioned me against that."

"Why?"

"Since the script is about two students murdering a teacher and getting away with it, I think he thought the school's board would be reluctant to see it performed with parents present."

That got a laugh from all three. The dean spoke up. "Since your film doesn't have titles yet, I didn't realize that you had acted in it, as well as directing, until I saw you this morning. Did you find that difficult?"

"Not as difficult as I had feared. I already had all the dialogue in memory, so I didn't have to worry about that. It was mainly a matter of organizing the setups and preparing in advance so that I wouldn't waste scene time."

"You seem to have shot everything in existing light," the dean said. "Why?"

"Because we had only two lights to work with. I used them, but it's probably hard to tell where." Peter cleared his throat. "May I ask a question?"

"Of course," the woman said.

"How many people here have seen my film or read the screenplay?"

"Just the three of us," she replied. "We watched it together."

"My father is very concerned that if

the film is widely seen that it might attract a lot of attention, and he doesn't think I'm ready for that. I tend to agree with him, so may I ask that you not discuss the film with anyone else and that you return the screenplay and DVD?"

The dean answered. "I think that's a very reasonable request, and we will give you our promise to do so, until you're ready to have it more widely seen."

"Thank you," Peter replied.

"Do you have any other questions, Peter?" the woman asked.

"I don't think so; I found answers to most of my questions before I got here."

That got another laugh.

"Anyone else?" the woman asked her colleagues, but both men shook their heads. "I just want to mention one thing, Peter," she said. "Do you know that we have places for only two hundred students in our program?"

"Yes, I do, and I appreciate how difficult that must make your decisions. I hope I'm accepted, but I certainly understand why I might not be."

"Thank you for coming to see us, Peter," she said. "We notify all our applicants at the same time, so you'll get a letter in due course."

Peter shook their hands and thanked them, then left the room.

When he had left, his inquisitors all chuckled.

"He's lying, of course," said the man who had not spoken during the interview.

"About what?" the woman asked, surprised.

"About his age," the man replied. "He's not eighteen; he's at least thirty-five."

They all had a good laugh.

Stone saw Peter coming down the hall and looked at his watch. He had been gone for only twenty minutes. The three of them got up and walked out to the parking lot. "That was quick, wasn't it?"

Peter shrugged. "I don't know."

"I was in there twice as long," Ben said. "How did it go?"

"They were all very nice," Peter said.

"Had they seen your film?" Stone asked.

"Yes, all three of them. They promised not to discuss it with anyone."

"Did they like it?"

"They didn't say."

They found a restaurant and had lunch. Stone thought the boys were unusually quiet.

33

When Stone got the boys home he went upstairs to the master suite and found Arrington in bed, reading a *New Yorker*. "How did it go for the boys?" she asked, putting down the magazine.

"I'm not sure there's any way to tell," Stone replied. "They were both asked a lot of questions, but Peter was in there only half the time that Ben was. We weren't sure what to make of that. Peter extracted a promise from them that they'd return his screenplay and DVD and not mention his film to anyone."

"That's a relief," she said.

Stone picked up the magazine. "Why are you reading a fifteen-year-old *New Yorker*?"

"I'm reading the profile of Vance I wrote for them."

"Oh."

"Did you ever read it?"

"No, I was jealous."

"I"m sorry."

"Why are you reading it now?"

"There was another phone call from somebody at the *Post,* wanting information about Vance. I didn't return it, but clearly there's something afoot. I thought one way to stop it was to say that I'm writing a biography of Vance, to include a memoir of our marriage and his murder."

"I think that's a terrific idea," Stone said. "Once you're in the new house you'll have time on your hands, and working again would be good for you."

"My thoughts exactly," Arrington said. "I talked with my old agent, Mort Janklow, and he thinks there would be a lot of interest in the book."

"If you do it, you're going to have to explain when Peter was born and why his name has been changed, and I don't think it would be a good idea to tell anything but the truth."

"I think you're right, but by the time anyone saw the book, Peter would be older, when it might not matter. If I publish after he's out of Yale and working at making movies, the publicity might even give his career a boost."

"The boy wonder stories would run after he wasn't so much a boy anymore," Stone said, "and if we can keep a tight lid on it until then, it would be a stunner."

"I'm glad we're of one mind on this. Oh, and I had a call from the architect today. Completion date on the house is next week, and there are some last-minute decisions to be made that I have to be on-site for, so I thought I'd fly down tomorrow."

"For how long?"

"Three weeks, maybe a month. I'll have to get everything out of storage and moved in, and I want to send some of mine and Peter's clothes up."

"Don't send anything he's already

outgrown," Stone said. "I've bought him some new things, but he's not done growing yet."

"Good point. Maybe there's no point in sending any of his things at all. I could give them to a charity down there."

"That might be best," Stone agreed. "I think I'll move him to a larger room, too."

"He's going to have a lot of books and computer equipment," she said.

"Then maybe the suite upstairs might be a good idea. It was intended for a servant couple when the house was built, and it's empty, except for some things stored there. He'll have a bedroom and a sitting room, and I could get some shelves and storage built in."

"That's the sort of thing he would love planning," Arrington said, "so get him involved."

"I wish his grandfather were still alive," Stone said. "He could build everything and do a finer job than anyone I could hire."

"It's a pity they didn't get to know each other," Arrington said.

Stone got undressed and got into bed. He pulled her onto his shoulder, and she got out of her nightgown. "What am I going to do without you for three weeks?" he asked.

"Or a month. I suppose the way you got along without me for fifteen years." She caught herself. "Well, maybe not *exactly* the way you got along without me. I can imagine the parade of women who've marched through this bed in the interim."

"Well, I had to do *something* with my time, didn't I?"

She snuggled closer and moved her hand to his crotch. "I suppose you did," she said, "but it makes me jealous to think about them."

Stone rolled on top of her and rested on his elbows, bringing their faces to within kissing distance. "I think I like you jealous," he said, kissing her.

She reached down and maneuvered him inside her. "Stop talking, please, and start fucking."

And he did.

The following morning he drove her out to Teterboro and got her settled on the G-III Gulfstream.

"I'm concerned about your having to see Timothy Rutledge again," Stone said. "Is there any way to avoid that?"

"Not without firing him, and that would resound in the county, and not to my credit. Also, it would make him even angrier, and I don't want to have to deal with that."

"Be careful of him," Stone said. "You're right not to want to make him angry; I think he has serious anger issues."

"I'll be very correct with him," she said, "but not friendly. I'll keep it cool."

"That's the idea," he said.

"You'll come down and see the place when it's together, won't you? And bring Peter?"

"Of course, if he can take a few days off from school."

"Maybe I'll have a little housewarming and introduce my new husband to the Virginia gentry. Can you ride a horse?"

"Yes, in a manner of speaking, but the last time I was aboard one was at summer camp in Maine, when I was sixteen."

"It's like sex; you never forget how. I don't suppose you have any riding clothes."

"No, but there's time to find a hacking jacket and some boots."

"Don't forget the breeches," she said. "I'd like to see your ass in those tight ones."

"All right."

"And get a helmet, too; we're safety conscious."

"I will be very safe."

The stewardess, wife of the captain, came aft. "We've got our clearance, and we're ready to start engines now," she said.

Stone kissed Arrington once more, then walked down the airstair door and away from the jet. The door closed behind him, the whine of the engines came up, and he covered his ears.

Shortly, the aircraft taxied to runway one, and a moment later, started down the runway, accelerating quickly. It lifted off, the landing gear came up, and in another minute it was out of sight.

Stone walked back to the car, feeling lonely already. He drove back into the city, wondering what he was going to do with himself. He'd become accustomed to being married and to being a father, and he was very conscious that his life had changed in a big way. He felt confident about the future, but not about the next month, with Arrington gone.

34

Kelli Keane got to work a little late, and the strong coffee she was drinking had not yet cured her hangover. The social part of this job, she thought, could kill you, especially when combined with the kind of sex life she was accustomed to. She was still wearing the clothes she had changed into last evening for going out.

Kelli went into a ladies' room booth, moistened some paper towels, removed her panties, and gave herself a going-over. That accomplished, she took a fresh pair from her purse and put them on. Now she felt better.

She came out of the booth to find Prunella Wheaton standing before the mirror, touching up her makeup. "Good morning, Prunie," she said.

"Ah, Kelli," Wheaton replied. "You're looking a little drawn this morning. Rough night?"

"Not rough, just long."

"I'm learning that you and I are more than a little alike," Wheaton said, "at least, when I was your age. I used to come into work after a night of fucking, with it showing on my face, just like you."

Kelli checked her face in the mirror and made repairs.

"Come and see me when you have reconstituted yourself," Wheaton said as she left.

Kelli walked down the hall to Wheaton's office, accepted hot coffee in her china cup, and sipped it gratefully. "I'm at a dead end on the Calder/Barrington story," she said.

"What's the problem?" Wheaton asked.

"There are two problems," Kelli replied. "First, I ran a check on a birth certificate with Vance Calder listed as father and got back a message saying, 'Document sealed by the court.'"

"Ah," Wheaton said, "you're not going to be able to break that seal, unless you have a records clerk willing to risk his job for a couple of hundred bucks."

"I was afraid of that," Kelli replied.

"What's the second problem?" Wheaton asked.

"I also ran a check, just for the hell of it, on a birth certificate for a Peter Barrington, and I found one." She removed a copy from her purse and handed it to Wheaton. "Have a look."

Wheaton read the whole certificate. The parents listed were Christine Carter Barrington and Stone Barrington. "It seems to be in order. What's the problem?"

"Look at the date of birth," Kelli replied.

Wheaton looked and seemed to do the math. "This makes the boy eighteen," she said, furrowing her brow, "and Arrington's name wasn't Barrington that long ago."

"But if the boy was born when your

source said he was, that is, after the marriage of Calder and Carter, he would be only sixteen now."

"That *is* baffling," Wheaton said, shaking her head and reading the certificate again. "But why would they want the boy born two years earlier? That would obviate Calder as the father and make the boy a bastard. Is it possible that Stone and Arrington had an earlier marriage and were divorced? And that the boy was two when she was remarried to Vance?"

"There's no record of either Arrington or Stone being married to anybody before the marriage to Calder, at least, not in New York or California," Kelli said. "I checked the records."

"The other thing is," Wheaton said, "as far as we know, Arrington and Stone were both living in New York for the four years prior to the marriage to Vance. So why would the birth be registered in L.A.?"

"I don't know, and the birth certificate doesn't list the address of either of them. Also, you can't live in L.A. without driving, and Arrington didn't get a

California driver's license until shortly after she was married to Vance."

"Maybe the boy's birth date is just a typo on the certificate," Wheaton said. "Why don't you check the hospital records and see if they match the year on the certificate."

"Which hospital was it?" Kelli asked.

Wheaton looked at the certificate again. "Uh-oh," she said.

"What?"

"I missed this the first time. The birth took place at the Judson Clinic, in Beverly Hills."

"I'll call them."

"Don't bother," Wheaton said. "The Judson Clinic is a *very* private hospital, the sort of place that *tout* Hollywood goes to when they want a quiet abortion, or a quiet detox, or a quiet breakdown. Vance was very private. There was no birth announcement in the papers, even, and it didn't make the columns. You won't crack the Judson."

"Well, shit," Kelli said in disgust. "I'm all out of options."

"Then get Arrington on the phone and ask her to explain all this."

"I called yesterday, and a secretary told me that Mrs. Barrington is writing a book about her marriage to Vance Calder, her marriage to him and his murder, and that she will have no comment to the press until the book is published, and maybe not even then. And if that isn't enough, she's out of town, and the secretary wouldn't say where or for how long."

"Well, at least you've got that little exclusive for Page Six: Arrington Calder Barrington is writing a tell-all book. Go with that. Maybe somebody will crawl out from under a rock, so make sure your byline is on the story."

Kelli set down her empty coffee cup. "Good idea," she said. "Thanks for the advice." She went back to her desk, wrote a paragraph, including the information that Arrington had, at first, been a suspect in her husband's death, and took it to the day editor.

"What's your source for this business about the book?" he asked.

"Her husband's secretary. She gave me that as a reason for Arrington's not speaking to me."

"Okay, I'll run it at the bottom of the page, but no byline."

"I need the byline, because it might generate a call from somebody who knows something."

"Knows something about what?"

"It's going to take me at least fifteen minutes to bring you up to date," Kelli said. "Have you got that much time right now?"

"Go," he said.

So, she pulled up a chair and laid out everything she had.

"Maybe it's just a typo on the certificate," the editor said.

Kelli explained why she couldn't check with the hospital. "So, there are only two people who know the truth about this: Arrington and Stone Barrington, and neither of them is talking."

"How about the boy?" the editor asked.

"He was pretty young at the time."

"That doesn't mean he doesn't know who his father is or the circumstances of his birth. Things like that get talked about in families."

"I've already had a shot at the boy,

and he cut me dead, wouldn't even give me his name."

"Oh, come on, Kelli; a girl as attractive as you are shouldn't have a problem getting an eighteen-year-old male to talk to her."

"Give me the byline, and I'll give the boy another shot."

"Okay," the editor said. He marked up the story and tossed it into his out basket. "Now get out of here."

35

Stone woke up at his usual time and reached, as he had become accustomed to, for Arrington's ass. His hand fell on a cold sheet, and he remembered that she was in Virginia. She had called the night before to let him know she had landed safely and to speak to Peter, but that wasn't the same as falling asleep or waking up with her. Stone felt something he wasn't accustomed to: loneliness.

Stone arrived at his desk without having shaken the feeling. Joan came in.

"That woman from Page Six, Kelli Keane, called again yesterday. I gave her the story about Arrington writing a book, and I think she bought it."

"Actually, it's the truth," Stone said. "Arrington plans to do just that."

"Boy, I want to read that one," Joan said, then went back to her desk. A moment later she buzzed: "Bill Eggers on line one."

Stone picked up. "Good morning, Bill."

"A better morning than you may know," Eggers said. "Hank Hightower called a moment ago and hired us to handle Steele Security—all of it. We'll have an agreement for him to sign before the close of business today, and he'll have fired his previous firm by that time, so we're getting ready to receive their files. His old firm will bombard us with irrelevant paper, and we'll have to sort it out for ourselves."

"You do understand, don't you, Bill,

that I'm just terrible at that kind of work?"

"Don't worry, that's what we have associates for. And speaking of associates, I think it's time we assigned one to you."

"I'd appreciate that, Bill. I'm getting tired of reading all the financial paper. It would be good to have somebody prioritize what I need to know."

"I'm going to give you a young woman named Allison Wainwright," Eggers said. "She's been here a year, so she's not green, and I think she'll be a good fit for you."

"Thanks, Bill."

"Shall I send her over to see you?"

"Sure; I'm here all day."

"You'll find her a little . . . different."

"What do you mean by that?"

"It's hard to characterize. You can make your own judgments. If you don't like the way it's going, I'll pull her and assign you somebody else."

"Okay."

"Talk to you later." Eggers hung up.

Less than an hour passed when Joan buzzed. "There's an Allison Wainwright to see you."

"Ah, yes. I forgot to tell you, she's an associate at Woodman & Weld, and Eggers has assigned her to me. Send her in, and then you can put her in the office next to yours."

"Okay."

There was a rap at the door, and Stone looked up to see an impeccably dressed young woman, with perfect dark hair and chiseled features. "Good morning," he said.

"Good morning. I'm Allison Wainwright."

Stone stood up, shook her hand, and waved her to a chair in his seating area, then sat down himself.

"Do you have any idea why I've been assigned to work here?" she asked.

"Bill Eggers thinks I need an associate. I've no idea why he picked you."

"I'm not sure I like the idea of being stuck in Turtle Bay," she said.

"The door you came in by works both ways," Stone said, "but before you leave, shall we talk a little?"

"Oh, all right," she said.

"Tell me about your background."

"Personal or educational?"

"Whatever you think is important for me to know."

She took a deep breath. "Born and raised in New York City, Spence School, then Mount Holyoke and Columbia Law." She hadn't needed a second breath.

"You look like all of those," Stone said.

"What do you mean by that?" she asked, sounding defensive.

"I meant it to be a compliment," Stone replied.

"Oh. What, exactly, do you expect from me?"

"For a start, I want you to read all the corporate paper that comes into this office from Strategic Services and, starting soon, from Steele Security, our new client, and brief me on the high points. In short, I want to be able to appear that I know about everything financial in both firms, without actually having to read the documents."

"I get the picture."

"I believe they'll be sorting out the files as they arrive from the client's previous firm, so you won't have to do that."

"What else?"

"I'll let you know when it comes up."

"Is your secretary my secretary, too?"

"Did you have a secretary in the Seagram Building?"

"Just somebody to handle the phones."

"Joan will do that for you here. We have a line that runs through the main switchboard, so you should probably route your calls through them; Joan will give you an extension number. My advice to you is, make friends with Joan."

"Why?"

"First, common courtesy; second, she's a very nice lady and extremely capable; third, she makes a bad enemy."

"All good reasons," Allison said.

"And if you're unhappy working in Turtle Bay, you can work from your own desk at W&W, but don't let your distance make more work for Joan, like calling her to come get a file. If you be-

come friends, she'll go out of her way
to help you."

"Okay."

"Allison, you seem to have some sort
of chip on your shoulder. You want to
tell me about it?"

"It's nothing to do with you, in spite
of what I've heard. I just thought that by
this time, I'd be doing more important
work."

"What sort of work?"

"More client contact."

"You've been with the firm for what, a
year?"

"Yes."

"There are people over there who've
been associates for twenty years or
more and have rarely seen a client, and
they're doing important work. My experience of Bill Eggers is that he likes to
see people succeed, and if you impress
him, you'll be given all the responsibility
you can handle."

"I've heard that," she said.

"Did you expect that you'd make
partner by now?"

"No, of course not."

"Why do you think Bill sent you to me?"

"I'm not sure," she said.

"Have you been having problems with people in Seagram?"

"A little, maybe."

"Well, there are fewer people to get along with here; maybe Bill thought it would be good practice for you to start small, before you go back to the offices."

"You haven't asked what I've heard about you," she said.

"I'm not interested in gossip. If you've heard something that concerns you, then bring it up now or later, and we can talk about it."

"All right. I've heard that you will screw anything that moves, and I'm not up for that."

Stone laughed. "Perhaps you haven't heard that I'm recently married."

"No, I hadn't."

"She's in Virginia, moving into a new house that she started a year ago, and she'll be gone the better part of a month, but your virtue is not in jeopardy. And we have a son who's in school at Knickerbocker Hall, on the Upper East Side. His name is Peter, and you'll meet him in due course. You'll find that he's smarter than you, just as he's smarter than I. It can be a little unsettling at first, but he's a good kid."

"I'll look forward to meeting him."

"One other thing: a gossip-type journalist has been sniffing around since our wedding, so be on your guard, and let me know immediately if somebody sidles up to you and starts asking questions. Our privacy is important to us."

"Of course."

"Any other questions?"

"I expect I'll have some soon."

"Try Joan first, then me. Go see her, and she'll get you settled. You'd be smart to take her to lunch one day soon."

"I'll do that." Allison got up and left Stone's office.

36

Kelli Keane got out of a taxi a couple of doors down the street from Stone Barrington's house, and stood opposite, stamping her feet in her boots and wrapping her long coat around her legs, trying to keep warm. It was seven a.m., and she was just going to wait until the kid went to school.

She was fortunate that Peter left the house only a few minutes later and walked up to Third Avenue, while Kelli kept pace with him on the opposite side of the street. He waited for a bus while she hailed a cab and got in. "Just wait here until the bus comes," she told the driver, "and when it does, follow it and don't get ahead of it."

"Follow a *bus*?" the driver said. "Whatever happened to follow that *car*?"

"Times are hard," Kelli replied. "More people are taking the bus."

The bus arrived, Peter got aboard, and the two vehicles moved in tandem up Third Avenue. Finally Peter got off and walked toward Second Avenue, and Kelli told the driver to turn right and stop. She watched as Peter ran up the steps of a large building and disappeared inside.

"Go down to that building and stop," she said to the driver, who did so. "What's the name of this place?" she asked.

"Knickerbocker Hall," the driver replied. "It's chiseled in stone over the front door."

"Oh, yeah." She gave him the address of the *Post*.

"You work at the *Post*? I thought you were a private eye," the driver said.

"You're a romantic, aren't you?"

"Sure; you want a demonstration?"
"Just drive."

Peter walked upstairs in the nearly
empty building. It was only seven-thirty.
As he was about to turn into the film
department, he heard piano music coming from the opposite direction. He
turned right instead of left, into the music department, and the music got
louder. Like a cross between Chopin
and Rachmaninoff, he thought, if that
was possible. He looked through a window in a door marked "Recital Hall" and
saw a very pretty girl seated at a nine-
foot grand piano, playing with enthusiasm and precision. He pushed open the
door, tiptoed in, and took a seat at the
rear of the little hall.

She finished the piece with a flourish
and, without looking up from the keyboard, said, "Come on down front;
you're bothering me way back there."

Peter walked down and took a seat
in the front row, only a few feet from
where she sat.

She began to play again, this time in

a jazz-inflected style. Peter thought he heard the left hand of Errol Garner and, in the right hand, traces of Nat Cole. She finished, and he said, "I don't recognize that."

"I'm just improvising," she said.

"The first piece, too?"

"Yes. I've never seen you here before. Who are you?"

"I'm Peter Barrington. I'm in the film school."

"I'm Hattie Patrick," she said, leaning over the lip of the little stage and offering her hand.

Peter thought she was even more beautiful close up.

"Are you new here?"

"Yes, I just started this term."

"Where were you in school before?"

"In Virginia. I moved to New York just before Christmas. I live in Turtle Bay. Do you know it?"

"Yes. I once saw it from a tall building on Third Avenue. The interior garden looks very inviting," she said.

"I'll give you a tour of the gardens sometime."

"I think we should wait until spring for that; everything's dead now."

"Do you compose or just improvise?"

"Composition is what I'm studying at Knickerbocker," she said. "Why do you ask?"

"Because I've made a film, which is nearly finished, but I don't have a score. Would you like to try writing it?"

"How old are you?" she asked.

"I'm eighteen," he said. "How old are you?"

"I'll be eighteen on Saturday," she replied. "You talk like someone a lot older, no slang."

"It's not the first time I've heard that," Peter said. "So do you."

She laughed. "It's not the first time I've heard that, either."

"If you're interested, I'll take you to a birthday lunch on Saturday and then screen the film for you."

"Screen it where?"

"At my house. Don't worry, my dad will be there to chaperone us."

She looked at him. "I'm not worried," she said. "I'd like that, but could I see the film before then? That way I might have some ideas about the score to talk about."

Peter took the screenplay and DVD from his leather envelope and handed it to her. "It looks best on Blu-ray."

"I've got Blu-ray in my room. I'll watch it tonight. What's it about?"

"You'll know tonight. Where do you live?"

"At Park and Sixty-third Street."

"Do you know the Brasserie restaurant in the basement of the Seagram Building, entrance on Fifty-third?"

"Yes, I've been there."

"May we meet at the Brasserie at twelve-thirty on Saturday?"

"Yes, that will be fine. You said your dad will be at the house. How about your mother?"

"She's back in Virginia for a couple of weeks," Peter replied, "moving us into a new house."

"Are you going to live there?"

"Only part-time. New York is home, now."

"Welcome to the big city. How do you like it so far?"

"It's everything I dreamed it would be," Peter said.

"You dreamed about living here?"

"Everybody who doesn't live in New York dreams about living here. I'm no exception. I can go to the movies as often as I like."

"The movies are your thing, are they?"

"I like the theater, too, but I'm crazy about movies. If you're not, I'll probably bore you rigid."

She laughed. "I like movies, and you don't seem in the least boring."

"That's the nicest thing anybody has said to me in the big city," he said. He glanced at his watch. "I have an appointment with some editing equipment. If you'll excuse me, I'll see you on Saturday."

"I'll look forward to it," she replied. She turned back to the piano and began to play again.

Peter left the recital hall and walked back to the film department, feeling a little light-headed. He felt some other things he hadn't felt before, too.

37

Alan Ripley switched off the light in his office and, in the gathering dusk, walked across the campus at Herald Academy in tidewater Virginia, kicking at little piles of leaves the wind had gathered. Autumn came late here, but now there was a real nip in the air. He wrapped his muffler tighter.

He climbed the stairs to his small apartment in the faculty residence and switched on the lights, then he lit the already laid fire and backed up to the hearth as it caught. When his backside got too hot to handle he poured himself a small scotch, settled in a leather wing chair near the fire, and picked up the le Carré novel he had been reading. He had just opened the book when the phone rang. He closed the book and grabbed the phone. "Hello?"

"Alan?" A vaguely familiar voice.

"Yes, who's that?"

"A voice from the past. It's James Heald."

Ripley was pleasantly surprised. "James? It's good to hear from you. I haven't heard that voice since we left Harvard."

"Good to hear yours, too."

"Where are you? What are you doing?"

"I'm teaching set design at the Yale School of Drama."

"Good for you. I'd heard you were working on Broadway at some point."

"Yes, but it was too fast a track for me, and the gaps between jobs were too long. I've been at Yale for nearly two years, now, and it suits me better."

"Congratulations. It sounds like a good place to be. How did you find me?"

"Well, I stopped n the dean's office for a minute last week and I caught a bit of your performance."

"Performance? What do you mean?"

"Your screen acting performance."

"You baffle me."

"Didn't you act in a student film down there?"

"Oh, Christ, yes. I'm sorry, I didn't make the connection. We don't really have a film department as such, and I acted as faculty adviser on a student project last year. I got roped into playing a part. That must have been what you saw."

"That's exactly what I saw, and just enough to get the gist of the plot. I must say, I was impressed. Perhaps you missed your calling."

"Well, if the recession ever catches up with music teachers, maybe I'll try Broadway or Hollywood."

"Did you know I went to Herald?"

"No, I didn't. I don't expect it's changed much since you were here."

"Probably not. I have to tell you that I'm surprised the powers that be down there allowed the film to be made."

"You baffle me, James. Why shouldn't they allow it?"

"Did anybody from above read the script?"

"No, I guess not. I haven't even read it myself."

"You were the faculty adviser, and you didn't read the script?"

"No, the boy who directed it came over all Woody Allen and insisted that the actors saw only the pages of the scenes they were appearing in. He was very secretive about the project. I wondered why, at first, but he assured me that there was no nudity, no sex, and only minimal, prep-school-boy bad language."

"Ah, now I begin to get it."

"Get what?"

"Well, after I saw the scene in our dean's office, I filched the script from his secretary's desk and read it."

Now Ripley was getting worried. "Was there anything alarming in it?"

"Nothing that would alarm the general public, since it's only a student film, but you should hope the headmaster never sees the film."

"Why on earth should I be concerned about that?"

"You obviously don't get it, Alan. The script fairly closely follows some real events at the school. It would have been before your time, of course—five or six years ago. I could see why you wouldn't have known. I can also see why the student wanted to keep his film under wraps. I take it you haven't seen the finished product."

"No, the boy left school early, and he was still editing, I think. He promised to send me a DVD, but he hasn't as yet done so."

"Mmmm, yes."

"James, exactly what real events does the film follow?"

"Well, as I said, it was before your time there, and after mine. I didn't hear about this until I attended my tenth reunion. There was some talk about it at that time."

"Go on."

"Well, the rough outline is something like this: a master diddles a student, student drops out of school, hangs himself while allegedly doing that sex thing that's supposed to generate an orgasm with partial asphyxiation—but suicide is a possibility."

"Good God!"

"Hang on to your hat, my friend, there's more."

"The investigation is cursory—small-town Virginia police, you know, but back at Herald, the boy's death brings attention to bear on a chemistry master. A few weeks later, the master is found dead in his study."

"Dead how?"

"The supposition is suicide, but the autopsy report does not give a cause of death. But the fellow *is* a chemistry master, after all, and the feeling is that he mixed up some sort of untraceable potion and offed himself."

"This is awful," Ripley said, downing the remainder of his scotch.

"Just one more thing: there was a suspicion in the air that one or more of his students, out to avenge their class-mate, may have concocted the potion and somehow introduced it into his sys-tem. The police questioned everybody, but they could find no evidence pointing to anyone in particular. By that time, the master's remains had been cremated, and his ashes scattered on the James River, so the whole business eventually petered out."

"James," Ripley said, "is there any way you can get your hands on that script, or the DVD?"

"Nope. The boy asked for both to be returned to him, and they were. He didn't want anyone to see it. Actually, that may not be a bad thing for you. And, if the headmaster gets wind of the flick, you might want to stick with only the facts you knew before this conversation, which I will keep to myself. After all, being dumb is better than being complicit."

"You have a point," Ripley said. "Tell me how this film came to be in your dean's office."

"The boy, this Peter Barrington, has applied for admission to the school, and the word is, he had a favorable interview. The dean did tell his secretary that the committee all thought his film was brilliant, the sort of thing that might do well at the indie festivals."

"You said Barrington?"

"Peter Barrington."

What the hell? Ripley thought. "His name wasn't Barrington when he was here. It was Calder."

"Like the sculptor?"

"Like the actor. So, if he's accepted, he would matriculate in the fall?"

"It seems so."

"Well, thanks for the heads-up, James."

"Not at all, Alan."

"At least I'll know what I'm up against if I have to face the headmaster monster."

"If you get up this way, let me know, and I'll buy you a bad lunch in our cafeteria."

"Certainly will, James. Take care." Ripley hung up and stared into the fire. *So now Peter Calder is Peter Barrington? Let's see, it's January*, he thought. *If I start looking now, I might just be able to find a new job before the fall.*

He poured himself a second scotch, a larger one.

38

Arrington drove from her rental house to her new property and turned down the long, oak-lined drive. Even from that distance she could see Tim Rutledge waiting for her on the front porch, a roll of blueprints under his arm. He stood stone-still, staring at her as she approached.

Arrington began to take deep breaths, trying to keep her blood pressure from rising. She parked her car out front, then gathered her purse and her briefcase and got out. She walked up the front steps purposefully, tucked her purse under one arm, and held out her hand. "Good morning, Tim," she said.

He looked at her hand contemptuously, then deigned to shake it briefly. "Good morning," he said. "Is that all you have to say to me?"

"I'm sure I will have a great deal to say to you, once we get to work, and it will be all business. I believe that has been made clear to you."

"Well, Barrington called and said he was your lawyer. That was news to me."

"He has been my attorney for just over a year, and I'm very pleased with him. I trust him to convey to others my exact intentions."

"Does that include your intentions toward me?"

"It does. Now, shall we get to work?" Without waiting for a reply, she inserted her key in the front door and opened it. She walked into the broad hallway that ran the length of the house, stopped and looked around. "Take notes," she said.

Rutledge produced a yellow legal pad and pen.

"The color of the wood stain on the

floor of the library is not the one I selected; it's not dark enough."

"I thought it should be the same as
that in the hall," Rutledge replied.

Arrington walked into the library, set
her briefcase on the top of a steplad-
der, opened it, and took out a stain
chart. She dropped it on the floor. "See
the X?" she asked. "That's the color I
want on this floor. Please see that it's
sanded and restained immediately. I
can see that there's only one coat of
varnish applied, and when the stain is
right, I want ten coats, as I specified
earlier. Same for the hall."

"All right," Rutledge said, making a
note.

"I do not want the move-in date
changed by so much as an hour, because the ten coats have taken so long
to dry. With the varnish I selected you
can apply two coats a day, one at eight
a.m., another at six p.m."

"All right," Rutledge said.

"Where is the shotgun cabinet?" she
asked, pointing at a gap in the beautiful
paneling, near the fireplace.

"The cabinetmaker made a serious

error, and I insisted he remake it. It will be installed tomorrow."

"When my furnishings arrive, you will find two very fine shotguns and two rifles that belonged to my father. Please be sure that they are securely locked in that cabinet. Where are the keys?"

"The cabinetmaker has them. He had to install the locks."

"Fine. I don't want those weapons stolen; they're worth a fortune."

"I understand."

He was beginning to sound more cordial, she thought.

"Listen to me, Arrington," he said.

She turned to face him. "Yes? Is this about the house?"

"It's about you and me. You can't treat me as if I'm some servant who works here, not after what we've done in bed."

Arrington drew back her right hand and delivered a swinging slap that connected with his face, staggering him. He stood, wide-eyed, staring at her.

"Don't you ever again speak to me in that manner, or about anything but this house. Is that perfectly clear?"

Rutledge rubbed his face, which had turned red with anger.

"As you wish," he said.

"And there's something you should know: Stone Barrington and I were married on Christmas Day."

Rutledge turned pale and was blinking rapidly. "Congratulations," he said weakly.

"Good," she replied. "Now, let's have a look at the living room floors." She led him through the remainder of her list of things to do in the house, then she curtly said good-bye, got into her car, and drove back to her rental house.

39

Stone had slept late on Saturday morning when the phone rang. "Hello?" He coughed.

"Poor baby," Arrington said, "I woke you. I thought you woke at dawn, regardless of the day."

"So did I," Stone replied, pressing the button to raise the head and foot of his bed to a sitting position. "How's it going down there?"

"Better," she said. "It was a mess when I got here, but I got it sorted out. The floors in the library and living room had been stained improperly, but that is being redone, and there were a dozen other things that needed attention. Moving-in day is next Friday."

"Do you want me to come down there and help?"

"You'd just be in the way. You don't know where anything goes, and I have a carefully worked out plan for where every piece of furniture and box should land. Anyway, I don't want you to see it until it's perfect."

"I can handle perfect," Stone said.

"What are you doing with yourself today?"

"Chaperoning Peter and a girlfriend."

"Girlfriend? What's this?"

"She's a music student at Knickerbocker, and he says she's going to score his movie. He's pretty excited about it. They're going to lunch at the Brasserie, then coming here to watch the film."

"And you're going to sit between them, right?"

"Maybe I'll watch it with them, or maybe just bundle them up in blankets and seal them in with duct tape. By the way, I read his script while he was having his interview at Yale, and I thought it was great."

"Be sure and look in on them several times," she said. "After all, he *is* your son, so he got half his genes from you."

"And the other half from you."

"That doesn't make me feel any better."

"Peter and I had the conversation about sex, you know. I told you about it."

"Well, I hope you didn't tell him anything he didn't already know."

"I don't think I did. In fact, about the only thing I could have told him was the only thing I've ever really learned about women."

"Which is?"

"That they like sex just as much as men."

"Good God! I hope you didn't tell him that!"

"He'll find out for himself in due course."

"Due course is why he needs watching."

"What would you do, if you were here?"

"I told you: sit between them."

"I don't think that's a possibility," Stone said. "Anything else?"

"Who is this girl?"

"Hattie something. She lives at Park and Sixty-third."

"At least she's from a good address. That makes me sound like a snob, doesn't it?"

"*Everybody* at Knickerbocker is from a good address."

"You know, I think this is Peter's first real date," she said.

"Unless something happened at Herald that you don't know about."

"Perish the thought! Anyway, they were watched like hawks by the faculty anytime there were girls on campus."

"Oh, I forgot to tell you: the woman from the *Post* called again."

"Prunie?"

"No, the younger one. Joan told her you were doing a book and that you would have nothing further to say until it's published. Joan thinks that put her off."

"I'm so glad. That sort of thing was a

constant threat when Vance was alive. We had to book at Beverly Hills restaurants under false names to avoid the paparazzi."

"New York is better about that, I think."

"Then why are they so interested in us?"

"Maybe we should hire a publicist," Stone suggested.

"But we don't *want* any publicity."

"I mean hire a publicist to keep our names out of the columns."

"How does that work? It sounds unnatural."

"The publicist puts out a press release saying that he's representing us, so all the calls go to him, if there's a question, and he gives them something innocuous, or just brushes them off."

"Vance never had a publicist."

"He had the studio, and they have a whole publicity department."

"You're right."

"If we were in L.A. they could handle it for us, but they're probably too far away. But things have been quiet, since

Joan brushed the woman off, so we probably don't need to do anything about publicity, until Peter is a famous director."

"Then he can get his own publicist. Oh, a delivery truck has just pulled up outside; I have to go. I love you!"

"Wait a minute!"

"Yes?"

"How did it go with Timothy Rutledge?"

"I managed very well, thank you. Bye-bye!"

"I love you, too," Stone said, but she had hung up.

Peter arrived at the Brasserie ten minutes early, was given a booth with a view of the front door, and sat down and waited nervously. Hattie was ten minutes late, and Peter had already had a glass of iced tea and needed to go to the bathroom.

He went to meet her as she descended the stairs from the door and escorted her to their booth.

"I *really* liked your film," she said, as she slid into her side of the table, "and I already have some ideas about what the score could sound like."

"Wonderful!" he said.

"Do you have a piano at your house?"

"Yes, but I'm not sure it's in tune. That's all right, though, I have an electronic keyboard."

"Do you play?"

"Sort of. I amuse myself with it sometimes."

They were brought menus and studied them carefully.

"What would you like?" he asked.

"I'll have the eggs Benedict," she replied.

"Good idea. So will I."

They ordered, and Peter sat back in his seat and looked at her. "It's the first time I've seen you when you weren't in profile," he said.

"And what is your opinion?" she asked, archly.

"Very high," he said. "I have a high opinion."

"That was just the right thing to say," she said, blushing a little.

They seemed stuck for words for a moment, so Peter said, "Excuse me, I have to go to the men's room."

And he did.

40

Kelli Keane sat at the bar at the Brasserie and toyed with her lunch. She had spotted Peter Barrington the moment he entered the restaurant, and he had made it obvious that he was waiting for someone. Kelli was delighted with the coincidence that she and Peter had chosen the same restaurant. She had been working too hard at this, she thought, and she deserved a break.

When the girl arrived Kelli saw how Peter hurried to meet her. This was obviously a first date, and he had probably met the girl at school. She was a pretty thing and fashionably dressed for a high school girl. This was the first time Kelli had had an opportunity to stare unblinkingly at Peter and take his measure. He seemed exceptionally mature for an eighteen-year-old, and she knew a lot about the subspecies, having started to date eighteen-year-olds when she was thirteen, and having lost her virginity to the second one, at thirteen and a half. She had had an abortion at sixteen, as the result of carelessness with yet another eighteen-year-old, and she had turned her attention then to twenty-one-year-olds, who seemed to have a greater appreciation of the pitfalls of the menstrual cycle.

Peter did not have the native slovenliness of the current crop of eighteen-year-olds, nor did he seem to need the appearance of stubble or a patchy beard to build his confidence. She was willing to bet that his room was very neatly kept.

The headwaiter drifted by and Kelli snagged him. "Hey, Geoffrey," she said.

"Kelli, how you doing? You want a table?"

"No, I'm fine at the bar. Tell you what I do want, though: see those two kids over there in the booth?"

"Yeah."

"There's a hundred in it if you can find out the girl's name and where she lives."

"Would you like to pay now or later?" he asked.

"Payment is on delivery," she said.

Bruce ambled over to where the young couple sat. "Good day, folks," he said. "Is this your first visit to the Brasserie?"

Both shook their heads.

"Well, we're very happy to have you as regulars. I'm Bruce, your mâitre d'." He offered his hand to the boy, who shook it and replied, "Peter Barrington."

He turned to the girl. "And you?"

"Hattie Patrick," she replied, shaking his hand.

"I'm very pleased to meet you both. Do you live in the neighborhood?"

"I'm at Sixty-third and Park," the girl said, "and Peter lives in Turtle Bay."

"Great. I hope we'll see both of you often." He strolled away, spoke to a couple of other diners for cover, then went back to the bar.

"Hattie Patrick," he said, "Sixty-third and Park."

Kelli slipped him the hundred. "Bruce, you're a dear, and very clever, too."

"He was nice," Hattie said to Peter.

"Yes, he was. Maybe we'll become regulars, like he said."

"Are you a regular anywhere else?" she asked.

"Only at the Knickerbocker cafeteria," Peter replied. "My dad hangs out at Elaine's."

"I've never been. Will you take me sometime?"

"Sure, I'd love to take you. We could ask my friend Ben along, but he's headed back to Choate Monday."

"Who are your friends at school?" Hattie asked.

"Just you. I haven't been there long enough to make other friends."

"I'm confused about something," she said.

"What?"

"You did say you graduated from your last school in December."

"That's right."

"How did that happen?"

"Well, I took a lot of courses and got ahead of the curriculum."

"While shooting a movie at the same time?"

"Yeah, we only worked a couple of hours a day on the movie."

"Are you just taking film courses at Knickerbocker?"

"I'm taking college-level French and American history, too."

"Are you going to college in the fall?"

"Ben and I have both applied to the Yale School of Drama."

"You want to be an actor?"

"I want to learn about acting. They have a directing program, too, and Ben wants to produce, and they have a program for that, even an MBA. When we get out of school we want to be partners in the making of films."

"That sounds very ambitious," she said. "I wish I had that kind of inner direction. I seem to just wander along, doing whatever seems like a good idea at the time."

"Studying musical composition seems to be a very directed choice," Peter said.

"I suppose so. That was a delicious lunch."

"Mine, too. Shall we go to my house?"

"Sure."

Peter paid the check, and they walked over to Turtle Bay. He let them into the house and hung up their coats, then they went into the living room where the old Steinway grand was.

Hattie sat down and riffed through a few chords. "Have you decided what the titles are going to be like yet?" she asked.

"I have a lot of shots of the school campus and the James River. I thought I might string together some of them under the titles."

"Good, that's what I was thinking,"

she said. She began to play. "I thought
I would begin with a slow passage,
sort of pastoral in nature, like this."
She played a few measures. "Then I'll
establish a simple theme that will return at various points in the film." She
played the theme, then another minute
or two of music, then stopped. "This is
where it says, 'Directed by Peter Barrington,'" she said. "Then the music
stops for a while. I think the score
should be kind of spare. I hated it in a
lot of old movies when the music was
there all the time. I don't think a film
needs music all the way through; it
should be saved for when it's needed
to augment the film, maybe heighten
the drama. Listen to this: it's when the
two boys are actually mixing the poison that they're going to give to the
master." She played a spikier, more
staccato passage.

"That's perfect," Peter said, in awe of
what he was hearing. "I'd be happy for
the whole score to be just your piano."

"There are a few places where we
could add a cello and a flute," she said,
"and I'd like a double bass in the more

dramatic passages. There are kids at school who could play those parts."

"Whatever you say. Play me the theme again."

She began the passage, and Peter was swept into it. He closed his eyes and listened.

41

Stone was in his office when, from upstairs, he heard the sound of the piano. It sounded very nice, he thought, and he was glad he had it tuned twice a year. After a while the music stopped, and Stone thought that, in light of his conversation with Arrington, he should find out why. He got up and went upstairs.

"Good afternoon," he said, startling the teenagers.

"Hello, Dad," Peter said. "I'd like you to meet Hattie Patrick, my friend from school."

Stone shook her hand. "Hello, Hattie. I liked what you were playing a minute ago."

"I hope we didn't disturb you," she said.

"Not at all."

"That was some of the music Hattie has written for the score of my movie, Dad," Peter said.

"Wonderful. Peter, if you have a moment, there's something I'd like to show you. Hattie, you can come along, too."

He led them to the elevator and they rose to the top floor. Stone switched on a hallway light, then they walked into a sunny room at the rear of the house, overlooking the gardens. "Peter, I think you need more space for the things your mother is sending from Virginia, and I thought you might like these two rooms. The bedroom is over there," he said, pointing.

"This is nice," Peter said. "Hattie, do you like it?"

"Very much," she replied. "You could make it beautiful."

"You'll need some bookcases, and

maybe a built-in desk for your computer station," Stone said, pointing.

"I can design those," Peter said, "and we can get someone to build them."

"I know a good cabinetmaker," Stone said. "He used to work for your grandfather. Make some drawings, and we'll get him in for a look."

"Okay. Let me look around some more, then Hattie and I are going to watch my film together and make some notes for the score," Peter said.

"Good," Stone said. "I'll be right next door." He hoped Peter got the message.

Stone left them there and went down to the master suite, where he opened the *Times* and started on the Saturday crossword, always the toughest of the week.

Kelli Keane got home to her little apartment on Third Avenue in the Seventies and immediately went to her computer. She opened a program that searched apartment buildings for the names of tenants or co-op owners, typed in Park Avenue and Sixty-third Street and the name Hattie Patrick. In a matter of seconds she had a hit at 576 Park, a prewar co-op building, and Hattie's name appeared along with those of her parents, Sean and Margaret. She thought the name Sean Patrick sounded familiar, so she Googled him and got the Patrick Group, a hedge fund that, according to their website, managed more than fifty billion dollars. Wow! Kelli thought.

For good measure she Googled Hattie and got more than she had expected. The girl was a star music student at Knickerbocker who had played piano recitals and earned good reviews at some of the city's better venues. She had been the piano soloist a year before in a performance of Gershwin's *Rhapsody in Blue* and *Concerto in F*, with the New York Youth Orchestra at Carnegie Hall. Wow! again.

Just on the off chance, she Googled Peter Barrington and got zip. She tried Peter Calder and got zip, too. It was as if the kid had recently arrived from another planet.

Peter and Hattie sat on pillows on the floor at the foot of his bed and watched his film come to an end. Hattie now had a full set of notes.

"I know what I want to write now," she said to Peter. "What I'd like to do is to record a rough track on film to make sure I've got the cues right, then I'll write some additional parts for cello, bass, and flute, and when I have the piano part perfectly recorded, we'll dub in the other instruments."

"That sounds perfect," Peter said. "How did you get so good at this so young?"

"The same way you got good at film-making," she said. "I studied, then prac- ticed all the time and played with other musicians whenever I could."

"That's not exactly how I got to be a filmmaker," Peter said. "I just went to the movies a lot, then made a movie. What are you going to do after gradua- tion?"

"I've been accepted at Juilliard," she said, "to study composition. I'm not really interested in a career as a concert artist; I want more freedom than that." She reached into her handbag and handed Peter a disc. "Here's a present for you."

Peter looked at the label. "*Rhapsody in Blue*? It's one of my favorites. So is *Concerto in F.* Can I put it on now?"

"No, it will just embarrass me," Hattie said. "Listen to it when you're alone."

"All right."

Stone knocked at the open door and came in. "Everything go well with the film?"

"Yes, Dad," Peter said. "Hattie's got what she needs now to write the whole score. And she gave me this." He handed Stone the disc.

Stone read the label. "Carnegie Hall!" he said. "That's very impressive."

Hattie turned pink.

"She embarrasses easily," Peter said. "She won't even let me listen to it while's she's here."

"I've heard it before," Hattie said, getting to her feet. "And now I think I have to get home and walk the dog. I take

him to Central Park about this time every day, and he'll be expecting me."

"I'll walk you down and get you a
cab," Peter said.

The two went downstairs and got
their coats.

Peter was back in ten minutes, and he
came into the master suite. "You want
to listen to Hattie's recording?"

"Sure," Stone said. "Put it in the
player over there." He pointed. He
tossed Peter the remote for the other
side of the electric bed. "Get comfortable," he said. Peter inserted the disc.

The music started, and Stone turned
up the volume to concert level.

The two pieces finished, and they were
both silent for a moment.

"That was breathtaking," Stone said
after a moment.

"It sure was."

"Did you know she was that good
before today?"

"I heard her improvise some stuff in a

recital hall at school, but I'm astonished."

"Is she going to pursue a concert career?"

"No, but she's going to study composition at Juilliard this fall. She says
she doesn't want a career as a concert
artist."

"I don't blame her," Stone said. "That's
quite a girl, Peter. Hang on to her, if you
can."

"I wonder if Yale has a music school,"
Peter said.

42

Stone was in bed the following morning with the Sunday *Times* when Peter came into the room. "Good morning, Dad," he said.

"Good morning, Peter. Did you sleep well?"

Peter looked a little sheepish. "Not all that well."

"Ah," Stone said, "thinking about Hattie?"

"Well, yes."

"Tell you what: Ben is off to Choate tomorrow morning; why don't you and I and Ben and Dino have dinner at

Elaine's, and you can ask Hattie to join us."

"Terrific!" Peter said. "She's never been to Elaine's, and she wants to go." He ran out of the room, then quickly returned. "I know that she usually has dinner with her parents on Sunday nights. May I ask them to join us, too?"

"Of course," Stone said. "Let me know how many to book for."

Peter ran out and returned in ten minutes. "Everybody's aboard. There'll be seven of us. I wish Mom were here."

"So do I." As if on cue, the phone rang. "Hello?"

"Hey, there," Arrington said.

"Hang on, I'll put you on speaker; Peter's here, too." He pressed the button and Peter came and sat on the edge of the bed.

"How's the house coming along?" Stone asked.

"Beautifully," she replied, "if I do say so. I did a brilliant job of packing at the old house, and everything is going right into place. We're hanging pictures tomorrow."

"Sounds wonderful," Stone said. "Peter has a new friend."

"Yes, I do," Peter said, then launched into a monologue about Hattie and how brilliant she was.

"Whew!" Arrington said when he finally paused. "That's the longest I ever heard anybody talk without taking a breath!"

"She's quite a girl," Stone said.

"Well, Peter, why don't you ask her down for our housewarming? It's next Saturday night. You can ask her folks' permission at dinner tonight, and tell them they're invited, too."

"That would be wonderful, Mom," Peter said.

"Come down on Friday, so we'll have all of Saturday and Sunday together," Arrington said. "You can fly back on Monday morning. Will the school let you do that?"

"I pretty much make my own schedule," Peter said.

"Stone, you'd better take Peter to get a new tux. His old one isn't going to fit. And don't forget to get some riding clothes for yourself. I'll have the perfect horse for you."

"I'll do that."

"I can't wait for you to see the house. It's going to look like it's always been here and we've always lived here. *Architectural Digest* is coming on Friday to photograph the place."

"Who's doing your PR?" Stone asked.

"I am. Paige Rense, the editor, is an old friend."

"Are they going to photograph us?" Stone asked.

"No, just the house."

"When will the piece run?"

"I don't know; not for some time, I expect. They have a long lead time."

"Well, I suppose everything will be more settled by then."

"Mom," Peter said, "I've got a new room upstairs." He told her about his plans for his suite.

"That sounds perfect for you, Peter. May I speak to Stone alone for a moment?"

"Sure. Good-bye, Mom. I'll see you on Friday." He padded back to his own room.

"Is he gone?" Arrington asked.

"Yes, we're alone." Stone picked up the phone. "What's up?"

"There's something I have to tell you about," she said.

"All right."

"Tim Rutledge will be around this weekend for the photo shoot and for the housewarming, of course. He's from an old family in the county, and everyone here will know him."

"Okay," Stone said. "I don't have a problem with that, as long as he behaves himself."

"Are you sure? I don't want any scenes at the party."

"It's not a problem for me," Stone said.

"Well, it's a problem for him. I'm afraid he didn't take the news of our marriage very well, and you may not find him exactly friendly."

"That's all right. I don't need to be friends with him."

"I want you to be nice to him, no matter what he says or does," Arrington said.

"I try to be nice to everybody," Stone said.

"Tim can sometimes be difficult," she said. "He's quick to anger, and sometimes intemperate in his remarks."

"So I may have to slug him, if he acts up?"

"Don't you dare. Remember, he's in tight with most of the people who'll be here, who are my neighbors, and I want you to exercise some forbearance. I don't want him to be able to say an unkind word about you that anyone would believe. Remember, you only have one opportunity to make a first impression, especially with the local gentry. I want you to be not just charming but gallant."

"All right, I'll wait until we're alone to slug him. You know, I think I still have my old cop's blackjack somewhere. I'll dig it out."

"Oh, stop it!"

"All right, all right, I won't harm a hair on his architectural head, and I'll charm the locals right out of their socks."

"That's better."

"Does Peter know him?"

"No, Peter was at school when I was

seeing him, so they've met only once, briefly. Be careful what you say about Tim when you're around him."

"Is there anybody else to whom I have to show forbearance?"

"Practically everybody," she said. "It's an inbred society down here, and they're not likely to display any genuine warmth toward a stranger. They'll be nice, because I'm a local girl, but believe me, they would have been much happier with me if I'd married Tim Rutledge."

"Well, I'm not going to give you up just to please them."

"You'd better not give me up for any reason!"

"You, my love, are a keeper," Stone said with feeling.

"And so are you," she said.

43

Kelli Keane got to work on time and ran into Prunella Wheaton on the elevator.

"Come see me," Wheaton said. "I may have a little something for you."

"Certainly," Kelli replied. She dropped her coat at her desk and walked back to Wheaton's office, looking forward to her delicious coffee.

"Come on in," Wheaton said. "Coffee's on."

Kelli took her usual seat. "You're looking lovely today," Kelli said. "As soon as I can afford it I'm going to start asking where you shop for clothes. To know now would just hurt."

Wheaton laughed. "The way you're going, that will happen soon enough, and maybe what I've got for you will help." She handed Kelli a cup of coffee.

"I'm all ears."

"I found out where Arrington Calder Barrington is."

Kelli sat up straight. "Oh? Spa? Mental hospital?"

"Neither," Wheaton said. "She's in Virginia, where she has been living during the years since Vance's death. She was born and raised in Albemarle County, and she's just built a house there. She's getting it ready for a housewarming next Saturday night."

"How on earth did you learn that?" Kelli asked.

"I had dinner with a friend last night, and he works at *Architectural Digest*. They're photographing it on Friday for the magazine, and my friend says it's going to be really something. It seems that a little over a year ago, Arrington bought Champion Farms, a racehorse breeding establishment in the county. A house had existed on the property since the mid-eighteenth century, but it burned down early in the 1920s. Arrington unearthed the plans for the house in the University of Virginia Library, and an architecture professor there drew plans for a nearly identical new house on virtually the same footprint as the old one, but with all mod cons, of course. It's going to be the showplace of the county."

"Wow, that sounds marvelous. Now, how am I going to get an invitation to that housewarming?"

"I think that's reaching a bit, my dear, but there is another way you can get a very good look at it."

"Tell me," Kelli said, eagerly.

"Well, first of all, you have a lunch date today with a handsome young man—in fact, the person I had dinner with last night. He's the son of an old friend of mine, and you're meeting him at twelve-thirty at the Harvard Club. Do you know where that is?"

"West Forty-fourth, next door to the New York Yacht Club."

"That's right," Wheaton said. "His

name is David Rutledge. Now go do yourself some good."

Kelli walked into the Harvard Club and surveyed the scene: to her left was a reception desk, and the door ahead of her, through which she now walked, opened into a large lounge with a fire-place and a lot of comfortable furniture strewn about. She looked around and saw a man coming toward her—tall, very slim, early thirties, dressed in a tweed jacket with leather elbow patches, a blue chambray shirt, and a brown knit tie. A thick mop of sandy hair fell across his forehead. He had his hand out.

"Kelli Keane?"

"And you're David Rutledge," she said, shaking his hand.

"Shall we go in for lunch?" He led her into the dining room, a gothic glory with an enormously high ceiling and a quiet buzz from the tables. A headwaiter seated them near the fireplace. "What would you like to drink?" he asked.

"Oh, just a glass of Chardonnay," she

said. "I do have to go back to work later."

He ordered the wine and a martini for himself, and they clinked glasses. She was showing some cleavage, and he was noticing. "Prunie speaks highly of you," he said.

"That's sweet of her. She says your mother is her old and dear friend."

"My grandmother, actually; they were classmates at Stanford. Tell me about you. Where did you spring from?"

"I sprang from West Chester, Pennsylvania, and I worked on the paper in Philadelphia right out of Bennington, then I came here last year. How about you?"

"Charlottesville, Virginia, Herald Academy in Jamestown, UVA School of Architecture, then an MBA at Harvard. I went to work at *Architecture Magazine* right out of school, then moved to *Architectural Digest* six years ago. I was promoted to executive art director right before Christmas."

"Congratulations! That sounds like a wonderful job."

They chatted on through lunch, played

who-do-you-know (nobody), then over a second drink warmed to each other.

She waited for him to bring it up, and he didn't, so finally she said, "Prunie tells me you've got an interesting shoot next weekend."

"Yes, we do." He told her about the history of the house. "The architect is a cousin of mine, Tim Rutledge. He teaches at UVA."

She pretended not to know about it. "It sounds beautiful," she said. "I just love that sort of thing. You don't need an assistant for the trip, do you?" she asked, trying to sound facetious.

"Oh, something might be arranged, if you play your cards right," he said, leering a little.

She leaned forward to give him a better view of her cleavage, an act, she had discovered, that tended to concentrate the minds of men. "I'm a pretty good card player," she said. "And I'll pay my own airfare. You can deal with the hotel arrangements."

"You're serious, then?"

"I am."

His eyebrows went up. "We're staying at a small country inn near the house, and I think they're pretty booked up."

"I don't mind sharing," she said, "as long as I'm not in the stable."

He shook his head. "Of course not. You can bunk with me, if that's all right."

"That's fine."

"Why don't we have dinner before we go down there?" he asked.

"I'd love to."

"Tomorrow night? Eight o'clock at Park Avenue Winter?"

"Sounds wonderful."

"Shall I pick you up?"

"I'll meet you there," she said. "You can see me home afterward."

"I'll look forward to it," he said.

"So will I."

44

Stone and his party took the big round table at the rear for their party of seven: Dino, Ben, Peter, Hattie, Hattie's parents—Sean and Margaret Patrick—and Stone. He seated himself between the parents. The chat was immediately warm and friendly, and it was clear to Stone that he and Arrington would get along as well with Sean and Margaret as Peter and Hattie were getting along.

They covered all the usual ground: Sean had emigrated from Ireland as a twenty-one-year-old graduate of Trinity College, Dublin, and had gone to work for a stockbroker. He was in business for himself at thirty and was, judging from the size of his hedge fund, very wealthy. Margaret was an Irish-American music student when they met, and it was she who had taught Hattie all her early piano.

"You must be very proud of Hattie's gifts," Stone said to her.

"Oh, yes!" Margaret replied. "I'm sorry she doesn't want to pursue a concert career, because that way I could follow her around and listen to her play all the time."

"I've heard some of the music she's composed for Peter's film, and I was very impressed with it."

"I understand your mother was a very fine painter," she said.

"Yes, she was," Stone replied. "and my father was an artist, too, but he expressed himself in wood. I hope you'll come to my house soon and see some of his work."

"We'd love to."

"My wife, Arrington, is in Virginia at the moment, moving into a house she has just built. She asked me to invite the three of you to her housewarming next Saturday night. We'll fly down on Friday afternoon in my airplane and return on Sunday afternoon or Monday morning, if you can take that much time."

"What a delightful invitation!" Margaret said. She leaned forward and explained it to Sean.

"Sounds great!" Sean said.

"We'll meet at Teterboro Airport, at Jet Aviation, at two p.m.," Stone said, "and there'll be room for everyone to stay in the house. The party on Saturday night is black tie, and the rest of the time is very casual. There are horses to ride, or tennis if you like."

"We'll all look forward to it," she said.

"We'll look forward to having you," Stone replied, winking at Peter, who had hung on their every word. Peter beamed, and so did Hattie.

Dino leaned across the table. "Ben's getting time off from school so he can come down, too. We're flying down with Mike Freeman and Bill Eggers."

"Perfect," Stone called back. "I was getting short of seats in the Mustang.

We've got one more, if Ben wants to ride with Peter and Hattie."

Ben nodded.

"Just be at my house at one o'clock," Stone said to the boy, "and don't forget your tuxedo."

The evening turned out to be a smashing success, and Stone felt that he and Arrington had made their first new friends.

On Monday afternoon Stone took Peter to the Ralph Lauren store on Madison and got him a tuxedo. It surprised him that the boy had moved up a size and from regular to long, and that the new size fit him perfectly. Stone found a tweed hacking jacket for himself in another department, and then they went downtown to a riding equipment store, where Stone bought riding boots, socks, and the tight-fitting pants that Arrington had requested. All their new gear would be delivered in time for their departure.

Kelli Keane woke early at David Rutledge's loft downtown and crept out of bed so as not to wake him. She had been there since Saturday night. She tiptoed to the beautiful bathroom, with its twin sinks, shower, tub, and bidet in a space as large as the bedroom in her apartment. He had done a spectacular job of transforming the formerly industrial space into a large duplex apartment of more than six thousand square feet.

She was in the middle of her shower when David joined her, and she was tall enough that they could easily make love standing up. She had lost track of how many times they had done it—or something—since Saturday night. David had left very little room for expansion in her repertoire. She was getting the feeling that this one was a keeper, and she had not been previously acquainted with that feeling. *Take it easy*, she said to herself, *and see how it goes*.

She scrambled some eggs for them, and he ate them hungrily.

"You're the first woman ever to spend a whole weekend in this apartment," David said.

"I don't believe that for a moment."

"I've only been in it for five weeks."

"I still don't believe it," she said.

He laughed. "Next weekend really ought to be fun. Oh, and by the way, the boss has sprung for the company jet, so we won't have to fly the airlines. It's always a pain in the ass when you have half a dozen cases of photographic equipment, plus personal luggage."

"That's great news," she said.

"A car will pick you up at seven Friday morning. That way, we'll have most of the day to work and the following morning, as well."

"Are we going to get an invitation to the big do on Saturday night?" she asked.

"We'll just have to see if that happens," he said, "but you might bring a suitable dress, just in case. It's a dressy event."

"I can do that," she said.

"If you're free this evening, I'll cook us some dinner."

"Oh, you cook, too? My God!"

"And bring your toothbrush," he said, smiling.

At work, Kelli made a beeline to Prunella Wheaton's office. Prunie poured her a cup of coffee. "I hear you had a very pleasant weekend," she said knowingly.

"How did you know?"

"Sweetie, you're going to have to get used to the idea that I know *everything*. No one can hide anything from me, if I really want to find out."

"I believe you, Prunie," Kelli said. "Yes, it was a wonderful weekend. That apartment!"

"Well, he trained as an architect," she said, "and he does work at *Architectural Digest*, doesn't he? He has to hold up his end, and the staff there always know where to find the most beautiful things."

"I've never known a man with that kind of taste and style," Kelli said. "You wouldn't believe the state of most men's living quarters these days."

"I expect it's not much worse than when I was your age," Prunie said, "and it's probably much better!"

45

Allison Wainwright came into Stone's office and laid a small stack of papers on his desk. "We're up to date on the financial reports from Strategic Services and Steele. These are the ones you need to see. Everything else is just boilerplate."

"Have a seat, Allison," Stone said, picking up the papers. He scanned them quickly, then handed them back to her. "Good job," he said. "That was exactly what I wanted you to do."

"They'll be easier to keep track of, now that we're caught up," she said.

There was a knock at the door and Stone looked up to see Herbie Fisher standing there. "Come in, Herbie," he said. "I'd like you to meet my new associate. This is Allison Wainwright. Allison, this is Herbert Fisher, our client, and, incidentally, a law student."

Herbie shook her hand. "Actually, Stone," he said, "I've finished with school. Graduation won't be until June, but I've completed the course work, and now all I have to do is bone up for the bar exam."

Stone noted how Herbie was looking at Allison and how she was returning his gaze. "Have a seat, Herbie," he said. "Excuse me for a moment. There's something I have to do." He left his desk and walked down to Joan's office and sat down.

"Are you here for the reason I think you're here?" she asked.

Stone nodded. "I thought I'd give them a moment to get acquainted."

"I'm glad. Allison is *very* horny; she's been complaining about it, and Herbie might be just the ticket for her."

"Maybe you're right," Stone said. "What do you think of Allison?"

"I like her," she said. "She sat right down and did that dirty job you gave her, and I never heard a peep of a complaint. I think she's very smart, too."

"Woodman & Weld wouldn't have hired her if she hadn't been both smart and highly qualified. The firm is among the two or three most desirable for graduates among all the New York firms."

"Do we keep her, then?"

"I have the feeling she'll move up pretty rapidly. Let's keep her out of the Seagram Building for as long as we can."

Joan smiled. "I was hoping you would say that."

"Peter and I are going down to Virginia this weekend for Arrington's housewarming, so scrub my calendar for Friday and Monday."

"Will do. How did Peter's Saturday date work out?"

"It worked out just fine, thanks. She's smart as a whip, a terrific pianist, and he's smitten."

"Ah, young love."

"Speaking of young love, I'd better get back in there, before Herbie and Allison end up on my sofa."

"Go."

Stone went back to his office and found Herbie and Allison talking rapidly and laughing. As he sat down his phone buzzed. "Bill Eggers for you," Joan said.

"Why don't you take Herbie to your office, Allison?" Stone said, then picked up the phone. "Morning, Bill."

"Good morning, Stone. I just got an invitation to Arrington's housewarming, and we're planning to go. Mike Freeman has asked us to fly down with him on Friday, and we'll come back Sunday afternoon."

"Great. I'm glad you can make it. By the way, Bill, I'm impressed with Allison Wainwright. Thanks for sending her to me."

"You're welcome, but the reason she's there is because of a contretemps with one of the partners, who shall remain nameless."

"Let me guess: he made a pass at her?"

"Without confirming or denying that, you are very perceptive. He's already looking for work elsewhere, and when he's gone I'll want her back."

"Then you'll have to fight me for her," Stone said. "Joan likes her, too, and that's not easy to come by."

"We'll see," Eggers said, "and we'll see you on Friday in Virginia. Arrington is putting us up, and Mike, too."

"See you then." Stone hung up as Herbie came back in.

"Allison is very nice," he said.

"When's the wedding?" Stone asked.

"Oh, come on, Stone. I'm not that bad."

"Oh, yes, you are," Stone replied.

Herbie turned red. "Well, we are having dinner this weekend."

Stone laughed.

46

On Friday morning Stone went down to his office, and Joan handed him a letter for Peter from the Yale School of Drama.

"I wanted to open it," she said, "but I didn't."

Stone called Dino. "Did Ben get a letter from Yale this morning?"

"Yeah," Dino said, "but I haven't given it to him yet. Eduardo called, though, and said there would be good news today."

"Peter got his today, too."

———

Early Friday afternoon, Stone packed Peter and Ben and their luggage into the car and drove out to Teterboro. The Patrick family met them in the lounge at Jet Aviation, and they walked to the ramp just outside, where the Mustang awaited them. There was half an hour of stowing luggage and doing a preflight inspection, and Peter walked around the airplane with Stone, as he pointed out various items for inspection.

Stone settled the Patricks and Ben in the four rear seats, and put Peter in the copilot's seat, then he closed the door, gave the group a briefing about seat belts, the emergency exit, and oxygen masks, buckled himself in, and started through his checklist. Peter followed him with the copilot's copy, and Stone pointed out each item on the instrument panel as he checked it. Finally, Stone called the tower for his clearance, wrote it down, entered the route into the flight computer, and got permission to taxi to runway one. Stone talked Peter through the whole procedure, then, when they were cleared for takeoff, explained what was going to happen. He pushed the throttles all the way forward and started down the runway. A minute or so later, at two thousand feet, they were handed off to New York Departure and began their climb.

"I want to learn how to do this," Peter said.

"When you're a little older," Stone replied. "In the meantime, you can read the flight and avionics manuals."

"I want to learn *now*," Peter said.

"You're learning how to fly to Virginia now," Stone replied. "In two or three years, you'll be able to do it yourself. Learning to fly goes better when you have a reason to have an airplane. You'll be at university, and you won't need to fly anywhere for a while."

"Oh, all right," Peter said. "Can I talk on the radio?"

"Listen on the way down, and you can do the radio work on the way back. Radio procedure is an essential part of flying, and the key to it is to know what the controller is going to say next. Soon, we'll get a clearance to a higher altitude, so you can expect that."

The controller called and cleared

them to their cruising altitude of thirty-four thousand feet, and Stone showed Peter how to change the altitude in the autopilot and start the climb.

"The autopilot really flies the airplane, doesn't it," Peter asked, "and you just tell it what to do?"

"Correct, but you also have to be able to do everything manually, if the autopilot fails for some reason."

"Has it ever failed?"

"Not in this airplane, yet, but in my old airplane I once had a complete electrical failure and had to hand-fly it into Teterboro, using a handheld radio."

"Wow," Peter said.

"They don't often let you do a visual approach at Teterboro," Stone said. "They like everybody lined up on the instrument approach. I had to declare an emergency to get permission for a visual that day."

An hour later they were descending into Charlottesville, and once on the ground they taxied to Arrington's hangar, where the Gulfstream was kept. One of the pilots was waiting for them with a large van. He stowed their lug-

gage and drove them to the house, forty
minutes away, while a worker put the
Mustang into the hangar with the G-III.

There was a buzz in the van when everyone saw the driveway, lined with a
dozen huge oak trees on each side, and
at the end, the house, perched on a little rise.

"This is very impressive," Sean Patrick said.

"Most of these trees predate the original house," Stone said. "Arrington
bought three or four other mature trees
and had them moved here to fill in any
gaps. They seem to have taken root
successfully."

Arrington met them on the front porch,
and introductions were made. "The
photographer and crew from *Architectural Digest* just left," she said to Stone.
"They seemed to get everything they
wanted." She led the party into the
house and gave them a quick tour of
the ground floor—a broad hallway that
ran through the house, with twin stair-
cases on either side; a big drawing room
and the dining room to the right; to the
left the library and the kitchen at the

rear of the house. When that was done she led everyone upstairs and showed them to their rooms, while staff delivered the luggage. She let everyone know that drinks would be in the drawing room at six-thirty.

"We're at the end of the south wing," she said, taking Stone's hand. She led him into the master suite, a sunny sitting room and bedroom, with a dressing room and bath on each side.

"It's gorgeous," Stone said, looking around. "You were right: the house looks as though it has always been here and we've always lived in it. Except for my empty dressing room."

"That will get filled as time goes by," she said.

"I'm sure it will," Stone replied.

"Now," she said, taking his hand and leading him toward the canopied bed, "we have two hours until drinks, and you're going to be very busy."

In a moment, they were naked in bed. "God, how I've missed you," she said.

"I know exactly how you feel," Stone said.

There was a knock on the door.

"Mom?" Peter called, and tried to open it, but she had locked it.

"Later, Peter!" Arrington shouted back.

"The other houseguests have arrived," Peter yelled.

"You're appointed host. The butler will find them rooms."

"How many bedrooms are there?" Stone asked.

"Ours, Peter's, and five more," she said, "but at the moment you may concern yourself only with this one."

At six-thirty the whole group, including Mike Freeman, Bill Eggers and his wife, and Dino gathered in the large living room, and the butler, who was introduced as Somes, poured champagne for everyone, even the children.

"Just one glass for you three," Arrington said. "With your parents' permission, Hattie."

"Just one," Margaret Patrick said.

"Sure," Dino echoed.

"Dino," Stone asked, "maybe now

would be a good time to deliver the mail?"

Stone and Dino each produced an envelope and handed it to his son. "We don't know what the letters say," he said.

Peter and Ben turned over the envelopes and inspected them.

"They haven't been opened," Dino said.

"We may as well," Peter said, tearing open the envelope and reading the letter.

"Read it to us," Stone said.

Peter held up the letter and read, "'Dear Mr. Barrington, I am pleased to tell you that you have been accepted to the Yale School of Drama for the fall term. Your friend Mr. Bacchetti has been accepted, as well.

"'I congratulate you both, and we look forward to seeing you this fall. You will receive a packet of information at a later date that you will need for enrollment and to help with arranging housing.'

"It's signed by the dean," Peter said.

"Mine says the same," Ben said. Both boys stood there, looking astonished.

"Now we have something to toast," Stone said. "To Ben and Peter, may they get everything their parents hope for from their education."

There was laughter and applause, and everyone drank.

"Excuse me," Sean Patrick said, "but our daughter Hattie has an announcement."

Everyone grew quiet. Hattie stood and, holding her champagne flute, said, "Before Christmas I applied to both Juilliard and Yale to study music. I was accepted to both, and I have chosen Yale for my studies."

Another uproar and more drinking. Peter and Hattie hugged each other, and she gave Ben a hug, too.

During the next hour they emptied four bottles of Krug '99, and then Somes called them to dinner, opening the double doors that led into the dining room. They were served a salad, then a silver cart was wheeled in and Somes carved two rib roasts for them.

When they were on coffee, Somes's

wife, Marlene, who was the chef, came in and was introduced, fetching a round of applause.

They walked across the hall to the walnut-paneled library and were served coffee and cognac.

"If it were summer, we'd do this on the front porch," Arrington said, "but in winter, it's nice to be by the fire."

Somes came in and put a couple more logs in the large fireplace.

They talked until after ten, then everyone went upstairs to their rooms.

"You're going to have to perform again," Arrington said, as she closed the door behind them.

"I'm up for a command performance," Stone said, taking her in his arms.

47

Stone was wakened by a sharp knocking on their bedroom door. "Mom? Dad?"

Arrington stirred. "I told him we'd all go riding this morning," she said.

"Right after breakfast, Peter," Stone called back. "Say, eight o'clock?"

"I'll meet you downstairs at eight," Peter replied, then went away.

"What time is it?" Arrington asked.

"Six-thirty."

"Then breakfast will appear momentarily." She got up, slipped into a dressing gown, and unlocked the bedroom door. A moment later someone knocked, and she opened the door. Somes came in pushing a hotel-style table on wheels, and he set it up before the fireplace in the sitting room, while Arrington and Stone brushed their teeth. They ate hungrily.

"I'm so glad the college acceptances came when they did," Arrington said.

"It worked out perfectly, didn't it? And Hattie had a nice surprise for us. I don't think Peter knew."

"We're not going to be able to keep them out of bed together, you know," Arrington said.

"I suppose not," Stone said. "Maybe we'd better yield to reality and get the three of them an apartment together in New Haven."

"Oh, I'm not sure the Patricks would go along with that," Arrington said. "You'd better let me feel things out with Margaret before you bring up that subject."

"I will leave the matter in your capable hands," Stone said, with relief.

They met Peter, Ben, and Hattie down-stairs at eight.

"My folks are still asleep," Hattie said. "I couldn't get them up."

"My dad, too," Ben said, "and I heard snoring from the Eggerses' room."

The five of them walked out to the stables, where a groom had saddled horses for them, and soon they were trotting along a trail, with Peter in the lead. Shortly, they broke out into open fields and were able to canter.

"No jumping of fences, anybody," Arrington called out. "I'm not having any-one's broken neck on my conscience," she said to Stone, who was riding along-side her, feeling more and more com-fortable on his mount.

"Are my riding pants tight enough?" he asked Arrington.

"Oh, I already checked them out," she replied, laughing. "They're perfect, and so is your ass."

They rode for most of the chilly morn-ing. Virginia was nowhere near as cold as New York, but it was nippy. Arrington gave them a tour of Champion Racing Farms, and they stopped at the big stable, met the horses, and watched them work out on the track.

"That big gelding out front is going to win the Derby for us this year," Arrington said. "His name is Valentino."

They were back at the house in time for lunch, which they had at a long table in the big kitchen, with another fire going.

After lunch, Arrington excused herself. "I have a party to get ready for," she said to her guests. "Everyone's coming at six."

"May I help?" Margaret Patrick asked.

"Are you any good with flowers?" Arrington asked. "The florist's truck will be here any minute."

"That is my métier," Margaret replied, and she followed Arrington from the room. Hattie tagged along, too, and so did Bill Eggers's wife.

Somes appeared. "Mrs. Barrington

won't allow cigars in the house," he said, "but we do have some port."

"By all means," Stone said, and the decanter was brought and passed to the left around the table. Ben and Peter were allowed a dram.

"So, Stone," Bill Eggers said, "are you going to leave the law and become a Virginia gentleman?"

Stone laughed. "I am unqualified for that role, by upbringing, education, and inclination."

"Well, you certainly have the property for it," Mike Freeman said.

"Yes, and I have the feeling I'm going to have a hard time keeping Arrington in New York for more than a few days at a time, especially when spring comes."

"That could be a good thing for a marriage," Eggers said. "My wife spends much of the summer in the Hamptons, and I go out on weekends. That way, she maintains her tan, and I get some work done."

"I may take some time off this summer," Stone said, "to take Arrington and Peter up to Maine."

"Oh, yeah," Peter said. "And you're going to teach me to sail."

"I am indeed. Ben, you and your father are invited, too."

"You're not getting me in a boat," Dino said.

"You never know, Dino," Stone replied. "You might even like it."

After lunch, the men drifted off to their rooms, and Stone had a look around the house, where the women were arranging huge quantities of flowers in crystal vases all over the ground floor. Some musicians arrived—a string quartet, it seemed—and set up in the main hallway, next to a Steinway grand.

Stone wandered upstairs, undressed, and stretched out for a nap. The riding had been tiring, and he had a sore ass. He stirred a little when Arrington came upstairs and crooked a finger at her.

"Oh, no, you don't," she said. "I'm going to take a very long bath and then take a very long time to get dressed. It's four o'clock, and I'm not sure I can get it all done by six." She vanished into her dressing room.

Stone lay on his back and gazed drowsily at the ceiling. He had no feeling of ownership of this place—not even a feeling of Arrington's ownership. Instead, it felt as if they had checked, en masse, into a very luxurious country inn. He dozed.

He was awakened an hour later by the string quartet, the sound making its way through the thick door. He struggled out of bed, showered and shaved, and got into his tuxedo. When he came out Arrington was sitting at her dressing table in her bra and panties, doing something to her hair. He exposed the nape of her neck and kissed her there.

"You know what that does to me," she said. "If you aren't careful, I'll have to start all over."

"All right, all right," he said. "I'll wait for you downstairs." He wandered down to the library, past the string quartet, who appeared to be rehearsing, or perhaps just playing for their own amusement.

He poured himself a small Knob Creek and took a chair by the fire, happy to have a moment to himself before the bash, with the music lending atmosphere.

48

Arrington walked into the library at the stroke of five forty-five and poured herself a Knob Creek.

"You're a bourbon drinker? I'm still learning about my new wife."

"I'm looking for a more instant buzz than champagne will give me," she said. "I can't face all these people sober." She sank into the chair opposite him.

"I've never seen you look more beautiful," he said. "We have to get a picture taken, since we'll never be this young again."

"What a nice way to put it!" she

laughed. "Don't worry, there'll be a photographer; in fact, he's already arrived
and is stationed outside, to get people
as they enter."

A car door slammed outside.

"Oh, oh," she said, tossing off the
rest of her bourbon, "here they come.
Why is someone always early? Haven't
they ever heard of fashionably late?"

"Fortunately, they are *your* friends,"
he said, "so I cannot be blamed for their
swinish conduct."

"I'll blame you if I want to," she said,
getting up. "Come on, time to play
host."

Stone made his bourbon vanish and
followed her into the main hall. The
quartet started up, on cue, with "Eine
Kleine Nachtmusik."

Somes opened the door, and the first
half dozen of their guests entered. Introductions were made, while a maid
made their coats disappear, and Stone
heard spoken, for the first time in his
life, the words "And this is my husband."

The seventh person through the door
was a tall, slender man with a head full

of graying hair and a supercilious expression.

"Stone, this is our architect, Timothy Rutledge. Tim, this is my husband, Stone Barrington." Those unfamiliar words again.

Stone extended his hand, and Rutledge gripped it lightly by the fingers, as if he were warding off a bone-crushing handshake. "How do you do?" he said, as if he didn't care how Stone or anyone else did.

"Good to meet you," Stone lied. "You've done a very fine job on the house." That was the truth.

One corner of Rutledge's mouth turned up slightly. "You're very kind to say so," he replied, as if kindness were a curse.

Arrington forestalled any more conversation between them by taking Rutledge by the arm and introducing him to someone else.

Once the flood of arrivals subsided from a river to a trickle, Stone grabbed a flute of champagne from a passing silver tray and circulated, mustering all the charm at his disposal. He was greeted, in most cases, by some warmth, and in others, by a trace of sleet. He would have to ask Arrington later what caused the dividing line. The eyes of the women invariably darted from console to chandelier to carpet, while the men, mostly, looked for a waiter bearing booze, and they didn't seem to care what kind.

A bit after seven, when Arrington judged that enough lubrication had been passed among her guests, she nodded at Somes, who produced a silver bell and walked around the house, singing, "Dinner is served. Dinner is served in the dining room!"

The string quartet sawed away on some Vivaldi while the guests rushed the dining room and the buffet on the groaning board. Half an hour later they were distributed around the ground floor on furniture, the stairs, and on the floor, scarfing up filet of beef or wild salmon and allowing Somes to repeatedly refill their flutes.

Stone shared a small sofa in the living room with a plump, beautifully coiffed Virginia matron named Vilia.

"A beautiful name," he said. "I've always loved the Lehár song."

"From my mother's favorite operetta," she said, smiling broadly at his recognition.

"I once saw a production of *The Merry Widow*, due to circumstances beyond my control, entirely in Finnish."

"And how did that come about?" she asked.

"Well, I was in Helsinki at the time, and I was one of at least two Americans in the audience. I know, because they sold us both the same seat. We compared tickets, and he wandered off somewhere." He looked up to see a woman passing the piano who appeared distinctly of New York and not Virginia. She was tall, slender, and wore a tight, low-cut black dress with a slit up her leg nearly to the illegal limit. She looked vaguely familiar, but out of context. He thought about it and couldn't place her. As he watched, she set down her flute and produced, from God knew where, an iPhone, and began snapping pictures of the room, in a manner more befitting a backyard barbecue than a haut monde Albemarle County soiree. She was joined by a lanky young man who reminded Stone of Rutledge, the icy architect, and who, apparently, told her to put away the electronics. She reclaimed her champagne and trailed him from the room, teetering on six-inch heels.

Kelli Keane was having the time of her life. She had been to some good parties, but never anything quite like this. There were men dressed in red hunting jackets, for Christ's sake, over their black ties, and women in ball gowns! Kelli had a very good memory, and she digested as many names as she could, for matching later with her photos. David was being a prick about the pictures, but she had snapped shots in every room before he stopped her. A change in the music turned her head.

Two members of the string quartet had exchanged a violin and a cello for a guitar and a banjo, and they were executing an enthusiastic reel. They finished to a big round of applause from the guests, then recovered their original instrumentation and began playing "Good-Night, Ladies," apparently the signal for the gentry to put down their glasses and get the hell out. The butler and three maids appeared, carrying armloads of coats and, miraculously, found their owners. Twenty minutes later, Kelli and David were in their rental car, headed back to the inn.

"You were naughty to take photographs," David said.

"Then I'll make it up to you by being naughty when we get to the inn," she said, stroking the inside of his thigh with her long nails.

Stone said good night to some guests then turned and spotted Arrington, who had been backed into a corner by Tim Rutledge, and Stone did not like the desperate expression on her face. Stone walked over to them, shouldered Rutledge out of his way, and held his arm out to Arrington, who took it and walked away with him. As they passed Somes, Stone said to him, through a clenched smile, "Find Mr. Rutledge his coat, *now*."

They walked into the library, now empty of guests. "What was *that* all about?" he asked.

"Oh, it was nothing," she said. "Just Tim being Tim."

Stone nodded toward the gun cabinet near the fireplace. "I hope those are loaded," he said.

"My father always kept them that way," she replied, "but you keep your hands in your pockets."

49

They lay on their backs in bed, naked, holding hands.

"Well," Stone said, "that seemed to go very well."

"Did it?" Arrington asked, sighing. "I hardly noticed. I didn't have the time."

"Tell me about Tim Rutledge," he said. "What did he want from you?"

"Guess," she said.

"Was that all?"

"Was that all?!"

"Not to undervalue your virtue, but somehow it seemed more complicated than that."

"He wants not just my virtue but my house and my fortune."

"Did you explain that those things were already committed?"

"I did so, and succinctly, but he wouldn't take 'No, not now, not ever, now get out!' for an answer. You arrived just in time."

"Are there any other former lovers lurking about that I should be wary of?"

"No, and he is included in that category because, for a year, you weren't around."

"I wasn't invited."

"Well, I was busy, I guess, and he was around. Constantly."

"Did you give him hope for the future?"

"I did not. On the contrary, I actively and explicitly discouraged any thought of the future."

"Good. Then I don't have to feel sorry for him."

"Oh, he'll have moved on to someone else by next week—probably a married woman, that being his specialty. He's known among the local matrons as 'The Prong.'"

Stone laughed.

"Oh, there's something I've been meaning to tell you," Arrington said. "We have a family plot in the local churchyard. You're welcome to join us."

"Is that where you wish to rest for eternity?"

"It's quite pretty, really."

"I always thought I'd like to be scattered somewhere."

"After cremation, I suppose."

"Yes, cremation obviates dismemberment."

"Scattered where?"

"Someplace beautiful. Off the dock at the Maine house would be nice."

"I liked that house," she said. "The cousin who bequeathed it to you had very good taste in houses."

"Yes, he did."

"You get bequeathed a lot of things, don't you? Houses, paintings, airplanes."

"I do. I'm fortunate in my family and friends."

"Do you want me to tell you about my will?"

"No, I'd rather know nothing, thank you."

"Not everything is in it. I'd better tell you a few other things. I'd been meaning to write a letter, and I may yet, but mostly it's about how you would deal with Peter in my absence, should that ever occur."

"I am statistically likely to precede you into the Promised Land, but go ahead."

"I'm concerned that Peter might have too much, too soon, and I like your idea of keeping things in trust until he's thirty-five, so I put that in there. You have the authority, however, to deal with that as you wish, up until he's thirty-five."

"Thank you. I'll try to keep a tight rein on things."

"I don't think that will be hard, since he never seems to think about money, unless it's in connection with his filming budget. I just don't want a truckload of cash dumped on him before he knows something about handling it."

"I understand, and I entirely agree."

They were quiet for a moment.

"Is that it?" Stone asked.

"I'm thinking," she said. "Give me a minute."

"All right."

"Give my jewelry, in reasonable amounts, to Peter's wife, when he marries. Funny, but I've been thinking about Hattie as Peter's future wife, which is silly, I suppose."

"We can wish for that," Stone said. "They seem very well suited to each other."

"But they're so young!"

"And getting older every day," Stone said. "He says she's smarter than he is."

"No!" Arrington said. "I've never heard him say that about *anybody*!"

"He's probably never met anybody who's that smart," Stone pointed out.

"There is that," Arrington admitted. "He's spent his whole life stunning me, on an almost daily basis, with his precocity."

"I'm beginning to get used to that," Stone said.

"Really? I never have."

"I still have difficulty thinking of him as a child."

"Well, he is. You'll see that in him, eventually. It comes out at the damnedest times."

"He's going to be gone before I get to know him fully," Stone said. "I want to spend some time with him in Maine this summer, teach him to sail. He already wants to learn to fly."

"Fly? He doesn't even drive yet!"

"Don't worry, I'm not going to let him even take lessons until he's at least eighteen. Once he starts at Yale, he'll be too wrapped up in work to even think about it."

"I hope you're right, though I think he has traits that will make him a good pilot. He's organized and detail-oriented, and, of course, he learns with blinding speed."

"We've had only one flight in my Mustang, coming down here, and he seems already to have grasped the avionics pretty well."

"That's the sort of thing he does." She yawned. "I'm sleepy," she said.

"Then go to sleep."

"No making love?"

"We'll save it until the morning."

"All right."

"I have a date to go riding with Peter and Hattie at eight. Do you want to come?" he asked.

"No, I'm going to sleep until lunchtime. That'll give the staff time to make the house pristine again. I don't want to see it until then." She yawned again, then her breathing became regular.

Stone was not far behind. He dreamed about Peter and Hattie and, maybe, a grandchild. Then there was something unpleasant, something shocking, but when he jerked awake he couldn't remember what it was. It took him an unusually long time to get back to sleep, and when he awoke the following morning he was tired, as if he hadn't slept at all.

50

Stone showered, dressed, and went downstairs to the kitchen, where he sat, alone, at the long table and waited for his breakfast to be cooked. Then Peter and Hattie joined him and placed their orders.

"Beautiful day outside," Stone said.

"Great day for riding," Peter replied.

Hattie was quiet.

"Did you sleep well, Hattie?"

"All right, I guess."

"Ready to greet the new day on horseback?"

"Sure."

"Did you two have a good time at the party?" Stone asked.

"Oh, yes," Peter said. "But I knew hardly any of those people."

"Don't worry, you won't have to spend any time with them. I think your mother had the housewarming just so that they wouldn't be angling for invitations to see the house."

"Get it all over at once, huh?" Peter said.

"Right."

"Hattie, did you meet anyone you liked?"

"Not really," Hattie replied, "but I met someone I *didn't* like."

"And who might that have been?"

"That architect fellow."

"Ah, yes. I don't think you'll be seeing him again."

"Why? Did someone shoot him?"

"Not yet," Stone replied.

Peter laughed. "Mom didn't seem to be very happy to see him."

"Had you met him before?" Stone asked.

"Just once. He came over when I was home from school last Easter to talk to

Mom about how the house was going. I didn't like him then, either."

They finished breakfast and left by the rear door to walk over to the stable. A groom had their horses saddled, and they mounted and walked down the trail through the woods, warming up the horses in the chill air before leaving the woods and cantering across the fields.

Kelli Keane got out of bed and tiptoed, naked, into the bathroom and drew a hot tub for herself. David was out like a light, exhausted from the naughty work-out she had given him at bedtime. She put her iPhone on the edge of the tub and eased into the hot water, then she turned on the phone and looked up the photographs she had taken at the party. These were too good for the *Post*, she thought; they'd never run more than one or two. Maybe she should query *Vanity Fair* for a piece. It couldn't run until after the *Architectural Digest* spread had run, so there wouldn't be any conflict with what David was doing. She needed something, though—a hook to hang the story on. The house wasn't enough, "Widow of Vance Calder" wasn't enough. Pity there hadn't been a fistfight among the prominent guests, something like that.

The three of them rode for nearly two hours, then pulled up under a tree and got down. Peter opened the picnic basket the kitchen had made for them and they had hot chocolate and cookies.

Stone thought about asking Hattie to come up to Maine for the summer but stopped himself. He should let Peter issue that invitation.

They remounted and started back toward the house, taking their time. From a hilltop they could see the horses from the racing stable being worked on the track. They walked their mounts for the half mile, cooling them before they would be given water, then turned them over to the groom and started for the

house. From that direction came a muf-
fled bang.

"What was that?" Peter asked.

"Sounded like one of those heavy
mahogany doors being slammed,"
Stone replied.

"Somebody must be mad about
something," Peter said. The trash from
the party was being removed by the
back door, so they walked around the
house toward the front door. They heard
a car start and drive away, apparently in
a hurry, but it was gone by the time they
reached the front porch. Stone turned
and looked down the drive between the
oaks and saw some sort of station
wagon turn onto the main road and disappear.

They entered by the front door, and
Stone stopped in his tracks. On the floor
of the main hall, a dozen feet from the
front door, lay a beautifully engraved
shotgun, a Purdy, Stone thought. Probably worth a hundred thousand dollars.
He turned to his left and looked into the
study. The glass front of the gun cabinet had been shattered.

"What's going on?" Peter asked from the front door.

"Peter, listen to me," Stone said. "Take Hattie, go into the living room, and wait there."

"What for?" Peter asked.

"Just do it." Stone had a terrible feeling, and he didn't want the couple there. He watched them go into the living room before he continued down the hall.

A huge flower arrangement on a table in the center of the hall blocked the view toward the rear of the house, and when Stone started around the table he saw a white pile of some sort of fabric farther down the hall. It looked like a pile of tablecloths, he thought.

Then, as he continued toward it, the shape became clear: it was a woman in white. Alarmed, he began to walk faster. Then he saw a blob of red on the clothes. Then he saw Arrington's face, turned toward him.

He ran and knelt beside her. Her eyes were open and he saw her blink, then she seemed to focus on him. She tried to speak but couldn't.

"Don't," he said, his face close to

hers. "Just breathe. I'll get some help." He felt for his phone on his belt, but realized he hadn't brought it with him. "I'm going to telephone," he said, and she managed to nod. Her chest was a mass of blood and tissue.

He ran to the rear of the hall where a phone was on a table and dialed 911.

"Nine-one-one," an operator said. "What is your emergency?"

"There's been a shooting," Stone said. "A woman is critically wounded. I need an ambulance and the police immediately." He gave her the address. The operator began to ask questions, but he hung up and ran back to Arrington, lifting her head and shoulders, in the hope that it would help her breathe better.

He held her head up. "Just breathe. Help is on the way." Her mouth formed a word, but no sound came out.

"Peter!" Stone called. "Come here, quickly. Hattie, you stay where you are."

Peter ran into the hall, saw his mother lying on the floor, and froze.

Stone beckoned for him to approach and kneel beside him.

Peter stared at his mother, speech-less.

Arrington's lips moved again, and it was not difficult to read her lips. "I love you both," she was saying, then her pupils dilated.

"Mom!" Peter said.

Stone felt at her neck for a pulse but found nothing. He lowered Arrington gently to the floor, then put his arm around his son. "She's gone," he said softly.

Peter hugged his father, and they both wept.

51

Kelli Keane was beginning to tire of the tub as the water cooled. Then she heard sirens approaching. She stood and wrapped herself in a towel for warmth, then looked out the high window over the tub.

From her left she saw two police cars and an ambulance burning up the dusty road past the inn. She could see them make a right turn at the next intersection. The Barrington house was down that road.

She hurried out of the bathroom and got into a sweater, some slacks, and her boots, then grabbed her coat and her handbag. She ran back to the bathroom for her iPhone, then, as she passed through the bedroom, David lifted his head.

"What's going on with the sirens?" he asked.

"Trouble at the Barrington place," she said, grabbing the rental car keys from the dresser. "I'm going up there."

"Wait for me," he was saying, but she was already gone.

Kelli jumped into the car and got it started, then raced out of the parking lot, spraying gravel. She made the turn at the intersection and put her foot to the floor. Up ahead, she saw the last of the three vehicles disappear into the Barrington driveway. She slammed on the brakes and turned sideways on the gravel road, but slid past the driveway, and a rear wheel ended up in a ditch. She got out and looked: no way to drive it out. She started running up the driveway.

By the time anyone arrived, Stone had got Peter into the living room and onto a sofa with Hattie, then had gone back to the hall and asked a woman in the kitchen for a tablecloth. He went back to the hall and gently spread the cloth over Arrington's body, then he went to the front door to wait. His heart was pounding in his chest, and he was determined to be calm. How many homicides had he attended during the ten years when that had been his career?

He saw the sheriff's cars pull up in front of the house and two young men got out. The ambulance was right behind them. He opened the door and let the deputies in.

"You called nine-one-one about a shooting?" a young deputy asked.

"Yes. The body is at the other end of the hall. Do you have a crime-scene unit at your disposal?"

"Yessir, the county has one."

"Please call them immediately."

The deputy ignored the request, walked to the shotgun, and picked it up.

"Put that down!" Stone commanded. "Don't you know this is a crime scene?"

The young man flushed and put the shotgun back where he had found it. "Jake, call the sheriff," he said to his companion, then started down the hall.

The second deputy pressed a speed dial button on his phone and put it to his ear. "Hello, Sheriff? This is Jake. I—"

Stone took the phone from his hand. "Sheriff, this is Stone Barrington speaking. My wife has been murdered in her home." He gave the man the address. "We need a crime-scene unit here at once. One of your men has already picked up a shotgun lying on the floor, so he'll have to be fingerprinted. You'd better come, too."

"Is there a suspect?" the sheriff asked.

"Yes, a man named Tim Rutledge."

"The Dr. Rutledge who's a professor at UVA?"

"The same. You should question him at the earliest opportunity. Oh, and find out if he drives a station wagon." He handed the phone back to the deputy.

"Yes, sir, that's pretty much the situation. No, I'm just going to look at the body now." He listened for a moment. "Yes, sir." He hung up the phone. "Milt, the sheriff says to stay away from the body and don't contaminate the crime scene."

Milt, who had already pulled back the tablecloth, put it back and walked back to the front door. "Okay," he said. "What happened here?"

Stone sat down in a hall chair. "Let's wait for the sheriff," he said. "I don't want to have to go through this twice."

Dino appeared on the upstairs landing, still buttoning his shirt. "What's happened?" he called to Stone. Mike Freeman and the Eggerses were right behind him, in various stages of dress.

"Dino, you come down here," he said. "Will the rest of you please wait upstairs until somebody comes to get you? Thanks."

Dino walked down the stairs, looking at the covered body, and came over to Stone. "Who is it?"

"Arrington. Shotgun." He nodded toward the weapon, then shook his head.

Dino put a hand on his shoulder. "Who?"

"Had to be Rutledge, the architect."

"Who are you?" the deputy Milt asked.

"This is Detective Lieutenant Dino Bacchetti of the New York City police department," Stone said. "Dino, deputies Milt and Jake."

Dino shook hands with the two young men, then pulled up a chair and sat next to Stone. "I'm so sorry, pal," he said. "I wish I could tell you how sorry."

Stone nodded, then took some deep breaths.

Kelli reached the front steps, then ran up them and peered through a window next to the door. She could see a shotgun on the floor, and she thought she knew what that meant, and she could see, farther down the hall, a pair of feet protruding from under a white cloth. The toenails had been painted.

She dug into her bag and found her New York City press pass and hung the cord around her neck, then she got out her iPhone and took a photograph of the corpse's feet through the window, using the zoom to its fullest.

The sheriff's car pulled up, and he got out and came up the steps. A young woman with a plastic card dangling from her neck ran over to him.

"Sheriff, I'm a reporter," she said, holding up the card, which had her photograph on it. "May I come inside? I'll stay out of your way."

The front door opened, and Stone Barrington came out and introduced himself to the sheriff. She snapped a shot of them shaking hands.

"Mr. Barrington, this young lady says she's a reporter and wants to come inside. Do you want her inside?"

Stone looked at the young woman and recognized her from the party. "Who are you?" he asked.

"I'm Kelli Keane from the *Post.* We've talked on the phone."

"No," Stone said to the sheriff, "I don't want her inside." He opened the door for the sheriff, then closed it behind them, leaving Kelli on the porch.

Kelli went back to the window by the door, switched off the phone's flash, and took as many shots as she could. Then she moved to the next window and saw the two young people sitting on a sofa together and took some shots of them.

52

Stone sat down in the hallway and began to talk to the sheriff. They were interrupted when the crime-scene team arrived and took their instructions from the sheriff, who then returned to Stone's side.

"I'm sorry about all this," he said to Stone, waving his hand at all the people in the hall.

"I'm a retired homicide detective," Stone replied. "I know what you have to do." He introduced Dino.

The sheriff listened as Stone related

the facts of his morning, carefully and fully. "That's it," he said finally, "right up to this moment."

"I'd like to talk with your son and his friend," the sheriff said.

"Come with me." Stone led him into the living room. "Peter, Hattie, this is the sheriff. He needs to ask you some questions."

"Separately," the sheriff said.

"Hattie, you come with me," Stone replied. "Peter, can you answer his questions now?"

"Yes, Dad," Peter said.

Stone led Hattie into the study, where they sat down on a sofa.

"I'm awfully sorry, Mr. Barrington," she said.

"Thank you, Hattie. I'm all right. How do you think Peter is holding up?"

"A lot better than I would be," she said.

Hattie's parents came into the room and expressed their condolences.

"Is there anything we can do?" Sean Patrick asked.

"I don't think so," Stone said. "The

sheriff will want to talk with you, I'm sure. I expect you'll want to go back to New York this afternoon, and Mike will have room on his airplane for you."

"I want to stay with Peter," Hattie said.

"We'd be glad to have you, Hattie," Stone replied, "but that's up to your folks."

They looked at each other and nodded. "You can stay on for the rest of the week, Hattie," her father said. "We'll arrange for you to get back."

"Please let me deal with that," Stone said. "I'll need a day or two to handle matters here, then I'll let you know when we can get Hattie home."

The Eggerses and Mike Freeman came in, expressed their sorrow, and everyone sat quietly. Shortly, Peter came in.

"Hattie, the sheriff wants to talk with you now," he said.

Hattie returned to the living room.

Two hours later the sheriff and his people had completed their work, and Arrington's body was being wheeled to the ambulance.

"I've sent people to find Dr. Rutledge," the sheriff said to Stone, "but so far, they haven't been able to locate him. He's not at home, and his car isn't there, either. You were right, he drives a Ford station wagon. Is that what you saw driving away?"

"It could have been a Ford," Stone said. "I couldn't swear to it."

"Mr. Barrington, I haven't asked you this yet, but I need to now. How was your relationship with your wife?"

"We were newlyweds," Stone said, "married on Christmas Day. We hadn't even had an argument."

"I understand. I'm aware that your wife was a wealthy woman. Can you tell me about her will?"

"I haven't read it," Stone said, "but Mr. Eggers over there wrote it, and he has my permission to tell you whatever you want to know." He beckoned to Eggers and asked him to speak to the sheriff. Fifteen minutes later the house was empty of law enforcement, and two maids were cleaning the hall floor where Arrington had fallen.

Somes came into the study, where everyone had gathered. "Ladies and gentlemen," he said, "we've prepared soup and sandwiches for everyone, and the table is set in the kitchen."

Stone saw the others to the table, then, unable to eat anything, went upstairs. He lay on the bed for an hour, trying to empty his mind of everything, which turned out to be impossible. Finally, he took a deep breath, got up, and went downstairs.

Everyone had gathered, and Arrington's pilots had come to drive them to the airport.

"I'm staying," Dino said. "I'll deal with the local law for you."

His son came over. "I'd like to stay, too, Dad."

"Ben, I think it's best if you get back to school," Dino said. "If there's a service later, you can come back for that."

"Thanks, Dino," Stone said.

When he saw his guests out, Kelli

Keane was still on the porch, shivering. "My car is in a ditch," she said.

"We saw it on the way in," one of the pilots said. "We'll get it out for you."

Everyone made their good-byes and got into the van. They had just driven away when another car pulled up to the house, and a priest got out and introduced himself.

"I'm Dr. Alfred Means," he said, offering Stone his hand.

Stone took him into the house, allowed him to offer a prayer, then they made tentative arrangements for Arrington's burial in the family plot, after the release of her body by the medical examiner.

The priest gave Stone the name of the local funeral parlor.

"I'll deal with them," Dino said.

"Thank you, Dino," Stone replied. "Peter and I are grateful to you."

That evening they gathered in the kitchen for dinner, and everyone seemed to have recovered a bit. Even Stone was able to eat and have a glass of wine.

"I guess we have some things to do this week," Peter said.

"Yes, we do," Stone replied. "Eventually, we'll need to decide about what to do about the house."

Peter nodded. "I guess we do."

Kelli Keane returned to the inn, wrote a story, attached some photos to the file, and e-mailed it to the *Post*'s weekend editor. She had decided to approach *Vanity Fair* with the story, but she wanted to get back to New York first. She and David got an evening flight back to the city.

Stone called Joan and explained things to her. "We'll have some sort of service later this week," he said to her, "so just wipe my calendar clean until at least the week after. You can reach me on my cell here."

"Don't you worry," she said. "Nothing will happen here that I can't handle."

"Call me every day," Stone said. "I'll want to hear your voice."

Stone fell into bed, exhausted, and sleep came more quickly than he would have imagined possible.

53

On Thursday afternoon a funeral service was held for Arrington at her family church. Nearly all those who had been at the housewarming turned up, suitably dressed and bereaved, and Ben arrived from school. Peter read the text, the priest did his ecclesiastical duty, and Stone spoke of her love of her son, her husband, and of Virginia. The pallbearers, including Stone, Peter, Dino, and Ben, carried the mahogany coffin out the side door of the building, into the churchyard, where a grave site had been prepared in the Carter family lot.

Arrington's remains were interred next to those of her parents. The attendees offered their condolences to her family and everyone went home. Stone handed the priest an envelope containing two checks: an honorarium for himself and a generous donation to the general fund of the church, then he drove everybody back to the house. It had begun to rain.

They ran up the front steps as the rain became a torrent. "I think we'll wait until tomorrow morning to return to New York," Stone said to them. "This weather will have moved through by then. Hattie, you can phone your folks and tell them you'll be home around midday tomorrow. They won't have to meet you; we'll drop you at your home."

"Thank you, Mr. Barrington."

"Hattie, I think we're good enough friends for you to call me Stone."

"Thank you, sir," she said.

"And no need for the sir," he said, kissing her on the forehead.

Hattie went to phone her parents.

"Peter," Stone said, taking out his notebook, "take a walk around the house with me." The two of them went upstairs and started with Peter's bedroom, making a list of what furniture and possessions he wanted to send to New York. They then looked over the whole house, Stone listing things—a mirror here, a chair there—that might work in his New York, Connecticut, or Maine houses.

"Who did Mom leave this house to?" Peter asked.

"I don't know, Peter," Stone replied. "I haven't read her will yet. We'll get together soon with Bill Eggers and go over everything."

"I don't want this house or the property," Peter said. "I'l l always think of it as the place Mom died."

"I understand. We'll look into selling."

The five of them dined at a table in the study, then went to bed.

The following morning Somes drove everyone to the airport and loaded their luggage into the airplane.

"What are you going to do with the Gulfstream?" Peter asked.

"I don't have any idea yet," Stone replied, "but I think it's more airplane than we need, since we already have the Mustang."

Peter nodded. "I think you're right." He walked Hattie into the hangar and showed her the interior of the larger aircraft.

Stone preflighted the airplane and got a clearance, then they took off into clear blue skies. They touched down at Teterboro at eleven, and Stone drove Hattie and the Bacchettis home.

"Do you want to have dinner tonight?" Peter asked.

"I think I'd better eat with my parents tonight," Hattie said. "How about tomorrow night?"

"Sure." He gave her a kiss and got back into the car.

"Hattie's quite a girl," Stone said. "You're lucky to know her."

Peter managed a smile, something he had not done often since his mother's death. "I know that," he said, "believe me."

An hour later Stone was at his desk.

Joan came in and gave him a big hug. "I'm so sorry," she said.

"Thank you."

"I know we're going to have a lot of work to do, settling the estate, and I'll do everything I can to help." The phone rang, and she answered it. "Bill Eggers for you."

Stone took the phone. "Hello, Bill."

"How did things go in Virginia?" Eggers asked.

Stone told him about the service.

"Can you lunch with me tomorrow in my office?" Eggers asked.

"Of course."

"I think we should go over Arrington's will and the estate."

"I'll bring Peter," Stone said. "I want him to hear all this from you, not me."

"I'm glad to have him." They agreed to a time and hung up.

Stone spent the rest of the day returning phone calls, catching up on paperwork with Allison, and replying to letters of condolence, including one from Herbie Fisher that was more legibly handwritten than Stone would have expected. "How's it going with Herbie?" he asked Allison.

"We're seeing a lot of each other," she said.

"Why don't you take over his legal work?"

"If he has no objection," she said.

"I don't think he'll have any objection," Stone replied. "Don't fill out a Woodman & Weld timesheet for that; Herbie is a special case. Give Joan your hours, and she'll handle it."

Stone made omelets for dinner for himself and Peter, and they went to bed early.

The following morning they met with a cabinetmaker to look at the plans Peter had drawn for his study, then they walked up to the Seagram Building to see Bill Eggers in his office, where a table had been prepared for them before the fireplace.

They finished lunch, then Stone took Arrington's will from his briefcase and handed it to Eggers. "Here's the original," he said. "Peter, your mother met with Bill to draw up her will, then I sealed it and put it in my safe."

"That's true, Peter," Eggers said. "Stone didn't want to have knowledge of her estate planning, and he asked for nothing."

"I understand," Peter said solemnly.

Eggers broke the seal on the envelope and opened it. "Most of it is boilerplate," he said. "Peter, that's just necessary legalese. Your mother left substantial sums to a dozen charities, coming to about twenty million dollars, but the heart of the will is what she bequeathed to you and your father."

Peter nodded.

"Stone, she left you approximately half of her liquid assets and the Bel-Air property. That's it. Peter, she left you the remainder of her estate—a little more than half of the total, including the Virginia property and horse farm and all the Centurion Studios stock."

"Wow," Peter said softly.

"Because of your youth, all this was left to you in trust. Do you understand what a trust is?"

"I think so," Peter replied. "It means

that someone will be in charge until I reach a predetermined age, and I won't be able to draw money from the trust or sell any property unless the trustees agree."

"That's correct," Eggers said. "Your mother felt strongly that you should not have unrestricted access to your inheritance until you are thirty-five years old, perhaps earlier, if the trustee agrees."

Peter nodded.

"Stone is the trustee, and should anything happen to him, I am his alternate. If something happens to me first, Stone will appoint my replacement."

"I understand. That's fine with me," Peter said. "One thing, I've already told my dad I don't want the Virginia property or the horse farm. I don't have any interest in the horse business, and hardly any connection with the house."

"I think we'll put it on the market," Stone said. "*Architectural Digest* will be running a feature on the place soon, and that might spark some interest."

"Let's not list it with a broker just yet," Eggers said. "Properties of this size often create interest among qualified buyers before they're listed, and if we can sell it directly, you wouldn't be paying a huge commission to a realtor."

Both Stone and Peter nodded agreement.

"There are some other things you should know," Eggers said, "and there's some good news. First of all, Arrington divided her liquid holdings into two accounts, roughly equal. She left the more conservatively invested account to you, Peter, and the more growth-related account to you, Stone, so there won't be any need to have to divide the assets."

"What's the good news?" Peter asked.

"First of all, you should know that the total value of Arrington's estate, as of this morning, is approximately two point six billion dollars. Stone, your share, including the investments and the Bel-Air property, comes to about eight hundred million dollars. It was Arrington's wish that you bequeath Peter your wealth inherited from her upon your death. Peter, if you should precede Stone in death, your trust will revert to him. Your trust from your mother will amount to ap-

proximately one point eight billion dollars."

Peter's eyes widened. "Then I'm a
billionaire?"

"Not until you're thirty-five," Eggers
said, smiling.

Stone spoke up. "Let me tell you how
we're going to handle this, Peter. We're
going to manage your trust through the
existing banking and investment pro-
grams, because they're doing very well,
and we're not going to touch the principal of the trust until it's turned over to
you, or until there is some other very
good, unanticipated reason. All of your
needs will be met from my personal
funds. When I die, I will bequeath you
the remainder of my inheritance from
Arrington."

Peter seemed to be speechless.

"Do you understand?"

Peter nodded. "Yes, I do. Thank you,
Dad."

"Now, you have to do something
hard, Peter," Stone said.

"What's that, Dad?"

"You have to forget that you're going
to be a billionaire and just live your life

like an ordinary person. That won't be as easy as you might think, but you should start by not telling anyone—and that includes Hattie and Ben—anything about your inheritance. You can just say that you have a trust, and that it won't be available to you until you're thirty-five. If people think of you as a billionaire, you'll find that they—even your very best friends—will have their perceptions of you altered by their knowledge of your wealth. I'm sure you want your friends to like you for who you are, and not what you have."

"I see," Peter said, "and I think you're right."

"Also, if anyone, such as your school or a charity, should ask you to donate money to them, tell them to call me, that you have no access to substantial funds."

"All right, I will."

"Any questions?" Eggers asked.

Both Stone and Peter shook their heads.

"Now the good news," Eggers said. "Due to an anomaly in the national budget created by the Bush tax cuts ten years ago, a folly of our Republican friends, there are no federal inheritance taxes on the estate of anyone who dies in this calendar year."

"You mean there's nothing to be paid?" Stone asked.

"No, not a cent."

"Wow," Stone and Peter said simultaneously.

54

Stone was back at his desk when Joan brought him the *New York Post*.

"You should see this," she said, opening the paper.

Stone looked at it. The headline read: Vance Calder Widow Slain in Virginia Shooting. There was only one photograph, a shot of the house down the driveway. He made a little groaning sound, then read the piece, which was bylined Kelli Keane and said that the police were looking for a person of interest. When he finished it he closed the paper and handed it back to Joan.

"Well, that was more restrained than I would have expected from the *Post*," he said. "This Keane woman came down to Virginia as the assistant to the art director from *Architectural Digest*."

"I thought so, too," she said. She handed him the *Times*, open to the page. "They're even more restrained, and Arrington's obituary is fairly brief."

Stone read the two pieces. One line in the obit said, "She is survived by her second husband, Stone Barrington, and a son, Peter, 18, both of New York." The implication was that Peter was Stone's son.

"It will be on the AP wire, of course," Joan said, "but they will pick up the *Post* piece." The phone rang, and she picked it up. "It's the sheriff, in Virginia," she said, handing him the phone.

It suddenly occurred to Stone that he had not given a thought to Tim Rutledge since speaking to the sheriff at the house. "Good morning, Sheriff," he said.

"Good morning, Mr. Barrington," the sheriff replied. "I just want to give you an update on Tim Rutledge. He left town the day of the shooting and left a note for his department head, saying that he was moving to California to take up a teaching appointment there."

"So, he's on the run?"

"He is. We've sent out a nationwide alert to police agencies. We don't think there is a teaching appointment in California, and he could be anywhere. He cleaned out his bank accounts last Friday, so that would indicate premeditation."

"I see."

"The shotgun was processed for fingerprints, and the only ones found were those of my deputy. Rutledge apparently wiped it clean. Shall I return the shotgun to you?"

"No, please give it to the butler at the house. He will send it to me in New York, along with some other items from the house that are being packed."

"Just one other thing," the sheriff said. "The autopsy on Mrs. Barrington revealed that one of her ovaries had been removed, and the remaining one was in the early stages of ovarian cancer. The pathologist says that it's unlikely that she knew. Whether she would have survived the illness would have depended on how long she waited to be treated."

"I see," Stone said. "She had an examination in December, but nothing was found."

"As the pathologist said, the cancer was in the early stages."

"What are the chances of finding Tim Rutledge?" Stone asked.

"That will depend on how well he prepared his disappearance. We know, since he cleaned out his bank accounts, that there was premeditation, but we don't know how long he was planning this. We're tracking his credit cards, but nothing has been charged as yet."

"How much did he take from his bank accounts?"

"About two hundred thousand dollars in cash, from checking and savings, and a cashier's check for half a million from investments, including an IRA. That check hasn't cleared the bank yet. When it does, we'll find out where he cashed it, and that might help us."

"So, he's not hurting for funds."

"No. He left the station wagon in his

parking spot at the university, so we think he has a second car, though there is not one registered anywhere in his name."

"Finding him may be harder than you think," Stone said.

"You could be right. In any case, I will keep you posted on any developments. May I have your e-mail address?"

Stone gave it to him. "Thank you for checking in, Sheriff." He hung up.

"Anything?" Joan asked.

"Nothing. The man is on the run, he's smart, and he's got money. My bet is he's already out of the country, probably in Mexico."

The phone rang again. "It's Sean Patrick for you," Joan said. She handed him the phone and went back to her office.

"Hello, Sean."

"Hello, Stone. Thank you for being so kind to Hattie while she was in Virginia."

"It was a great comfort to Peter to have his friend there," Stone said.

"We were both very taken with Arrington, and we're sorry we won't have her as a permanent friend."

"Thank you."

"Stone, when we left to fly back to New York with Mike Freeman, one of your pilots was kind enough to show me your Gulfstream jet. Mike thought you might want to sell it."

"I think so, Sean. The Mustang is adequate for my purposes."

"My partners and I have been looking for an airplane to buy, and I think a G-III might suit us very well."

"It's a very nice airplane," Stone said. "Arrington bought it a little over a year ago, and it had had only one elderly owner up until then, so it's a low-time airplane. I'd be happy to send you copies of the paperwork she used to make her decision. Mike advised her on the purchase, so he knows a lot about it, too."

"Thanks. I'd like to see the paperwork and perhaps have our consultant on the purchase go down to Virginia and see it."

"Of course. If you like the airplane, you might consider hiring the crew, too. Arrington was very pleased with them."

"I'll keep that in mind. Have you given

any thought as to what you'll do with the house and farm?"

"We'll sell it, I think."

"I'm not in the market for such a place, but I have a lot of very wealthy clients, so I'll mention it here and there."

Stone reminded him to read the *Architectural Digest* piece, and they said good-bye. Stone asked Joan to make copies of the aircraft material and messenger it to Sean Patrick.

"I think I'm going to go upstairs and lie down for a while," he said to her.

"Aren't you feeling well?"

"Just very tired," he replied. He went upstairs and stretched out on the bed. He'd been having these periods of feeling exhausted since Arrington's death, and right now, he couldn't face any further work for the day.

55

Stone and Peter got ready to go to Elaine's for dinner and met downstairs.

"I'm going to go pick up Hattie," Peter said. "We'll meet you there in a few minutes."

Stone gave him some cash. "We need to open a bank account for you and set up an allowance."

"Thanks, Dad, I'd appreciate that."

"Joan will set it up on Monday."

They walked to Third Avenue together and took separate cabs.

Peter wondered what this was about. Ordinarily, the doorman in Hattie's building would have put her in a cab, and she would have met them at Elaine's, but Hattie had said she wanted to talk about something.

He got out of his cab at her building, and she came outside. He opened the door for her.

"Can we walk for a little bit?" she asked.

"Sure," Peter replied. He paid the driver and got out. She slipped her hand into his, and he put both in his coat pocket. They walked up Park Avenue in silence for a couple of minutes.

"There's something I have to tell you," she said.

"All right."

"No one else knows, and you have to keep it a secret."

"Of course."

Hattie took a deep breath and let it out. "I'm pregnant."

Peter stopped and turned to face her. "But we haven't . . ." He stopped, his mind reeling.

"It was someone I went out with be-

fore I met you," she said. "It only happened once."

Peter thought about that. "I want to
help," he said.

"Thank you," she replied. "I've already
decided to have an abortion, and I won't
brook any arguments about it. If you
find that unconscionable, I'll understand, and you can go your own way."

"I want to help," he said again. "Does
the guy know?"

"No," she said, "and he's never going
to."

"Good," Peter said.

"I've looked this up on the Internet,
and I've found a clinic up on First Avenue in the Nineties."

"What kind of clinic?"

"Licensed, part of a nationwide family planning organization."

"Have you been there yet?"

"No." Her lip trembled. "But I have an
appointment after school on Monday.
Will you go with me?"

"Of course," Peter said, squeezing
her hand. "I'll be with you every step of
the way."

"The way I understand it is, first, I

have an interview, then the procedure is scheduled—there's a waiting list—and I have to be accompanied by someone."

"That will be me," he said.

"After the procedure I'll be kept there for a few hours, until they know I'm all right, then I can go home. But I don't want to go home."

"You can come to my house," Peter said. "I'll take care of you there, then take you home later."

"What about your father? I don't want him to know."

"There's a way into the house through the garden. He's usually in his office, so I can take you upstairs."

"We have to face the possibility that something might go wrong. In that case I'll have to go to a hospital."

Peter thought about that. "I don't see any way that we can keep you out overnight. If you need to go to a hospital, I think you'll have to tell your parents."

"I don't want to do that," she said.

"I understand, but you have to think of them, as well as yourself."

"I know, but I'm afraid."

"I know you love them, so think about

what you're afraid of—disappointing them in some way?"

"Yes."

"If I'm facing something I'm uncomfortable about, what I do to handle it is, I think about the worst-case scenario," Peter said. "What is the worst thing that could happen? Then I figure out what I would do if the worst thing happened. Once I've decided that, I feel a lot better. What's the worst thing that could happen in this case?"

"For my parents to find out what I've done."

"Let's think about what that would mean," he said. "What would they say to you?"

"They would be shocked, especially my father."

"Of course, but how would they react after that?"

"Once the initial shock was over they would be sympathetic," she said. "And they'd want to know who the father was."

"Would you tell them?"

"No, I wouldn't."

"Do you think they would punish you in some way?"

"Peter, I'm eighteen; they can't spank me."

"Would they ground you? Place some sort of limitations on you?"

"They can't do that, either. If they treated me like a child, I'd move out."

"How would you support yourself?"

"I have a trust fund. I could get by very nicely on the income from that."

"You couldn't take money out of your trust without the permission of your trustee, right?"

"Right."

"Who is the trustee, your father?"

"No, it's a bank. They would let me take money out of the trust for living expenses and my education."

"I can help, too."

"I wouldn't want you to do that."

"You have to let me decide what I want to do," Peter said. "I have a bank account in Virginia that receives automatic deposits for my prep school fees, but I left prep school early, so there's something like fifty or sixty thousand dollars in that account. I can write checks on it."

"I wouldn't want to touch that money."

"It's my money now; my mother is dead. Just think of it as a safety net."

"All right, I'll think of it that way." She smiled. "I feel better now."

Peter took her in his arms and held her for a moment. "Don't you worry about a thing," he said. "We'll make this work."

56

The group met at Elaine's, and Stone's first thought after they sat down was that both Peter and Hattie were unusually subdued. Normally, they would be talking a mile a minute, and instead, they were staring at their food or just into the middle distance. But, in the circumstances, what did he expect? He was pretty subdued himself.

"Have you kids thought about where you're going to live at Yale?" he asked, just to get a conversation going.

Peter spoke up. "I thought we might

look for a three-bedroom apartment," he said.

"Hattie," Stone said, "you're going to have to speak to your parents about that."

"I already have," Hattie replied. "They're good with it, as long as I have my own room. After all, lots of college dorms are co-ed, so it's not very different from that."

"I'll want to hear that from them," Stone said.

"Of course," she replied, then went back to staring at her food.

"I think you should look sooner, rather than later," Stone said. "I've looked at the Yale website, and starting in May, housing begins to disappear fast."

"We could take the train up there one day and have a look around," Peter said.

"You forget," Ben interjected, "I have a driver's license."

"All right," Dino said, "you can take my car. If you were seen on campus in that tank of Stone's, you'd ruin your reputations. I think you should stay overnight in a hotel, too. Hattie can have her own room and you and Peter can bunk together."

"Sounds good," Peter said.

"Yes, fine," Hattie echoed. Everybody stopped talking again.

"When do you want to go up there?" Stone asked.

"I don't know," Peter said, "maybe in two or three weeks?"

More silence. Stone gave up.

Peter took Hattie home in a cab. "Tomorrow, after school," he said.

"Right," she replied. "We can play hooky one day for the procedure."

They kissed, and she went inside.

Stone heard Peter come in, and he went to the boy's room and sat down. "How are you doing?"

"Okay, I guess," Peter replied. "How about you?"

"I think we're both still pretty shaken up," Stone said.

"I think you're right," Peter said. "I never expected anything like this to happen. I thought you and Mom would grow old together."

"We thought so, too," Stone said.

"Have they caught the architect guy yet?"

"Not yet," Stone said. He told Peter about the call from the sheriff. "They'll get him, don't worry."

"Then there'll be a trial, right?"

"Yes, there will."

"And you and I and Hattie will have to testify?"

"Maybe not all of us; maybe I can do it alone. That will depend on the district attorney's case."

"Nobody actually saw him there, did they?" Peter asked.

"No."

"And his fingerprints weren't on the shotgun."

"No."

"So what evidence do they have against him?"

"It sounds as though it would be circumstantial."

"Does that mean there's less of a chance of conviction?"

"Not necessarily. The man did run,

after all, and took all his money with him. That's damning. If he did it, he won't have an alibi, unless someone is willing to lie for him."

"Would someone do that?"

"It sometimes happens," Stone said.

David Rutledge got home from work and found Kelli sitting at the dining table, tapping away on her laptop. She had been living with him since they got back from Virginia.

"How's your piece going?" he asked, kissing the top of her head.

"It's practically writing itself," she said.

"Drink?"

"Please. Scotch."

David went to the built-in bar and poured them both one. He brought the drinks back to the table and set them down. "Good news. We had to pull a piece, so we're running the Virginia spread in the next issue."

"The one that closed today?"

"Yep."

"That's wonderful!"

The phone rang. David walked into the living area and picked up the extension on the coffee table. "Hello?"

"Listen carefully," a familiar voice said. "Are you alone?"

"No," David replied.

"I'm around the corner from your apartment in a bar. You know the place?"

David identified the voice now. "Yeah, I guess I'll have to come in. Be there in ten." He hung up.

"Be where?" Kelli asked.

"At the office. I forgot to check some pages before I left, and we have to go to press tonight. I'll be back in an hour or so."

"You want me to cook dinner?" she asked.

"Can you actually do that?" he asked back. She never had before.

"I can make very respectable spaghetti Bolognese," she said.

"Okay, I'm game," he said, putting his coat on. "I'll pick up some Alka-Seltzer on the way home."

She threw a pencil at him.

"You need anything else?"

"You can pick up a head of romaine lettuce and some bread," she said.

"Okay." He closed the door behind him and got on the big freight elevator.

David walked into the bar and spotted the back of his cousin's head immediately, in a booth at the rear. He shucked off his coat, hung it on a hook, and sat down. "Hello, Tim," he said, because he couldn't think of anything else to say.

"Aren't you going to ask what I'm doing here?"

A waitress came, and David ordered a scotch. "You're running, aren't you?"

"I didn't do it," Tim said.

David said nothing.

"They're trying to hang it on me, though."

"Who's trying?"

"The sheriff, the university—everybody."

"If you didn't do it, why did you run?"

"I didn't have a chance. I got a call from somebody who told me she was dead. It was the first I knew of it."

"Who called you?"

"You don't want to know that," Tim replied. "It's better if you don't."

"All right."

"Will you help me, David? You're all I've got."

"What do you want me to do?"

"Can you put me up for a few days, until things cool down and I can move around more freely?"

"I can't, Tim; my girlfriend has moved in with me, and she works for the *New York Post*."

"Oh, Jesus, don't tell her anything, then."

"I don't know anything," David said. "Do you need money?"

"No, I'm okay there."

"Then I suggest you move into a hotel. Not near here, please; uptown somewhere."

"Can you suggest a place?"

"No, I'm not going to suggest anything, Tim. I won't go to jail for you."

"I just got into town; I haven't found a place yet. Do you know a hotel called—"

David stopped him with an upraised

hand. "I don't want to know the name," he said.

Tim took a cell phone from his pocket and pushed it across the table. "I bought two of these," he said. "They're untraceable." He handed David a card. "Here's my number."

David looked at the phone for a long moment, then he put it and the card into a pocket.

"It's set on vibrate, and the voice mail is already set up, so we can leave messages."

"Do you know a lawyer in Virginia, Tim? A criminal lawyer?"

"No. I mean, I have an attorney, but he doesn't have a criminal practice."

"Call him on your new cell phone and ask him to recommend one, then go back to Virginia and let him turn you in to the sheriff. That's your best move, Tim, believe me."

Tim nodded. "I'll do that in a few days," he said. "There's something else I have to do first, then I'll go back to Charlottesville."

"What do you have to do here?" David asked, curious in spite of himself.

"It's better you don't know," Tim said, setting down his glass. "I'll leave first; finish your drink before you go home." He put a twenty on the table, got up, got into his coat, and left.

David took ten minutes to finish his scotch, then got into his coat and went to the neighborhood deli for the lettuce and bread.

God, David thought as he walked home, *I wish he hadn't called.*

57

Kelli Keane arrived at work and immediately went to see Prunella Wheaton. She placed her manuscript and copies of the photos she wanted to use on her desk, then plopped herself down.

Prunie handed her a cup of coffee. "First draft?" she asked.

"Final draft, before I send it," Kelli replied.

Prunie picked up the piece and began to read. Kelli finished her coffee and tiptoed around the desk for another cup, not wishing to disturb her mentor.

She hadn't expected Prunie to read the whole thing at once.

Prunie finished, and restacked the sheets on her desk.

Kelli waited, holding her breath.

"Comprehensive," Prunie said.

Kelli flinched. That was it? She had worked her ass off on that piece.

"Concise, highly readable—in fact, unputdownable. Excellent."

Kelli let out her breath. "What a relief!" she said.

"Did you think I wouldn't like it?"

"I hoped you would."

"You've done an outstanding job. It covers all the bases, doesn't criticize anybody, and, I assume, it's accurate."

"I can back up every statement in it."

"I like the photographs, too, particularly the one of the corpse in the hall with a foot sticking out from under the blanket."

"That was as close as I could get," Kelli said.

"You didn't quote Barrington on anything."

"He wouldn't talk to me."

"And the shot of the boy and girl consoling each other was perfect. You didn't use her name in the piece."

"I don't know her name," Kelli lied, "but I'm not sure I would have run it anyway. She's a high school kid, and I don't think anyone will recognize her from that shot."

"That's very sensitive of you," Prunie said.

"Who should I send it to at *Vanity Fair*? Graydon Carter?"

"No, don't jump the line. Let me send it to a senior editor I know, and if she likes it she'll send it to the executive literary editor, and if he likes it, he'll send it to Graydon. That way, everybody gets credit for liking it."

"That sounds smart."

"I assume you have another copy?"

"In my computer."

Prunie typed a letter to the *Vanity Fair* editor on her personal stationery, then wrote a name and address on a slip of paper and handed it to Kelli. "Messenger it over, and don't use a *Post* messenger. There's a service downstairs in the building, and keep a receipt. I assume you didn't write any of this at your desk here?"

"No, I did it all at home, and on my personal computer. And I gave the initial story about the killing to the paper."

"Good. Now get going."

Kelli downed the rest of her coffee, went back to her desk, found a non-*Post* envelope, took the package downstairs, and shipped it.

Tim Rutledge checked out of the New Jersey motel where he had stayed the night and drove into Manhattan. He dropped his luggage, except for one bag, at a small hotel on West Forty-fourth Street, parked his car in the Hippodrome Garage, then walked the block back to the hotel, carrying his largest duffel.

He checked into the hotel, having earlier phoned a reservation, and a bellman took him upstairs to his room. It was of a decent size, decently furnished, with a flat-screen TV, a comfortable bed, and chair. He unpacked his clothes, then opened the large duffel.

He removed and put away the clothes in that bag, then put on a pair of latex gloves from a box he had bought at a drugstore, then finally took from the duffel an elongated package, wrapped in sturdy brown paper and packing tape. Using his pocketknife, he cut away the paper at one end, then shook the contents out onto his bed.

The contents consisted of a used, 12-gauge Remington police riot gun, with a truncated, eighteen-and-a-half-inch barrel. He had bought it from an individual at a gun show in Virginia, before he had driven north out of the state. He found the box of double-ought shells he had bought. And oaded the weapon, leaving the chamber empty. He wouldn't need more than one or two rounds, he figured.

He took some tissues and wiped the shotgun clean of any stray prints that might have found their way to it, then returned the loaded weapon to its paper wrapping, now a sheath, from which he would fire it. Therefore, there would be no gunpowder residue on his hands or clothing, and, of course, no fingerprints on the shotgun or the shells. When he had completed his mission, he would dispose of the weapon in a dumpster at some construction site and it would vanish into a landfill somewhere.

Should the shotgun ever be found, it could not be traced to him. His mission satisfactorily completed, he would then drive his car to California. He had always wanted to drive across the United States, and, with his new and quite legal passport and Virginia driver's license, obtained a few weeks ago, he would be safe from an unexpected arrest. He had already begun to grow a beard, and it was looking quite attractive, he thought.

After a look at California he would drive across the border to Tijuana, and thence down to Baja, where he would, eventually, move the funds he had mailed to a bank in the Cayman Islands to a neighborhood Mexican bank, then buy a little house.

He would then begin his new career as a novelist, the mysterious E. Gifford,

and he just knew he would be successful at it.

Kelli had just left the *Post* building for
the day when her cell phone buzzed.
"Hello?"

"Kelli Keane?"

"Yes. Who's this?"

"This is Karen Kohler at *Vanity Fair*.
Prunie Wheaton sent me your manuscript this morning."

"Oh, yes."

"Everybody here loves it," she said. "I
walked it through the office, and nobody could put it down. We just had to
cancel a piece in the next issue that
couldn't pass fact-checking, so we can
slip it right in, instead of waiting for the
usual two or three months."

"Wonderful!"

"Do you have an agent?"

Kelli gave her the name and phone
number.

"Well, assuming we can make a deal,
and if the piece gets through fact-
checking with no major changes, you'll
see it in the next issue."

"That's great news, Karen," Kelli said.

"There's one more thing we need, though."

"What's that?"

"A decent photograph of this suspect, Tim Rutledge. A head shot will do, but get the best one you can."

"I'll get right on it," Kelli said.

"I'll call you in a day or two to come over here so we can go through the fact-checking and my notes. Can you bring your laptop and make any changes on the spot?"

"Sure, I can."

"I'll be in touch, then." The woman hung up.

Kelli flung herself in front of a taxi and headed for home. She couldn't wait to tell David.

58

Peter met Hattie after school, and they walked down to Second Avenue and got a cab uptown. He took her hand. "Are you still sure this is what you want to do?"

"Are you against it?" she asked, looking alarmed.

"No. If it's what you want, I'm all for it. I just want to be sure you're sure."

"I'm sure," she said.

They got out at the corner nearest the clinic and walked upstairs. There was a friendly-looking waiting room with landscapes on the walls and current magazines, not all of them for women. Hattie gave the assumed name she was using to the receptionist and came and sat next to Peter.

"I've got the titles finished and in the movie," he said. "It's as good as it's ever going to be now." He told her this to keep her mind off where she was.

"That's wonderful. What are you going to do with it?"

"Nothing, just yet. Dad thinks I should wait a couple of years before submitting it to anyone."

"Why?"

"He thinks the publicity it might produce wouldn't be a good thing for me right now."

"I'm not sure he's right," Hattie said. "The Sundance festival is soon, and I think your film ought to be in it. If you wait a couple of years, someone else might do a similar film, and that would take away from yours."

"I hadn't thought of that," Peter said.

"Anyway, you'll be at Yale by the time the film gets released, and that's a kind of insulation."

"You could be right," Peter said. "I'll talk to Dad about it."

"Miss Springer?" a woman's voice said.

Hattie didn't react until Peter squeezed her hand.

"Oh, yes," she said, standing up.

"Please follow me."

Hattie kissed Peter on the forehead and followed the woman from the room.

Peter sat and thought about what Hattie had said, and he realized that sending the completed film to Centurion would be an enormous relief to him. It was the natural thing to do after completing the work. He began to think about the details of doing that.

Kelli Keane arrived at the Condé Nast building and found the floor for *Vanity Fair*. Karen Kohler appeared in reception, shook her hand, gave her a broad smile, and took her to her office in the editorial department.

"Now," Karen said, sitting behind her desk and waving Kelli to a seat, "here are my notes." She handed Kelli a neatly typed sheet of paper.

Kelli read them. "I've no problem with any of these," she said. "I can fix them in ten minutes."

"Good. Now, there's one more thing."

"What's that?"

"There seems to be a discrepancy in the age of Arrington's son, Peter. She and Vance Calder were married about seventeen years ago. How could they have an eighteen-year-old son? They hadn't even met until she did the *New Yorker* profile on Vance."

"I believe the boy is Stone Barrington's son. They were seeing each other before she met Vance. I have a copy of the boy's birth certificate from L.A., showing him to be eighteen, and Barrington is listed as the father."

"Both Arrington and Stone were New Yorkers," Karen said. "Why would she have her child in L.A.?"

"I haven't been able to nail that down," Kelli replied, "and believe me, I pulled out all the stops. I'd like that part of the piece to remain the same, because it reflects the information I have confirmed, not what I'm guessing. Also, I don't want to embarrass an eighteen-year-old boy by discussing his parentage in a national magazine. To be clear, I'll put it this way: I won't give you the piece, if that's what you want to do."

Karen held up a calming hand. "Take it easy. If you feel strongly about it, we'll leave it as it is. Knowing our readership, we may get some letters to the editor about the matter, but we can deal with that when it happens."

"Thank you," Kelli said, opening her laptop. "If I can use the edge of your desk, I'll make your corrections now."

"Great. We're going to press tonight."

Kelli opened her laptop and went to work.

Peter was staring blankly at a magazine when Hattie came through a door and sat beside him.

"All done?" he asked.

"No, I'm afraid not. They've examined me and told me I can have the procedure in ten minutes. Apparently, another girl had second thoughts and canceled her appointment. If I don't do it now, I'll have to wait another two weeks before they have an opening, and I don't want to do that."

Peter thought about it for a few seconds. "That's fine. Just call your mother and tell them you want to do dinner and a double feature with me, and you'll be home by eleven."

"All right," she said. "With the rest period, this will take about four hours. Why don't you go to a movie or something, then come back for me?"

"All right," he replied.

"Wish me luck."

"You'll be fine."

They kissed, and she went back through the door.

Peter sat, a little breathless, and planned how they were going to do this. He checked his watch, then he left and walked down to the multiplex cinema on East Eighty-sixth Street. He had half an hour's wait before the movie he wanted to see started, so he had a snack nearby, then returned for the film.

———

When Peter came out of the movie it was dark, and he still had another hour before Hattie could leave the clinic, so he walked slowly back in that direction, window-shopping, taking his time.

When he arrived at the clinic he sat down in the waiting room. A woman opened a glass partition. "You're Ms. Springer's friend, aren't you?"

"Yes," he replied.

"I'm afraid there's been a complication, and she's been taken to the emergency room."

Peter's heart jumped into his throat. "Where?"

"She's at Lenox Hill Hospital," the woman replied.

Peter ran down the stairs and looked desperately for a cab. It had started to rain, and there were none.

He began to run. Lenox Hill was in the upper Seventies, he wasn't sure which street. He alternately sprinted, jogged, and walked, and the sweat was coming through his clothes.

He asked a cop for directions and got them, then he stood and caught his breath for a minute and called home.

"Hello?"

"Hi, Dad."

"Peter? Where are you? I was expect-ing you home from school."

"Hattie and I went to a movie, and we want to go to a double feature now, so I'll grab a bite between movies."

"Is that all right with her parents?"

"Yes, she's already talked to them."

"All right, I'll see you later."

Peter ended the call and began to run again. He still had two blocks to go.

59

Tim Rutledge stood in the rain across the street from Stone Barrington's house and huddled under the flimsy umbrella he had paid a street vendor ten dollars for. As he watched, the light in a street-level window went off, and a woman emerged from the adjacent door and locked it. She put up her umbrella and hurried up the block toward Third Avenue.

Rutledge waited for her to disappear around the corner, then he crossed the street, went down a couple of steps, and peered through the window where

the light had gone off. There were two
or three pieces of office equipment with
small screens that gave off enough of a
glow for him to make out a desk, filing
cabinets, and a pair of chairs. The
woman must be Barrington's secretary,
because his residence and office addresses were the same, with an A added
to the office street number. He tried the
door, but it was securely locked.

Rutledge looked up the block and
saw a police car coming, so he ducked
under the steps to the upstairs residence until it had passed. On the other
side of the steps was a garage door
that, apparently, belonged to the house.
He stepped back to the sidewalk and
looked at the first-floor windows. Lights
were on somewhere to the rear of the
house, but he saw no sign of life. A light
burned over the front door.

Turtle Bay, he knew, had a common
garden, surrounded on two sides by
rows of houses. The Second Avenue
side was made up of a row of shops,
and the Third Avenue side was taken
up by an office building.

Rutledge walked around the block

until he stood at a point even with the rear of Barrington's house. Some of these common gardens had an entrance opening to the street, and he walked down the block slowly, looking for one. He found a heavy, wrought-iron gate and could see a corner of the gardens through that, but it was locked, and he knew nothing about picking locks. He walked down to Second Avenue, then up Barrington's street again. He was going to have to catch him entering or leaving his house, but he had no way of knowing when that might be.

He finally gave up and went down to Second Avenue to find someplace to eat.

Peter found the emergency room entrance to the hospital and went inside. The waiting area was packed with people waiting for treatment, many of them wet. He went to the admitting desk, and a woman in scrubs looked up from her desk. "May I help you?"

"Yes, please. I'm looking for a young

woman who was brought in by ambulance."

"Name?"

"Springer."

The woman consulted her computer screen. "I'm sorry, we don't have a patient named Springer."

"Try Patrick."

The woman looked at him oddly. "She has two names?"

"She might have used either."

The woman checked her computer again. "First name?"

"Hattie."

"Yes, she came in about two hours ago and is being seen by a doctor."

"May I see her?"

"Not until she's admitted," the woman replied.

"Will she be admitted? Will she have to stay overnight?"

"I won't know that until the doctor who is seeing her makes his report on her condition."

"May I visit her before she's admitted?"

"You'll have to wait until I get her

chart back and see if there's an admitting order. Have a seat, and I'll call you. What's your name?"

"Peter," he said.

"Last name?"

"Just Peter." He went and found an empty seat, one that allowed him to look down a hallway. He had been there for five minutes when a large double door opened, and two ambulance drivers wheeled in a patient on a gurney, pushing it down the hallway and taking a right turn.

Peter got up and followed the gurney. He found himself looking through a window in a pair of double doors at a row of treatment tables, some of them occupied by patients. Behind the treatment tables was a row of cubicles, most with patients on tables, some with curtains drawn. As he watched, a man on an examining table sat up, and an orderly brought over a wheelchair. The patient got into the chair, and the orderly took his chart from the foot of the table and put it in the man's lap. Peter stood back to let them pass through the double doors. Apparently, the man was being discharged.

He pushed open the door and walked briskly into the room, wanting to appear as if he knew where he was going. He walked along the row of cubicles and, four or five down, found Hattie, lying on a table, half sitting up. She looked relieved when she saw him.

He went and stood next to her. "Are you all right?"

"Yes, I'm fine. I was bleeding, but it stopped over an hour ago. The doctor said he would discharge me in a few minutes, and that was half an hour ago."

Peter pulled up a chair. "I was scared," he said. "I came back from the movie, and they said you were in the emergency room."

"I wanted to call you, but they took my bag away when they put me in the ambulance, and when I got here they wouldn't let me use my cell phone."

A very young man in scrubs and a white coat walked into the cubicle. "How are you feeling?" he asked Hattie.

"Just fine, thank you. I'd like to go home."

He picked up her chart, made some notations, and signed it. "I'll find an orderly and have you wheeled out."

"I can do that," Peter said.

"Okay." He left and came back with a wheelchair. Hattie got into it, and the doctor handed Peter her chart. "Stop at the discharge window and check out with them, then take her all the way to the street in the chair. You can leave it there. You, young lady, are to go home and rest. If there's any recurrence of the bleeding, you're to call an ambulance and return here. Is that clear?"

"Yes, Doctor."

"You should be okay to go to school tomorrow," he said. "Good night."

Peter pushed the chair into the waiting room and got her checked out. Hattie wrote a check for her bill. "I didn't want to use my parents' insurance card," she said, as Peter pushed her toward the exit.

The rain had let up a lot. "I'll get us a cab," Peter said.

"I don't want to go home yet," Hattie said. "I'm hungry. Let's get something to eat."

"Are you sure?"

"Yes, I'm sure," she said, standing up and taking his hand. "And I'm not pregnant anymore."

60

David Rutledge looked at the first copy of his magazine's new issue and thought the Virginia shoot had turned out very well. As he scanned the piece he felt a pang of conscience. He had not done the right thing, and he regretted it. What had he been thinking?

He picked up the phone and dialed 411. A minute or so later he was talking to the sheriff of Albemarle County.

"What can I do for you, Mr. Rutledge? Are you related to Tim Rutledge?"

"Yes, I am," David replied. "He's my cousin."

"Is there anything you can tell me about his whereabouts?"

"Yes. He's in New York."

"How do you know that?"

"He called me from a bar near my home in the city, and I met him for a drink."

"And when was this?"

"The night before last."

"And why didn't you call me immediately?"

"I don't think I was seeing the situation clearly; I reacted as a family member, and not as a citizen. I'm sorry for that."

"Do you have any idea where he is now?"

"From our conversation I believe he might have moved into a hotel somewhere uptown."

"I don't know your geography there," the sheriff said. "What do you mean by 'uptown'?"

"Uptown from where I live. I live downtown."

"That doesn't help me a lot. Do you have an address?"

"No. He asked to stay at my place,

but I declined to have him do that. He asked me to recommend a hotel, and I declined to do that, too. My impression was that he wanted to be uptown somewhere."

"Perhaps near where Mr. Stone Barrington lives?"

"Perhaps; that name didn't come up. He did say he had something to do in the city, though."

"And what might that be?"

"He wouldn't say."

"Our theory of this case is that he shot Mrs. Barrington because he was jealous, a jilted lover. Apparently, Mr. Rutledge and Mrs. Barrington had some sort of relationship before she was married, while he was working on her house."

"I see. I didn't know anything about that relationship. Before the housewarming I hadn't seen Tim since last summer."

"Do you know how Mr. Rutledge traveled to New York?"

"No, I don't."

"He didn't say anything about having a car?"

"No, I don't think so."

"All right, Mr. Rutledge, thank you for your help in this matter. Will you please call me immediately if you see or hear from your cousin again? You might be saving a life."

"Yes, I will."

"And if you do speak to him, try to find out where he's staying."

"All right." The sheriff hung up, and so did David.

Stone was at his desk when Dino called. "How you doing?" he asked.

"I'm okay, I guess."

"I just got some news you need to hear."

"Tell me."

"The sheriff down in Virginia called the chief's office and told him he'd had a tip that Tim Rutledge, the suspect, is in New York. I just got the e-mail."

Stone sat up straight. "What else?"

"Nothing else. He may be staying in a hotel. That's all the informant had."

"Thank you for letting me know," Stone said.

"I think you should go armed for a while."

"I think you're right," Stone said.

"What time does Peter get out of school?"

"Usually between three and five, depending on what he's doing there."

"You want me to send a car for him?" Dino asked.

"Thanks, Dino, I'd appreciate that." He glanced at his watch; it was nearly four o'clock. "I'll call him and let him know." He gave Dino Peter's cell number.

"Consider it done."

"You're a good friend." They both hung up, and Stone called Peter's cell and got voice mail. "Peter, it's Dad. I've heard from the police that Tim Rutledge may be in New York, and I don't want you on the street until that's been dealt with. Dino is sending a police car to bring you home from school. They'll call your cell when they're outside. Don't leave the building until then." Stone hung up. He felt something he'd never felt before: worry about his child's safety.

He resisted the impulse to go to the school himself.

Joan came in with something for him to sign. "You look funny," she said.

"Tim Rutledge is apparently in the city."

"Jesus, I thought he'd be in Mexico, like you said."

"I was wrong, apparently. Dino is sending a car to pick up Peter at school."

"That's good."

Stone picked up the phone and called Mike Freeman at Strategic Services.

"Hi, Stone, how are you?"

"A little worried, Mike," Stone said.

"What's wrong?"

Stone explained. "I think I'd like someone armed to be with Peter for a few days."

"Certainly. Do you want him picked up at school?"

"Dino's sending a police car for him. Could you have someone here tomorrow morning at seven-thirty to drive him to school? He can use my car."

"Of course. There'll be two men, and they'll be our best."

"Thank you, Mike."

"Did Sean Patrick call you about Arrington's G-III?"

"Yes, he did. We sent him copies of everything we had on the airplane, and he's sending someone down to Virginia to look at it and interview the crew."

"That would be Milt Kaplan. I recommended him, and he'll see the worth of the airplane immediately. If Sean turns out not to want it, we could lease it from you until it sells."

"That's a nice thought, but as a board member, I wouldn't want you to spend all that money when you already have two airplanes."

Mike laughed. "All right, I'll take your advice." They chatted for a moment, then said good-bye.

Joan buzzed him. "Peter's on line two," she said.

"Peter?"

"Yes, Dad. I got your message. There's a police car outside right now."

"Good. Get in it and come home."

"Can I drop Hattie off on the way?"

"Sure, that's fine."

"I'll be home in half an hour or so."

Stone hung up feeling relieved.

61

At half past four Peter came into Stone's office, shucking off his coat. "Anything new about Rutledge?"

"No," Stone replied. "Don't be too worried about this."

"Dad, if *you're* not too worried, what am I doing traveling in a police car? I'll never hear the end of this at school."

"Well, from tomorrow, you'll be traveling in the Bentley, and you'll get still more guff about that, I'm sure. Two of Mike Freeman's men will be riding with you. And yes, you can pick up Hattie on the way to school and take her home after that."

"Thanks, Dad. There's something I want to talk to you about."

Stone walked over to the leather sofa and sat down. "Take a pew and tell me about it."

Peter fished in his bag and came up with a bundle of DVDs, secured with a rubber band. "My movie is finished; the titles and Hattie's score are in. It's called *Autumn Kill*."

"Intriguing title," Stone said.

"That's what I was going for. I've thought about this a lot, and I don't want to wait a year or two to try and get it released. I want to do it now."

Stone shook his head. "Peter, I've already explained why I think you should wait."

"I know, and I've considered your points very carefully. The thing is, I'll be at Yale by the time the film is in theaters, and that will give me some insulation. Also, I can just decline to talk about it. I'm concerned that if I wait, some other similar film might come along that could lessen its chances for success."

"You mean with a similar plot?"

"I mean something as simple as another film that takes place at a prep school. I have something original, and I don't want to have it look like a copycat because some other filmmaker does something that looks like it."

Stone thought about it and thought that, chances were, Peter was as right as he. "All right, but I think you have to offer it to Centurion first."

"That makes perfect sense to me."

Stone thought a little more. "You're going to need an agent to represent you in this. Since I'm on the Centurion board, I have a conflict of interest."

"All right, but how do I find an agent?"

Stone picked up the phone on the coffee table. "Joan, please get me Morton Janklow."

"Who's Morton Janklow?" Peter asked.

"The best agent I know."

There was a click on the line. "Stone, how are you?"

"Very well, Mort."

"I was very sorry to hear of Arrington's death."

"Thank you."

"What can I do for you?"

"I have a new client for you, if you want him."

"Who would that be?"

"His name is Peter Barrington; he's my son."

"Hang on, did you say 'son'?"

"I'll explain that part on another occasion," Stone said. "Let me explain what he needs, and you can tell me if you're interested."

"All right, go ahead."

"Peter is in his last year of prep school, and he's been accepted at the Yale School of Drama, where he plans to study directing. He's made a film called *Autumn Kill* and I'm going to messenger it over to you right now."

"Okay. What's it about?"

"It's better if you see it cold, I think. If, after ten minutes, you can switch it off, I'll be very surprised. Leo Goldman at Centurion saw an incomplete version and immediately wanted to buy it."

"Is Centurion who you want to sell it to?"

"I think we owe them the first refusal. I'm on their board, so I don't want to deal directly with Leo."

"Do you have any idea what you want for the film?"

"I'll tell you what I think would be ideal: We sell the rights to the film for a limited period and take some cash, plus a percentage of the gross."

"A limited rights deal is not what a studio wants," Janklow said.

"I understand, but let's start there."

"I'll be at home tonight, so I'll watch the film and call you in the morning."

"Thanks, Mort. It's on its way."

Both men hung up, and Stone buzzed Joan. "I want to messenger something to Janklow & Nesbit, a rush." She came in and he gave her two discs.

"You're sure Mr. Janklow is better than someone on the coast?" Peter asked.

"He has a deal with Creative Artists Agency. If he feels they can help, he'll go through them, but I thought I'd leave that up to him."

"Okay," Peter said. "Now I'm starting to get nervous."

"Don't be. You already know that Leo wants your film. The rest is haggling."

Peter laughed. "Oh, something I forgot. If the film is released, I think we'll have to come to some arrangement with the various unions and pay the actors and others at least union scale. I paid each actor a hundred dollars and got a release from everybody."

"Smart move," Stone said. "The studio will know how to handle that."

Peter stood up. "I've got some reading to do," he said. "I'll see you at supper."

At half past five Joan buzzed him. "Mr. Janklow on one."

"Hello, Mort?"

"Stone, I've watched the first twenty minutes of the film, and I'm rapt. And, guess who just called me about another matter? Leo Goldman. I mentioned that I have a new client, and when he heard who, Leo went quietly nuts."

Stone laughed.

"I'm overnighting the DVD to him, but he's already made an offer, which I did not accept."

"What's the offer?"

"Ten million dollars for all the rights, plus five percent of the gross. Don't worry, when he sees what I'm seeing, with titles and a score, we'll do better."

"What did he say about a limited license?"

"Exactly what I thought he'd say, but wait until tomorrow. I'll hear from him by noon his time, maybe sooner, if he's really excited."

"When you talk to him again, tell him he has to make the various unions happy about the release, at his expense, and he has to pay Hattie Patrick, who wrote the score."

"Good point."

"Thank you, Mort. I'll look forward to hearing from you."

"How old is your boy?"

"Eighteen."

"I want to meet him."

"Of course; we'll arrange that."

"He must be very smart, if he got into Yale."

"You have no idea," Stone said.

62

Shortly after noon the following day, Stone got a call from Morton Janklow.

"Leo got back to me," Janklow said. "We're at twenty million and ten points."

"Wonderful. How about the rights issue?"

"Seven years. I think that's good. Peter will end up owning his film outright."

"That's perfect, Mort."

"Leo is okay with dealing with the unions, and he likes the score, so he'll pay Hattie Patrick a hundred grand. If Peter wants to give her or anybody else points, it has to come out of his end."

"You've done a great job, Mort."

"I'll send Peter our representation contract to sign, and make sure he understands our commission is fifteen percent."

"I'll explain the facts of life to him."

"If I know Leo, we'll have contracts in a couple of weeks, and after we iron out the fine print, we should have a check in a month or so."

"Thank you again, Mort."

"When the contract is finalized, bring Peter to my office to sign, and he can meet some of our people."

"I'll do that." Stone said good-bye and hung up.

Joan came in holding a letter. "This came from Bill Eggers," she said, handing it to Stone.

"This is an outline of Arrington's estate," Stone said.

"That number," Joan said. "Is that now yours?"

"Yes, except Peter gets it when I die."

"Then I never have to worry about paying your bills again?"

Stone chuckled. "I'm sorry, but you do. I'm not touching this money."

"I always thought you were nuts," Joan said, "but now I know it."

Stone laughed. "I want these numbers kept strictly between you and me," he said. "I don't want anyone else to see them."

"Sure thing," Joan said, then returned to her office.

Stone called Bill Eggers. "Thanks for your letter, Bill," he said.

"It's just a summary of what I talked about with you and Peter."

"I don't want the money," Stone said.

Eggers was quiet for a moment. "Stone, listen to me: I understand that your feelings are still raw about Arrington's death and that you feel you shouldn't profit from her passing."

"That's very understanding of you, Bill. It's exactly how I feel."

"There's something you're not considering, though."

"What's that?"

"Arrington's feelings on the matter. When I first met with her about her estate planning she told me that you would feel this way."

"She knew me well."

"She also told me that, if I could keep you from doing something foolish about the money, you would eventually come to your senses. It was her wish that you have the money; she wanted that very much, and you have to take her wishes into consideration."

"If she'd asked me, I'd have told her how I feel about her money."

"She already knew; that's why she didn't ask you."

"If she knew that, why did she make this will?"

"Because she was smarter than you, Stone. She knew that, in time, you'd understand her wisdom and accept it."

"That hasn't happened yet," Stone said.

"Give it time, Stone. Take a year or two, then think about it again. You'll find satisfying uses for the money. Now I want you to promise me you won't do anything rash, that you'll consult me before you start disposing of the money, even to Peter. Just let it sit there and grow."

Stone sighed. "Oh, all right. I'll check with you before I give it all away."

"By the way, you need to make a decision about developing the Bel-Air property as a hotel and let Mike Freeman know. He's got investors and a management company on hold."

"Good point," Stone said.

"I think developing the property is a good idea," Eggers said. "I can't see you living in Bel-Air, and if you need to go out there, you'll have a house on the hotel grounds."

"I don't really want that," Stone said.

"Then the hotel can rent it in your absence."

"All right, I'll talk to Mike about it."

"Stone, maybe you should take a vacation. How long has it been?"

"I don't know, years, I guess, but Peter's in school. When he's out for the summer I'm going to take him up to Maine for a while and teach him to sail."

"An excellent idea. Another idea: as I recall, you have the lifetime use of the house there, and then it reverts to the foundation, according to your cousin's will."

"That's correct."

"My bet is that the foundation would

be very pleased if you bought the house from them now. Then they won't have to wait for you to die to get their property. They'd only sell it then, anyway. That would be a good use of your inheritance, and Peter will always have the house."

Stone brightened. "You're right, Bill, that would be a good use of the money. I'll get in touch with them and make an offer for the property."

"Good man. Now I have to go back to work."

"Thank you, Bill. I feel better now."

"Just remember your promise." Eggers hung up.

Stone didn't wait. He looked up the name of the foundation president, called him and made him an offer for the house. The man said he'd discuss it with his board and get back to Stone.

Next, Stone called Mike Freeman.

"Good morning, Stone. My men are on the job."

"Yes, I know, Mike, and thank you. I called about something else, though."

"What can I do for you?"

"Arrington left me the Bel-Air property. I want to proceed with the hotel development."

"I'm delighted to hear it," Mike said. "I'll let the investors and the management company know."

"Mike, you obviously think this development is a good investment, or you wouldn't be involved in it."

"I think it's an outstanding investment," Mike said. "Otherwise, I wouldn't be putting Strategic Services' money into it."

"How much, total, do we need to raise to complete the project?"

"Half a billion dollars," Mike said, "plus the property purchase. You could lease it to the company to make it easier for them."

"How much is Strategic Services investing?"

"A hundred million."

"I'll invest two hundred million, and that way, you and I will keep control of the project. I'll keep title to the land and lease it to the company."

"That's wonderful, Stone. I'll get in touch with the others and put it to them, and we'll make you an offer on leasing the property."

"Good, Mike," Stone said. "Get back to me, and we'll work it all out." He hung up, and reflected on his day's work. Making these decisions had actually made him feel better, and not just about the money. To his surprise, he felt something he hadn't felt since Arrington's death: enthusiasm.

63

Peter got home from school a little early and came in through Stone's office entrance, closely followed by his two security men. Hattie was with them.

"Thanks, fellas," Stone said to the guards. "You're done for the day. Same time tomorrow morning."

The two men said good-bye to Peter and Hattie and left.

Peter flopped down on Stone's office sofa, and Hattie sat beside him and held his hand.

Stone reflected that he was going to have to reintroduce the subject of sex to Peter. These two couldn't stay out of bed with each other for much longer; that was obvious.

"So, Peter, now that you've finished your film, what's your next project?"

"I want to write a play, so that I'll arrive at Yale with something to show them."

"Really good idea," Stone said. He fished around among the papers on his desk and found the representation contract that Mort Janklow had sent over. "There's something here for you to sign," Stone said, handing it to Peter.

"What is it?"

"It's a representation contract with the literary agency of Janklow & Nesbit. I've been over it with Mort and made a few small changes. The most important thing you have to know is that the agency's commission is fifteen percent."

"It used to be ten percent, didn't it?"

"Times have changed. Sign both copies at the bottom and date them."

Peter did so.

"Good. That means your first commission payment to Mort will be three million dollars."

"What?"

"That's fifteen percent of twenty million dollars."

"What are you talking about, Dad?"

"Twenty million dollars is what Centurion Studios are paying you for your film, if you approve."

Peter's mouth dropped open.

"Oh, and it's not an outright sale; you're licensing them the rights to the film for seven years, then you can either extend the license for a further payment, to be agreed upon, or the rights revert to you. Centurion will square everything with the unions before the release. By the way, Hattie, they're offering you one hundred thousand dollars as a fee for writing the score."

"Yes!" Hattie shouted, and she and Peter exchanged a high five.

"When are they going to release the film?" Peter asked.

"That's still to be determined by the studio, but don't expect it to be the Christmas movie at Radio City Music Hall."

"Why did they pay so much?" Peter

asked. "I was hoping for maybe half a million."

"Three reasons: first, because they like it and they know it would have cost them twice that to produce it themselves; second, because they think they will make a lot of money on it; and third, because you have a very good agent."

Peter and Hattie were hugging.

Tim Rutledge stood outside the house in Turtle Bay and watched the two large men hustle Peter Barrington and a young girl into the downstairs law office. A couple of minutes later, the men put the car into the garage, then left, walking toward Third Avenue. Rutledge took a deep breath, held it for a moment, then exhaled in a rush. Now was the time; it wouldn't get any better. He would be in Mexico tomorrow.

He unbuttoned his coat to access the shotgun, which hung by a strap from his right shoulder. The weapon was loaded and racked; all he had to do was release the safety and fire, after he had had a few words with Mr. Barrington.

He wouldn't kill Barrington, just his son. Then the man could live the rest of his life with his grief. He started across the street toward the downstairs door of the house.

Inside, the doorbell chimed, and Joan reached for the button that released the door. She was expecting Herbie Fisher, who had requested a meeting with Stone. She pressed the button.

She heard the door open, and a man she had never seen walked in, pulled back his coat, and pointed a shotgun at her. "Be quiet," he said. He walked to her desk, unplugged her telephone, and took it with him. "If you leave this office, I'll kill you, too," he said, then he disappeared down the hall toward Stone's office. Now Joan knew exactly who he was, and there wasn't time to dig out her cell phone and call the police.

Stone looked up and saw a man coming down the hall, carrying a shotgun in a firing position. He stood up as he recognized Tim Rutledge—bearded, but himself, nevertheless.

Peter and Hattie jumped to their feet, too.

"Good afternoon, Mr. Barrington," Rutledge said.

"Good afternoon, Mr. Rutledge," Stone replied. "How much time would you like to do?"

Rutledge looked confused. "What?"

"One to five for assault, five to twenty for manslaughter, or life without parole for first-degree murder?" Stone was playing for time; he didn't know what else to do. "Also, New York State has the death penalty."

Rutledge took a moment to sort that out, and Stone saw Joan come out of her office and begin to creep silently down the hall.

"I'm going to kill your son," Rutledge said.

"And why would you want to do that?" Stone asked, edging toward Peter.

Hattie reflexively stepped between Peter and the shotgun.

"Get out of the way, young lady," Rutledge said, "or I'll kill you, too."

"No, you won't," Joan said from the hallway, and before Rutledge could turn and look at her there was the roar of a gunshot, and he lurched forward and fell on Stone's desk, splashing blood and gore over the desktop.

Stone reached over the desk and plucked the shotgun from his hands, then unhooked the strap and racked it until it was empty.

Joan walked into the room, still pointing her .45 semiautomatic ahead of her, ready to fire again, but Rutledge slid slowly to the floor, taking Stone's business papers with him.

"What the hell is going on here?" a man's voice said.

Stone looked up to see Herbie Fisher standing in the doorway. Allison was standing next to him.

Stone stepped over Rutledge's body and took the .45 from Joan. "Sweetheart," he said, "would you call Dino and ask him to send some people and an ambulance over here? And would you tell him to order them not to clog up the whole block with their vehicles? It would upset the neighbors." He took a couple of deep breaths and worked on getting his heart rate down.

Joan picked up her phone from the floor, where Rutledge had set it, and walked quickly back to her office.

Peter spoke up. "I guess we won't need the security guys tomorrow," he said.

64

Stone sat in his office with Herbie and Joan. The police and the body had departed, and the special cleaning crew had done its work with the bloodstains. Peter and Hattie were upstairs in his room. Stone pressed a large scotch on Joan, then poured one for Herbie and a bourbon for himself.

"You look okay," Stone said to Joan.

"Strangely enough, I *am* okay," she said. "I'm glad I didn't have too long to think about whether I should do it."

"You saved all our lives," Stone said, "and in appreciation, I'm going to make a very large contribution to your pension fund. I'm counting on you never to retire, though, because then I'd have to shoot myself."

Herbie laughed aloud and took another sip of his scotch. "Maybe this isn't the best time," Herbie said, "but I came here to apply for a job as an associate."

Stone smiled. "I think you must have passed the bar."

"Top of the list," Herbie said. "I didn't tell you, but my law degree was with honors."

"That's better than mine," Stone said. "As for the job, we're jam up full here, what with Allison helping, but I'll recommend you to Bill Eggers at Woodman & Weld, without reservation. Anyway, you need to work in a bigger firm, not just in my office."

Herbie beamed. "Thank you, Stone."

"Joan, take a letter to Eggers as soon as Herbie leaves. I don't want to embarrass him with praise."

"You mind if I ask who the guy was that Joan offed?" Herbie asked.

Joan choked on her scotch a little.

Stone explained.

"Well, I'm glad he's off the streets," Herbie said.

"So am I," Stone said.

When Herbie had left, Stone dictated a fulsome letter of recommendation to Bill Eggers, then signed it. "Messenger it over, and write Herbie a check for the unused portion of his retainer. What is it, half a million?"

"Give or take," Joan said. "I take it you've changed your mind about your inheritance."

"I have," Stone said, "and being out of debt to Herbie is a good cause."

Two weeks later, Stone took Peter up Park Avenue to Janklow & Nesbit and introduced him to Mort Janklow and his principal associate, Anne Sibbald. Kind words were spoken about Peter's film, and he blushed. Then Leo Goldman arrived with Peter's contract. A little signing ceremony took place, and Leo handed a check for $20,000,000 to Mort.

Mort will deduct his commission, then
wire transfer the remainder of your funds
to your bank account," Stone said to
his son. "And as soon as you get home,
you have to write a check for five million nine hundred and fifty thousand to
the Internal Revenue Service."

"Ouch!" Peter said.

"Get used to it, Peter," Mort said.
"You're going to be writing a lot of
checks to the IRS."

"And, Peter," Leo said, "I have a surprise for you: your film has been accepted for the Sundance Film Festival."

Somebody found a bottle of champagne, and Peter's success was toasted.

On the way home Peter said, "What do
you want me to co with the money?"

"I think you should open a brokerage
account with the Chase Private Bank
and let them recommend how to invest
it, then buy yourself a nice gift."

"I'll have to think about that," Peter
said.

"I'm not going to have anything to do
with the money you earn," Stone said.
"I want to see what you do with it."

"Thank you, Dad," Peter said.

"Thank you for asking," Stone replied.

That weekend, Ben Bacchetti took the
train down from Choate, picked up his
father's car, and drove himself, Peter,
and Hattie to New Haven, to look for
housing for themselves. Joan had re-
served three rooms for them at a local
hotel.

The following day Peter called home.

"Hello?" Stone said.

"Hi, Dad."

"Everything okay?"

"Yes. In fact, it's better than okay."

"How so?"

"We found the perfect apartment for
us—three bedrooms, living/dining room,
kitchen, and a nice study."

"What's the rent?"

"It would be around five thousand a
month, if we were renting," Peter replied. "It's a new building, to be completed in a couple of months. We saw

the model apartment, then took a look at the top-floor unit to get an idea of the space. I've decided to buy the apartment."

Stone thought about that for a moment. "That might be a good use for some of your money, and you'll probably make a profit on it when you leave Yale. How much is it?"

"It would normally sell for around a million and a half, but they're asking a million two, because of the recession. I'll buy the place, and Peter and Hattie will split the monthly maintenance payments."

"Offer them a million, then settle for a million one," Stone said. "Give them a check for ten percent and bring home the contract for me to read before you sign it."

"Great, Dad, I'll do that. Something else."

"What?"

"As soon as I get home I'm going to take driving lessons and get my license, then I'm going to buy a car. I'll need it around here."

This, Stone thought, was as inevitable as sex with Hattie. "All right," he said, "but if you get a speeding ticket the keys are mine."

"Agreed," Peter said.

That night after dinner at a New Haven restaurant they returned to their hotel, and Hattie led Peter to her room. There, she did some more leading, having had slightly more experience than Peter, and from that point on, Peter led.

At home the following day, Peter gave Stone the contract for the condominium. "How did you know they would take a million one?" he asked his father.

"I didn't, but you always have to try. You have to remember that developers these days have excess inventory and not enough buyers. They need the cash, and with you as a buyer, they don't have to wait for mortgage approval."

Stone read the contract and found it acceptable. "Sign it, and I'll find a New Haven attorney to close the sale for you as soon as the apartment is finished and has been inspected. You'll need to speak to our insurance agency about insuring it, too."

"I hadn't thought of that," Peter said. "Dad, I'm also going to buy Hattie a piano, a Steinway, as a surprise."

"That's a very generous gift, Peter, but you should take her up to Steinway Hall and let her choose it herself. A piano is a very personal thing for a pianist."

"Hattie's going to decorate the apartment," Peter said. "How much should I budget for that?"

"That's up to you," Stone said, "or perhaps, up to Hattie. My advice is, buy nice things, but don't go crazy. In four years, you may not want anything you buy now, except for Hattie's piano."

"That's good advice," Peter said.

65

Stone lay back in the cockpit seat of the twenty-nine-foot Concordia and watched the sun fall toward Penobscot Bay.

Hattie was at the helm, Peter was looking after the foredeck, and Ben Bacchetti and a girlfriend occupied the opposite seat. Dino was below, washing and putting away the plastic glasses.

They had been in Maine for nearly a month, and all the kids had become comfortable with sailing the yacht. Hattie called for a jib, then turned into the wind, sliding expertly up to Stone's dock.

He looked at the house and thought how beautiful it was when viewed from the water. He had bought it from the foundation, and one day it would be Peter's.

The kids made the yacht fast, folded the mainsail onto the boom, and tied on the cover. They folded and bagged the genoa and dropped it down the hatch into the forepeak.

Half an hour later, they were assembled in the living room, freshly scrubbed, and half an hour after that they were feasting on lobster, prepared by Mary, the housekeeper and cook.

Peter spoke up. "I'm glad we all learned to sail," he said. "Let's do this again next summer."

There was a chorus of agreement, except from Dino. "I'll be a passenger next year, too, and let you kids keep doing the work."

"That works for me, too," Stone said.

The next day they flew home to New York, and a couple of days after that, Stone and Dino rented a van, and the boys loaded it with theirs and Hattie's belongings. Dino drove the van, and Stone rode with him, while the boys rode in Peter's new Prius. Hattie rode with her parents. Peter and Hattie had already made three or four trips to New Haven to receive the furnishings they had ordered, including Hattie's piano, and to oversee the painting and wallpapering.

When Stone and Dino walked into the apartment, they were impressed. "It looks like grown-ups live here," Dino said.

"I like the pictures," Stone said. "And the piano."

They ordered in Chinese food for lunch, then Hattie played a couple of pieces for them on her new Steinway.

Finally, Stone, Dino, and the Patricks had to leave; it was time for the children to start their new lives at university.

Driving back in the van, Stone said, "I remember the day I moved out of my folks' house and into the dorm at NYU. I remember the freedom I felt, and I guess that's what the kids are feeling now."

Dino nodded, but he seemed too choked up to talk for a while. Finally he said, "At least Ben's out of his mother's grasp."

Stone laughed aloud. Then he wished Arrington could have been there on that day. Who knows, he thought, maybe she was.

AUTHOR'S NOTE

I am happy to hear from readers, but you should know that if you write to me in care of my publisher, three to six months will pass before I receive your letter, and when it finally arrives it will be one among many, and I will not be able to reply.

However, if you have access to the Internet, you may visit my website at www.stuartwoods.com, where there is a button for sending me e-mail. So far, I have been able to reply to all my e-mail, and I will continue to try to do so.

If you send me an e-mail and do not

receive a reply, it is probably because you are among an alarming number of people who have entered their e-mail address incorrectly in their mail software. I have many of my replies returned as undeliverable.

Remember: e-mail, reply; snail mail, no reply.

When you e-mail, please do not send attachments, as I never open these. They can take twenty minutes to download, and they often contain viruses.

Please do not place me on your mailing lists for funny stories, prayers, political causes, charitable fund-raising, petitions, or sentimental claptrap. I get enough of that from people I already know. Generally speaking, when I get e-mail addressed to a large number of people, I immediately delete it without reading it.

Please do not send me your ideas for a book, as I have a policy of writing only what I myself invent. If you send me story ideas, I will immediately delete them without reading them. If you have a good idea for a book, write it yourself, but I will not be able to advise you on how to get it published. Buy a copy of *Writer's Market* at any bookstore; that will tell you how.

Anyone with a request concerning events or appearances may e-mail it to me or send it to: Publicity Department, Penguin Group (USA) Inc., 375 Hudson Street, New York, NY 10014.

Those ambitious folk who wish to buy film, dramatic, or television rights to my books should contact Matthew Snyder, Creative Artists Agency, 9830 Wilshire Boulevard, Beverly Hills, CA 98212-1825.

Those who wish to make offers for rights of a literary nature should contact Anne Sibbald, Janklow & Nesbit, 445 Park Avenue, New York, NY 10022. (Note: This is not an invitation for you to send her your manuscript or to solicit her to be your agent.)

If you want to know if I will be signing books in your city, please visit my website, www.stuartwoods.com, where the tour schedule will be published a month or so in advance. If you wish me to do a book signing in your locality, ask your favorite bookseller to contact his Penguin representative or the Penguin publicity department with the request.

If you find typographical or editorial errors in my book and feel an irresistible urge to tell someone, please write to Rachel Kahan at Penguin's address above. Do not e-mail your discoveries to me, as I will already have learned about them from others.

A list of my published works appears in the front of this book and on my website. All the novels are still in print in paperback and can be found at or ordered from any bookstore. If you wish to obtain hardcover copies of earlier novels or of the two nonfiction books, a good used-book store or one of the online bookstores can help you find them. Otherwise, you will have to go to a great many garage sales.